DREAMS FALL LIKE RAIN

ANDREA MAXAND

BELL THE CAT BOOKS

For my father
Thomas C. Maxand

NEW YORK CITY
1995

CHAPTER 1

I should be asleep.

But instead, I'm at the cramped Brooklyn offices of *Rags to Bitches*. My editor called early this morning and promised me a juicy assignment, so of course, I said I'd be here. But I'm restless. I'm no longer sure if this *Rags to Bitches* gig is following my dream, or if I'm just stuck in a rut. Getting up early *could* be worth it, though. Maybe Tom will finally give me the chance to chase something big.

I'm not surprised he's late to his own meeting. This magazine runs on passion, not punctuality. When I first applied, it was the name that caught my attention. *Rags to Bitches: An Independent Take on Music, Art, & Culture.* But everyone just calls it *Rags to Bitches*. Or sometimes just *Bitches*.

I started out here during my freshman year of college, mostly as a way to see bands play for free and because it made sense with my journalism major. But despite graduating over a year ago, I'm still here.

To pass the time, I take inventory of Tom's sparsely decorated walls. The only music memorabilia is a Bruce

Springsteen poster—an old one—from the *Born in the U.S.A.* era. Everything else in here is sports related.

Tom finally gets in about ten minutes later, and plunks a cup of the office coffee down in front of me. "Hey, Frankie," he says. "Thanks for coming by on such short notice."

"Thanks for the coffee," I reply, as he takes his seat across from me. The office coffee isn't great, but one of the things I love about this job is having a boss who would go out of his way to grab me a cup. Tom's a genuinely nice person, and he knows more about every mainstream, midlevel, and obscure band than anyone I've ever met.

"So what's this amazing assignment?" I ask.

He grins at me. "You're not going to believe it."

"Tom. Is this going to be your friend's jazz/punk/thrash/metal fusion band again? Because I've already covered them, like, three times."

He laughs—a delighted, raucous sound. "No, no. Not this time. But that would be funny, wouldn't it?"

"Not for me."

"No, probably not," he agrees, but he's still chuckling. "Okay, you ready? You want to hear what band you're going to interview?"

"Ready anytime."

"Fern on Fire."

I'm actually speechless. Fern on Fire is *huge*. As in chart-topping, internationally famous, shrouded in rock n' roll mystique huge. They're not the kind of band that *Rags to Bitches* typically covers. But that's only half the reason why I've temporarily lost my ability to speak.

"Told ya' you wouldn't believe it," Tom says gleefully.

"Doesn't Tyler want to cover this one?" I manage, when I finally recover my voice. "He's such a massive fan."

Tom nods. "He wanted to. But he won't be here. Family emergency, and he can't get back to the city in time."

"When's the interview happening?" I ask.

He grins wide. "Tonight."

"Holy shit!" I yelp. "I can't pull that off, Tom. I work this afternoon, and I'd have to listen to their album a bunch of times, and then I'd have to do some research...."

"You can absolutely do it," Tom interrupts. "In fact, I think it's perfect that you're not a super fan, like Tyler. You'll ask better questions."

"Better questions? I only have a few hours—I have no idea what I'd even ask them."

Tom tilts his head to the side, like he's finally hearing me. "Look, Frankie. I want you to do it, and I really think you *can* do it. But if you don't want this, just say so. I'll find somebody else." He pauses for a beat, then gives me a knowing smile. "So...do you want it?"

Do I want it? He has no idea how loaded that question is for me. It's about so much more than accepting a challenging, high-profile assignment on short notice. But as I sit and consider his question, the answer comes to me in a rush of certainty.

"Yeah," I say. "I want it."

"I knew you would." He reaches inside his desk and pulls out an eight-by-ten manila envelope then taps it with his finger. "Your pass for tonight is in here, and the location of the show."

"Show?" I ask.

"Yep. They're playing a small, intimate show for a select group of fans. So you get there, interview them, then stay for the show if you want. I'm assuming you want to?"

"Yeah, I want to." I give him a quizzical look. "How

come they're letting us interview them? I mean, we're not exactly—we're not at their level."

Tom leans forward. "Don't tell anyone, but I think our illustrious editor-in-chief, was, at some point, banging the band's bass player. So maybe he figured he owed her one? Or maybe they're still banging. It's a mystery. The main thing is, they're giving us an interview. I mean, *I* still can't believe it. But it's real."

I take a few moments to digest that information. "So... when do I show up?"

"Seven o'clock. Tell the person at the door who you are, and they should hook you up with the band's tour manager."

I reach across the desk and take the envelope. "Anything else I need to know? Any angle you want on this?"

Tom gives me this smile that I usually love to see, because it means he has full confidence in me. "I trust you. Come up with your own angle. Oh—one more thing. Don't freak out if the singer doesn't show up."

I lick my lips, nervous. "The singer? You mean, uh, Rex Thornton?"

"That's the one. Word is ever since the tell-all interview he did last summer, he's not down with talking to the press. And I mean, I love us, but we're motherfucking *Rags to Bitches*, not *Rolling Stone*. He might be there, but don't be surprised if he isn't."

"Okay," I shrug. "It should be interesting either way."

"That's the spirit. Any more questions for me?"

"Yeah. Do you have a copy of their latest CD I can borrow? So I can actually listen to it before the interview?"

I leave Tom's office with a copy of Fern on Fire's latest record. I'm reeling—and not from excitement over a "juicy" lead.

What I didn't tell my boss is that six years ago, I knew Rex Thornton. I knew him well. Or at least, it felt like I did at the time.

When Tom called this morning, I thought I was getting up early for an amazing opportunity. Instead, I've just had my past dumped right on my lap, here in the present. I left Rex behind a long time ago. But now, as I exit the building, it's hard to think about anyone else.

PACIFIC NORTHWEST

1989

CHAPTER 2

I pound on Erick's door. Loud, muffled music is playing inside his room. It's a Saturday morning, and we're out of bread and milk. Our mom is still asleep, so I'm making a trip to the nearby convenience store.

Erick yanks his door open, and stares at me. "What?" he snarls.

He's wearing his usual uniform of sweatpants and a heavy metal T-shirt. Today the band is Judas Priest. The shirt's black. All of my little brother's shirts are black.

"We're out of bread and milk," I tell him. "I'm going to the Food Mart. Can you think of anything else we need for breakfast?"

He shrugs. "How would I know?"

"Just asking, so you don't complain about it later when I don't get that one thing you really needed to have."

Erick makes a face at me. Whatever song he's listening to launches into a guitar solo. He jumps to the center of the room and starts playing an invisible guitar, banging his head back and forth so fast and so hard it makes me queasy. Clearly, he's done with me.

"Bread and milk it is!" I yell, over the din of the music.

I head out and hop on my bike, speeding downhill to the convenience store that's about a mile away. It's an easy ride there, but it'll be a tough haul coming back up. For the umpteenth time, I wish I could just take Mom's car, but she doesn't like me to drive it unless I've asked her first. She also doesn't like it when I wake her up.

I've decided I'm going to buy myself some orange cream cupcakes once I get to the Food Mart. It'll be my reward for having to make this trip on a Saturday.

The early October morning is chilly, the brisk air billowing my flannel shirt. I should have worn a jacket, but I was in a hurry. There's hardly anyone out, even though it's already close to ten am. Saturday mornings are slow around here. Outside the store, I chain my bike to the rack and lock the padlock.

Inside, the clerk is listening to the radio on a small boombox behind the front counter. He has it set to one of those stations that plays all the current hits. I grab a shopping basket and wander the aisles. I'm only here for three things: bread, milk, and the cupcakes, but I'm in no hurry to get back home.

Suddenly, there's the sound of deafening rock music playing on a car stereo in the parking lot. The music is so loud it momentarily drowns out the store's boombox. The car is loud too, and it shudders in protest as its owner turns it off.

I feel more than hear the person when they enter the store. Whoever it is has loud energy. I don't mean he's making lots of noise. I mean he's the kind of person who takes up tons of space without making a sound.

All at once I'm nervous, and I speed up my shopping. I find the bread and pop a loaf in my basket. Then I pause by the section with donuts, cakes, and other processed baked goods. But I don't see the orange cupcakes.

The person with the loud energy comes up behind me, and whoever it is starts humming along with the boombox, which is playing Rod Stewart's "Downtown Train." The humming is deep and masculine.

"Can't find what you're looking for?"

It's weird, but the dude with the loud energy has a soft speaking voice. Not weak. Just quieter than I would have expected. I turn to look at him.

He's got long, unruly hair, down to his shoulders, and it's this crazy strawberry blond color. He's wearing a black leather jacket over a T- shirt, and tight black jeans with a hole in one knee. He looks like he had a rough night. Even so, he's crackling with energy that's hard to ignore.

In high school, I hated guys like him. He's the type of guy my best friend, Ronnie, would have gone for. The kind of guy who'd make her forget to study for tests, so she'd be desperate to copy off my paper on test days. The kind of guy who smokes gross-smelling cancer-causing cigarettes. Who drives a loud, ugly car.

My feelings about boys like him haven't changed, I just haven't run into many of them since graduation four months ago. This particular dude seems older than the ones I remember—he might even be in his twenties—but he's wearing their uniform, so he's one of them.

"I'm just looking for cupcakes," I mutter, then go back to surveying the baked goods. I figure he'll go away and take care of his own business. Whatever that is.

Instead, he moves closer to me, so he can examine the array of pre-packaged sweets. He points, and his leather jacket brushes my arm.

"There."

Before I can stop myself, I blurt, "But I want *orange* ones." Like it's any of his business what kind of cupcakes I want. Now that he's closer, I can smell the faint odor of cigarettes. Typical. He's exactly the kind of dude Ronnie would go nuts over. Also the kind of dude my little brother looks up to. As soon as Erick goes to junior high, someone like this guy will probably drag him down the deadbeat path.

The guy seems oblivious to the fact that I'm judging him, however. Instead, he kneels down and sticks his hand behind a row of chocolate cupcakes. Then he pulls something out from the very back, straightens up, and hands it to me. A package of orange cupcakes.

I'm reluctantly impressed. "How'd you know those were back there?"

"Sometimes they don't do a good job re-stocking." He shrugs, and smiles. "But I got lucky." He has a surprisingly sweet smile. It touches his eyes, which I notice are an unusual color—a sort of pale green.

"Well, thanks." I put the package in my basket. "I uh...I need to get milk."

"Don't let me stop you." Now he sounds cocky. Like he knows that I think he's hot. But I don't. I don't think he's hot at all. He might have a great smile, but that's as far as my appreciation of him goes.

I roll my eyes at him, then turn around and head for the small refrigerated section to grab the milk. By the time I get to the checkout counter, he's already gone. I can sense the absence of his energy in the store. The checker bags up my three items, and I go outside to my bike.

He's there, leaning against the driver's side of his car,

smoking a cigarette. It's a 1970s muscle car painted a hideous shade of purple. Predictable. Hilarious.

He's watching me, but I ignore him and kneel down by my bike to unlock it. As I straighten up, I see him take a long drag of his cigarette. Then he turns his smile on me again and asks, "Need a ride anywhere?"

I gesture wordlessly to the bicycle.

"Your bike would fit in the trunk," he says.

"No, thanks. I need the exercise." I swing my leg over the bike and hang the plastic grocery sack on one of the handles.

"Kind of a bumpy ride home with all that shit you're carrying," he observes.

I shrug. "I do it all the time."

The guy shrugs, too. "Well, I tried to help." He lobs another smile in my direction, although this time there's something knowing behind the sweetness. Then he takes one last drag of his cigarette, drops it on the ground, and stubs it out with his foot. He turns around to open his car door.

"You shouldn't leave your cigarette on the ground like that," I burst out. "You're littering. It's gross and...inconsiderate of others."

He casts his eyes down at the pavement, which is literally strewn with a multitude of cigarette butts. Then he looks back up at me and squints.

"You need to chill out, sweetheart."

I glower at him, but he just gets in his car and starts it up. As it coughs and roars to life, he rolls down the window. "Enjoy your cupcakes!" he yells over the rumble of his engine. "And you're welcome."

Then he switches his car stereo back on, and a

cacophony of drums, bass, and guitars drowns out my voice as I yell, "I already said thank you!"

He puts his hand to his ear, like he can't hear me, and grins again. Only this time it's a more devilish sort of grin. Then he peels out of the parking lot, leaving behind a small cloud of exhaust.

CHAPTER 3

I'm heading out the door of our house to meet Ronnie, who's waiting for me in her car outside. But then I spy my mom in the kitchen. She's leaning against the kitchen counter, sipping a diet soda. I stop.

"Hey, Mom."

"You going out?" she asks.

"Do you mind? You didn't say you need me to watch Erick tonight."

She shrugs. "Don't let me stop you."

Her tone sounds noncommittal, though, and I don't trust it. "Are you sure it's okay?"

"Yeah, I'm sure. It's fine."

I hesitate, then hear Ronnie honk her horn outside.

"I gotta go," I tell Mom, then rush out the door before she can change her mind.

Ronnie wants to go to Seattle to see some rock band she's nuts about. Somehow, when we graduated from high school, I thought she would get over her fascination with long-haired, leather-jacketed deadbeats. But nope. She's just as into those guys as ever. I know she's dragging me to

Seattle because she has a crush on some dude in one of the bands we're seeing. I'm going with her to be a good friend. And, whatever. I like live music, too, even if I have a feeling this show won't be my thing.

I get in Ronnie's car and see she's dressed up. Black knit mini skirt, tights, and a shirt that emphasizes her boobs. She's made up her eyes with dark kohl eyeliner, mascara, and blue eyeshadow. She looks good. But it's clear we're approaching the evening from two different angles.

She groans as I get in her car. "Holy shit, Frankie, that's what you're wearing?"

I glance down at my jeans, long-sleeved tee, and hoodie ensemble. Then I look back up at Ronnie and grin. "I like to wear layers at shows. If it gets hot in there, I'll be prepared."

"Ms. Practical," she sighs.

"Ashamed to be seen with me?"

"Oh, shut up. If you don't want to meet anybody, then you don't want to meet anybody."

"I don't want to meet anybody," I confirm. "Just think of me as your wingman. That's my function."

"Thanks for coming with me," she says, dutifully.

Her thanks are genuine. I know she'd prefer it if we walked in the door dressed as two hot chicks, but having a friend with you is always better than going alone. It's more than that, though. Ever since we met, me and Ronnie have always had each other's backs. I can count on her—often more than I can count on my own family.

We park several blocks away from the club. When we get there, we show our fake IDs at the door. I'm still not comfortable having one, but if I want to hang out with Ronnie, it's a necessary evil.

The venue isn't very big. I figure it fits about two hundred people, and it's dark and stale-smelling inside. But it's packed. Loud music is playing through the club's sound system, and there's a band on stage breaking down their gear.

"Which band are we seeing again?" I yell to Ronnie.

"Fern on Fire!" she yells back.

"Fern on *what*?"

"FERN ON FIRE!"

What a strange name for a band. "So they're next?"

"Right!" She takes my hand and drags me into the crowd, pushing toward the front, near the stage.

I'd rather hang out in the back of the room, but this is all part of being a good friend.

The next band is hauling their gear on stage, and Ronnie's already paying rapt attention. As usual, I'm not sure what she sees in any of these guys, because the band seems unremarkable to me. Just another bunch of grimy dudes with long hair, trying to look tough. There are three of them, which could be interesting. Four guys seems to be the standard for most bands. A trio would at least be something different.

I study Ronnie. She has her eyes on the guy setting up his gear at the left side of the stage. He's got a mane of dark hair that he keeps flipping back from his face while he sets up his bass rig. In fact, he does it so often, it's kind of funny.

So, Ronnie digs the bassist—as in, *really* digs him. She can't tear her eyes away from him. I smirk and stop watching her, deciding she needs some privacy.

The guitarist and the drummer begin riffing together, testing out their sound levels. There's something about the way they play that's not just confident, but also visceral and compelling.

I've seen so many bands with guys who think they're Eddie Van Halen, but aren't. Or bands who try to ape the styles of other famous bands. I could be wrong, but I have a gut feeling this band might legitimately have its own thing.

Just as I notice there's no one standing in front of the mic positioned at the center of the stage, another guy walks out. He goes straight toward the mic and adjusts the stand up to his height.

He has long, reddish-blond hair, and when he looks straight ahead, I realize he's the guy I met at the Food Mart a week ago.

"Okay, I'm good," he says. "Let's do it."

His voice is just how I remember it, surprisingly soft for someone who looks so rough around the edges.

The band starts to play a deep groove. Their sound is rude. Loud. Sludgy and sexual. I'm bad with genres, but the guitar is grinding, and the rhythm section is solid. No, more than solid. They're sick. I don't think I've ever heard a band that's so perfectly in sync with each other.

So far the singer hasn't done anything. He's just standing there with his head down, listening to the band like the rest of us. Like he's absorbing their collective power.

Then the guitarist plays a lead-in, and he starts to sing.

His voice is resonant and powerful. Kind of blues-y. It's impressive that you can hear him over his super loud band, but he's more than a powerful singer—he exudes a fierce, hypnotic vibe. He doesn't move much while he sings, but he has this immense focus you can feel. It's almost a physical thing.

I hate to admit it, but this time, at least, Ronnie has great taste. This is captivating music, and every band member is uniquely talented. They've created their own sound. Their set goes by fast, and I'm disappointed when it ends.

When the singer thanks everyone for coming, the softness of his speaking voice in contrast with the power of his singing strikes me again.

Ronnie grabs my arm, and her eyes are snapping with excitement. "Let's go meet them!"

"Huh? Oh, no! Are you crazy?"

"Totally. Come with me!" She yanks on my arm. I'm afraid she's going to storm the stage or something, but instead she drags me to the ladies' room, where she starts reapplying her make up. It's so dark in there I don't know how she can see what she's doing.

I stand around, awkward, trying to stay out of the way of women coming and going. I'm not dressed like any other female here. Ronnie had the right idea with her mini skirt, tight top, and teased out hair.

I have my long brown hair pulled back in a ponytail. Between that and my hoodie, I almost look like someone's kid sister. I should be relieved the door guy didn't get suspicious when I gave him my fake ID.

Ronnie turns to me. "Want me to do your makeup?"

I wave my hands in front of my face. "No. I'm not here to meet anyone. Remember?"

She gives me a knowing look. "You sure? I saw you watching the singer."

I start to explain about the convenience store thing, then decide it's pointless. "Well, he'll just have to take me the way I am," I say, throwing out my arms. "It's the real me or nothing."

"You're so weird sometimes." She grabs my arm midair. "Let's go."

She's vibrating with about ten different kinds of excitement. I have no idea how we're going to meet these guys, but if anyone knows how to make it happen, Ronnie does.

She drags me outside the club, into the alley next to it. We're skulking past a small row of dumpsters, and just as I'm starting to think my friend has completely lost it, I see them. The band. They're just behind the club, hanging out. There's a few cars parked back there, including a purple GTO, and the guys are all smoking, talking, and laughing. Just them. I don't know what I expected. A bevy of girls, all dressed like Ronnie? Girls she'd have to fight to get close to her precious bass player? But there are no other girls. Just the band.

And suddenly, the fact that we're approaching them seems ridiculous. Maybe even dangerous.

"Hey, Ronnie," I say, pulling on her arm this time. "Why don't we just go back to the car and—"

"You're coming with me!" she hisses in my ear.

She propels me forward with swift decisiveness, and all at once we're in the circle of guys. I'm almost shoulder to shoulder with the singer.

There's a moment of uncomfortable silence. Then the singer smirks and takes a drag on his cigarette.

"Hey, Theo, looks like the groupies you ordered finally got here."

"Here we are!" Ronnie laughs, and at the exact same time, I say, vehemently, "I am *not* a groupie."

All the guys crack up.

"We don't have groupies," the guitarist says, looking in my direction. "So don't worry."

"It was a joke," the singer adds. Then he looks at me with recognition in his eyes. "Hey. Don't I know you?"

At that moment, there's an instant shift in the universe. Without a word, Ronnie deftly turns her back, which leaves me with the band's singer. It's like she's drawn a dividing line. She starts talking to the other three guys, making all of them laugh. Maybe they're being polite. Or maybe they think she's funny. Or maybe, they're laughing because they think she's hot.

And to be fair, Ronnie is pretty hot. A lot of the time, I think she's kind of embarrassing, but that's probably because we're such different people.

"I *do* know you," the singer says to me. "You're the chick who got on my case for littering at the Food Mart."

"That's me," I say, unsmiling. Now that he's not onstage being amazing, he's the same annoying guy I first thought he was.

He takes a long drag on his cigarette and sort of squints at me. His eyes glitter through the slits of his eyelids. "So how were those orange cupcakes?"

"Good," I admit. "You know, I *did* thank you for those. Right after you found them?"

Now he treats me to a full grin. "I know that. I was just giving you shit."

"Oh." I feel dumb. I always take things too seriously.

He blows a plume of smoke out of the corner of his mouth. "You got a name?"

"Umm...yeah. Frankie."

"Frankie?" he repeats, sounding incredulous.

"It's short for Francesca. But nobody ever calls me that."

He puts out a hand, then says slowly, "Hey, Francesca. I'm Rex."

I take his hand. *Rex.* That's not a name you hear every day. In fact, I don't think I've ever met anyone with that name.

He lets my hand go, and nods beyond me. "Looks like your friend is having a good time."

I turn around. Ronnie is no longer entertaining all three band members. She's managed to attach herself to the bass player, winding herself into him. And he's winding himself right back. It's dark, so it's hard to see, but I'm pretty sure his hand is inside her skirt, on her ass.

"Hey, Theo!" Rex yells.

The bass player looks up and over at us. "Yeah?"

"You want the car?"

"Are you offering?"

Rex reaches in his pocket and lobs a key in Theo's direction. He catches it one handed, then urges Ronnie forward. She starts giggling as they run for Rex's monstrous purple car. When they get there, they disappear in the back seat.

"You okay?" Rex asks. He's grinning at me, like he knows I'm bothered by the idea of Theo and Ronnie fucking in his car.

I am bothered, but mostly because it means I'm stuck. "Ronnie's my ride home," I say, casting a glance over at the car, then looking back at him.

"Ronnie—that's your friend's name?"

"Right."

"Don't worry about it," he assures me. "Someone will give you a ride home."

I really don't want one of these dudes to drive me home. Hopefully Theo sucks at sex, and Ronnie will be ready to leave soon.

The guitarist walks over to us and looks at Rex. "You gonna go in and catch the headliner?"

"Me and Francesca here were thinking about getting an omelette," Rex drawls.

I stare at him. *Omelette?* What the hell is he talking about?

The guitarist smiles and gives a resigned sigh. "You want me and Noah to go back inside and represent?"

"Do you mind?"

"Nah, we got it covered." Then he points at Rex. "But next time any groupies show up, it's your turn to represent."

"I'm not a groupie," I repeat.

Rex puts a hand on my shoulder. I sort of jump with surprise, then look at him. His grin is one part sweet, one part devilish.

"C'mon," he says. "Let's go get an omelette."

CHAPTER 4

Rex and I are sitting in a booth at this all-night diner sharing an enormous omelette. It was dirt cheap. Everything on the menu at this place is cheap. Our omelette is stuffed with sausage and cheese and a blend of peppers and onions. I've barely eaten any of it, and I'm already full.

It's kind of uncomfortable, being here with Rex. We're strangers. I don't know what to say to him. Mostly he's eating, and he's eating like he hasn't had anything to eat all day. Who knows, maybe he hasn't.

But when he's not occupied with the food, he's watching me. I'm half-flattered, half-unnerved by it. Does he really think I came out tonight to have sex with someone in his band? With him? Maybe he does think that. That's definitely why Ronnie came here tonight, and I'm her friend. So it would make sense to think that's why I came here, too.

As if he's been reading my thoughts, he says, "So, if you're not a groupie, what are you?"

I shrug. "Ronnie's wingman."

"What do you do when you're not Ronnie's wingman?"

ANDREA MAXAND

Maybe he's sincere. Or maybe he's trying to see if there's an angle he can work with me. I figure if he's even a little attracted to me, or bored, or horny enough, he's going to try to get what he can.

Still, his question kind of floors me. Who *am* I when I'm not being Ronnie's friend? "I'm not sure," I say, after a few moments. "Guess I'm trying to figure that out."

He grins. "I bet that whole groupie thing was weird for you, huh? Especially if you've never been with anybody."

It takes me a second to figure out that he thinks I've never had sex. "I've *been* with somebody!" I protest.

"Oh, yeah?" His grin seems to deepen. "Who?"

"High school. Boyfriend." And it's true. Jason and I were having sex all through senior year. But now I'm blushing like a proverbial virgin, and the vibe between me and Rex has gone instantly intimate.

He leans forward. "Still with the boyfriend?"

"We broke up after graduation." His eyes know and see too much. I need to change the subject. "So, umm...do you think maybe Ronnie would be..." I search for a word, "...*free* by now?"

"Yeah, okay," he laughs. "We can go."

When we get the bill, I try to help pay, but he waves me off. "It's less than five bucks," he says. "You didn't even eat anything."

Walking back to the venue, we don't talk much, but I feel like I know him now. I don't, of course, but I have this odd sense of connection to him that I didn't have before. I'm not sure I like that.

When we get to the parking lot, Theo, Ronnie, and the band's drummer are nowhere to be seen. There's just the guitarist, who looks like he's been waiting for us.

"Hey, Todd," Rex calls out. "Where is everyone?"

"Me and Noah loaded up the van. He drove it home and parked it in his mom's garage."

"Awesome. Now we don't have to load it tomorrow night."

Todd taps his temple with his finger.

"Where's Theo?"

"He and that chick split."

I start to panic. "Whose car did they take?" If Ronnie has abandoned me here with these guys, I will not be forgiving her for a long time. Next time she wants to bang a bass player, she can find someone else to be her wingman.

Todd looks at me. "I think they took hers. White Civic hatchback?"

"Fuck. Yeah, that's her car. Fuck."

"I'll take you home," Rex offers.

"I live all the way up north."

"So does he," Todd says.

"Yeah, it's no problem." Rex points at Todd. "Gotta take this guy home first, though."

"I'll get a cab." I don't know why I'm so dead set against Rex taking me home. My sense is these guys are basically all right. Not angels, but not criminals, either. I should be safe enough. But this wasn't how tonight was supposed to turn out. Ronnie wasn't supposed to abandon me here. I'm having a hard time accepting that she did.

Now, Rex just grins at me. "Don't be stupid. C'mon."

He starts walking toward his car, and Todd follows him. I stay where I am. Do cabs even come to this part of the city? Is there a pay phone nearby? How long will I have to wait for a cab?

Rex is already in the car. Todd turns around and smiles at me. "You coming with us or not?"

Fuck, fuck, fuck.

ANDREA MAXAND

"Yeah." I sigh and walk toward the car. "Okay."

Todd gets in the back seat. "You can ride shotgun," he says.

At first, I'm annoyed. He's trying to force me to be near Rex. Then I remember Theo and Ronnie just had sex in the backseat and decide I prefer to sit in front.

"Thanks." I slide onto the front bench seat, and avoid Rex's eyes as I start searching for the seatbelt.

Pretty quick, I figure out there's no shoulder belt in his car. I look for a lap belt, but don't find one. So I scoot over on the seat. Maybe I'm sitting on it? Then I feel Rex's arm go across me, as he reaches down, and pulls out the seatbelt.

"Sometimes it gets stuck between the door and the seat."

His voice is neutral, but the sensation of his body so close to me is producing a not-so-neutral response. I know myself well enough to know I'm turned on. I figure it's because this car was in service as a sex-mobile less than an hour ago. I'm responding to leftover sex vibes or something. I fasten my seatbelt as Rex starts up the car.

"Really loving the eau-de-quickfuck in the backseat," Todd says, as we leave the parking lot.

"Wanna sit up front?" Rex asks.

"Nah, I don't want to crowd the groupie."

I can tell he's teasing me. Still, I turn and give him a look.

"She has a name, you know," Rex says. "This is Francesca."

I start to remind him that no one calls me Francesca. My family has called me Frankie ever since I can remember. When I met Ronnie, it felt like my name was meant to be. We were Ronnie and Frankie, the two girls with the sort-of boy names.

26

But the truth is, I like how it sounds when Rex calls me Francesca.

I let it go.

"My apologies," Todd says, not sounding sorry at all. "Hi, Francesca. Welcome to the vehicle of stink."

"Is it really that bad back there?" Rex laughs.

"I'm sure the right person would revel in it. I'm just not that guy." Todd taps my shoulder, and I turn around. He's offering his hand, so I take it.

"I'm Todd, by the way," he says.

"Nice to meet you," I reply. Then I catch a whiff of what he means and screw up my nose in distaste.

Todd bursts out laughing. "She's catching on!"

"Shit, really? Man, this is like, the third time." Rex sounds kind of upset and kind of not.

"Fucking and farting," Todd informs me solemnly. "It's kind of Theo's thing."

I laugh. I can't help it. I think of Ronnie and her starry eyes, watching Theo on stage like he was some kind of god. And then I imagine her crawling into the car with him and getting farted on for the duration of their sexual encounter. She fucking deserves it for leaving me stranded.

"He's always been a man of many talents," Rex quips.

"Our apologies on behalf of your friend," Todd adds.

Rex groans, then laughs. "I'll hit it with a can of Lysol tomorrow. Until then, man, crack a window, will you? I think the smell is traveling up here." He looks over at me. "Bet you wish you took a cab, huh?"

"I'm okay," I say, meeting his eyes. Something passes between us, and again I have that eerie feeling of connection to him. Like I already know him.

The car gets a little cold after Todd cracks the window, but the fresh air is a relief. Rex drops him off at an apartment complex in the Queen Anne neighborhood. It's one of those buildings that looks kind of like a motel, where the door to every unit is on the outside.

"See you tomorrow, man," Rex says as Todd gets out of the car.

"Yep. Bright and early, as usual." He sticks his head back inside. "Nice meeting you, Francesca."

I decide I like him. I'm not sure why. It's a gut feeling. "You too," I say. He slams the door shut and goes toward the apartment complex, swinging his long hair back over his shoulder.

Now I'm alone with Rex. Other than the uncanny feeling of familiarity, I'm not sure what I think of him.

"You cold?" he asks, surprising me. "I can turn the heat up." Without waiting for my answer, he reaches over and cranks up the heater. I feel the hot air blast out of the vents in front of me.

"Thanks," I say.

We both go quiet, but it's loud between us. I become super aware of his hands on the steering wheel. He has long, tapered fingers. Behind the wheel, he's completely relaxed, like driving is one of the ways he chills out.

"So, you just graduated from high school, huh?" he says. "Trying to figure out what to do with your life?"

"Pretty much," I agree. "How about you? When'd you graduate?"

"Few years ago."

"Are you still trying to figure it out? What to do with your life, I mean?"

"Nope." He looks over at me. "I'm doing it."

"You mean the band?"

He nods, once. "We all feel the same way. We're in it, one thousand percent."

"Well, you guys are super good," I tell him. "I hope you make it."

Rex looks over at me again. "Did you ever see us play before?"

"No. Never."

"What did you think?"

"I liked it," I tell him. "I liked it a lot."

It's the truth, and it was easy to say. But after I say it, something about Rex seems to shift. He was relaxed before, but now he seems lighter and happier.

"I'm glad you had a good time," he says. "Mind if I play some tunes?"

"Go for it," I tell him. I figure music will drown out any awkwardness between us.

And it does do that. As soon as loud metal music starts blasting from his speakers, there's no point trying to talk. But it doesn't make me less aware of him. Instead, it makes me more tuned into him. Like I'm feeling him respond to every nuance of the music we're listening to, almost on a subliminal level. It changes how I perceive it. Makes me hear it differently. Appreciate it more.

When we get near the Food Mart, he turns the music down so I can direct him to my mom's house.

"This is it," I say, pointing out our modest rambler.

Rex pulls the purple monster to a stop outside our front walkway. "Sorry if the music was too loud," he says.

"It's fine. I mean, it sounds like the stuff you play. Kind of? It makes sense if that's what you listen to all the time."

"I like other music too," he protests.

"Yeah? Like what?"

"Like..." he thinks. "Like David Bowie. Like Prince." Then he grins. "Barry Manilow."

"You do not like Barry Manilow." I laugh. "No way."

"Okay, maybe not. But definitely Bowie and Prince and a bunch of others. And yeah, okay, a lot of metal."

"Well, umm," I say. "Thanks for the ride."

"Hey, listen. Francesca."

"Yeah?" I look at him. His face is partly in shadow, partly lit from the streetlamp that's near our house. It makes him look pretty spectacular.

"I know we just met and everything," he says, "but could I have your number?"

I must look stunned, because he half smiles and adds, "You know, in case I need a wingman sometime?"

"Umm, sure," I recover. "Got anything to write with?"

"Uhh..." He gives me a dopey grin.

"I think I have a pen." I open my bag and dig around in it. "Found one." I hold the pen aloft. "Don't have any paper though."

"Write it on my arm." He pushes up his sleeve. I scoot a little closer to him and take hold of his arm. It's thin, but muscular. His skin is warm under my fingers as I hold his arm steady so I can write.

"Make it so I can read it," he says.

"I will."

I feel him watching while I carefully ink my number on his skin. It makes no sense, but I'm getting turned on again.

"Should I write my name, too?" I ask, once I've put the last digit on his arm.

"Nah, I'll remember."

"Okay." I pull back. "Well, that's it." I scoot toward the passenger door and click it open. "Thanks again for the ride."

His eyes gleam at me through the dark. "See you soon."

I get out of the car and walk up to our house. As soon as I open the door, I hear his car roar away, leaving a smelly cloud of exhaust behind. I go inside but don't turn on a light.

As my eyes adjust to the darkness, I stare at our small entryway, adorned with only a cheap bookcase and a spider plant.

"He probably won't call," I mutter.

And probably, he won't. He'll go to sleep, get up, and forget about my number on his arm. The next time he takes a shower, it'll wash off, and that will be that.

CHAPTER 5

I wake up to someone tapping on my door.

Groaning, I roll over in bed, then look at my alarm clock. Nine in the morning. It was around one am when Rex dropped me off last night, but I was wide awake, so I stayed up and read until three. I was planning to sleep in, since I don't have to be at work until later this afternoon. I stuff my pillow over my head, but I can still hear the tapping.

"What is it?" I yell out, pissed.

"Hey, can I come in?" It's Erick. Obviously. My mother wouldn't deign to be awake this early on a Saturday.

"Fine, okay." I sit up in bed as he opens my door.

My brother is eleven. He still hasn't had a major growth spurt, but lately, his voice has taken on this husky quality, like it's about to change. I figure I'll wake up one day and he'll be taller than me with this deep man-voice. But so far, that hasn't happened.

He shuts the door behind him with an air of importance, as if he expects to have a serious conversation. It kind of cracks me up, but I try to keep my face neutral.

"What's up?"

He comes all the way over to my bed and sits on the edge. That's unusual. Sitting on my bed when we talk is something he used to do when he was younger, but he hasn't wanted to be this close to me in at least a couple years.

"Hey," Erick says. "Hey, can I ask you something?"

"I let you in, right?"

He gives me a withering look, and I try even harder not to laugh.

"Yeah, sure," I sigh. "Ask me whatever you want."

"Did Ronnie drop you off last night?"

"Umm, no," I say. "Ronnie decided to stay with a friend in Seattle."

"Yeah. Yeah, so then did you get dropped off by this guy in a big purple car?"

Now I do laugh. "Were you spying on me?"

Erick's tone gets self-righteous. "I was up watching TV. His car was really loud, and I had to see what was going on. What if he was someone dangerous?"

"Okay," I relent, "I guess that *kind* of makes sense. And yeah, you're right. I did get dropped off by a guy in a purple car."

"So, the purple car guy, do you know him?" Erick seems all excited, but I have no idea why.

"Not exactly. I met him at this show I saw last night with Ronnie? He was nice and gave me a ride back."

Erick is popping with crazy energy as he stares at me. "Do you even know who he is?"

I wonder what's got into my little brother. "Is he some-body I'm *supposed* to know?"

"The lead singer of Fern on Fire drives a purple car just like that."

33

That *is* Rex's band. The question is how Erick knows any of this. Now I stare at him. "The lead singer?"

He nods vigorously. "Rex Thornton. Is that who brought you home?"

"Umm, yeah," I admit. "I guess that actually is who brought me home." I'm mystified. Erick doesn't go to shows. He would if he could. But the all-ages music scene in Seattle is basically dead because of a restrictive ordinance that makes it almost impossible for venues to hold events for people under eighteen. I can't think of how my brother would know about Rex or his band. Or his car, for that matter.

Erick starts to pace around my room, agitated. "How'd you meet him? I mean, have you known him for a long time?"

He is really freaking me out. How does he know about Fern on Fire, and why is he so amped about them? Sure, they were crazy good last night, but they weren't attracting the kind of attention a famous band attracts. The only people who even tried to talk to them after the show were me and Ronnie.

"How do you even know who he is?" I ask.

"They were on this local radio show? And they played some stuff from a demo tape of theirs and it was *so* killer. They were talking a lot, and Rex said he lives around here. So I figured out where his house is and...you know. What car he drives?"

Oh God. My brother is as bad as Ronnie.

"You've been stalking him?"

Erick stares at me like I'm missing the obvious. "They're *super* good, Frankie. And his mom's in the phone book, so it was easy. He only lives, like, five miles away."

"Okay," I say. "I don't care how easy it was to find him. That's still stalking."

My brother is dismissive. "People stalk famous people all the time."

"He isn't exactly famous," I point out.

"But he will be." My brother sounds one hundred percent certain, as if he's an authority on the subject at age eleven.

Still, I kind of agree with him. The truth is, I felt the same thing last night. Rex's band is good enough to get signed. I don't think last night's crowd came out for them, but they won almost everyone over by the end of their set. Including me. In fact, last night's show had the feel of seeing a big thing before it actually happens.

"Maybe," I say.

"I'm so jealous," he groans. "I bet they killed it."

"They were pretty amazing," I admit.

"I'm so fucking jealous."

Erick's not supposed to swear. But I overlook it. Then I try to placate him. "Maybe they'll play an all-ages show sometime. If they do, I'll take you."

My brother gives me another withering look. "No one plays all-ages shows in Seattle." Then his eyes go sly. "Are you still using a fake ID?"

I give him a warning look. "You're not supposed to know about that. And Mom definitely shouldn't know about that."

"Could you get me one?"

"Erick, even if I could, no one would believe you're twenty-one. Maybe in a couple years?"

"I wonder if Mom already knows about your fake ID?" he muses. I can sense the veiled threat. If I don't get him a fake ID, maybe, just maybe, he'll let Mom know that I have one.

"Even if she does know," I say, "I think we need to maintain the polite fiction that she *doesn't* know, in order to preserve our familial equilibrium."

There's an even more veiled threat in my words. I'm telling him if he rats on me about the fake ID, I might not smooth things over for him with Mom. Which is definitely something I do for him. All the time.

"Stop showing off with your big words," Erick mutters.

But I know I've won. He won't tell Mom about the fake ID.

"So will you tell me if Fern on Fire *does* play an all-ages show?" he asks. "I mean, in case they do?"

"Count on it."

In our unspoken brother/sister language, I know we're good now. So does he. He gets up and says, "I think Mom wants you to make breakfast."

"Do we not have cereal? Toast?"

Erick shakes his head. "We're out again." He slips out of my room without another word.

I stare at the door for a few minutes after he leaves. Then I heave myself out of bed, and shuffle to the kitchen to find something to conjure up for breakfast. There is no way I'm biking down to the convenience store this morning.

CHAPTER 6

Almost a week later, I haven't heard from Rex. I'm not surprised. I never really expected him to call—I didn't even bother telling Ronnie he gave me a ride home the night she abandoned me.

I've been avoiding her. Kind of. I don't think she's noticed, though. When she calls, all she wants to talk about is Theo. Apparently, after their first night together, he invited her to the band's next show. And that was it. Now they're a "thing."

Based on how long Ronnie's relationships usually last, I figure she'll be back at loose ends in a couple months. Give or take a few weeks. Maybe by then I won't be so pissed at her. In the meantime, I have enough to keep me busy. Like my job.

I work for this independent fast food-style restaurant. Even though the business has an official name, everyone just calls it the chicken shack. Customers call it that. Even employees and management call it the chicken shack. I don't love working there, but it's how I'm saving money for college.

After the dinner rush on Monday, I'm standing at the cash registers with one of my coworkers. It's late evening, so things are slow. We've already re-stocked the condiments and cleaned every surface, visible and hidden, so now we're just loitering and listening to the canned music in the dining room.

And then Rex walks in.

He's wearing sunglasses, but he takes them off as soon as he steps inside. It's such a cliched rock star gesture that I want to laugh, but he pulls it off, even though it's dark outside. It feels weirdly natural from him. As he walks up to the front counter, he seems to fill the whole dining room with his presence.

He stops in front of me. "Hey. How're you doing?"

"I'm doing well." He hasn't said my name, and I'm actually not sure if he recognizes me. So I do what I'm trained to do: I take his order. "What can I get started for you this evening?"

His eyes glitter at me with amusement, then he looks up at the menu board above my head.

"I hear the fish and chips are good." He kind of squints at me. "Are they?"

"Best fish and chips in town!" That's what we're supposed to say whenever someone asks if a menu item is good. It always feels ridiculous if a customer asks about, say, the mashed potatoes, which I happen to know are made not from scratch but from a mix. They're definitely not the best mashed potatoes in town.

Rex grins. "I'll take an order of that, and, uh...a large Coke."

I step in back and call out, "Fish and chips!" to the fry cook. During busy times we print up the orders from the register and put them on an order wheel. But I've learned from experience that when it's slow, it's better to shout the order to the cook. That way I know if he's paying attention.

I hear him yell, "On it!" from the kitchen. Then I go back to my register and ring up Rex's order. "That'll be four-fifty."

He hands over a five-dollar bill, and I give him back two quarters with his receipt.

"Your order number's on there," I tell him, pointing to the receipt. "We'll call it out when it's ready."

"Hey," he says, with this earnest look in his eyes.

"Yeah?"

"I'm sorry I didn't call you."

Okay. So he *does* know who he's talking to.

"Umm. Yeah?" I fold my arms across my chest. I hate that he's seeing me in my work uniform, which is blue polyester pants and a blue pinstripe polyester shirt, topped off with a matching blue visor. It's truly hideous.

"Yeah," he nods. "Your number kind of sweated off my arm while I was sleeping." He seems a bit sheepish about this, then he straightens up and looks directly at me. "Anyway, Ronnie told me you work here. So...I came here."

I'm not sure whether to be freshly angry with Ronnie or grateful to her.

"Yep," I say. "This is definitely where I work."

For a moment I'm afraid the conversation will just trail off into an eternal awkward silence. We'll be trapped in this moment forever. Neither of us will ever say anything, ever again.

And then he asks, "What time do you get off?"

"Eleven."

"Can I pick you up then?"

I never go out after work. I'm always tired, and I smell like greasy food. I usually want to go right home and take a shower, and I'd kind of like to shower if I'm going to be hanging out with Rex.

"I rode my bike here," I hedge.

"I'm positive it'll fit in my trunk," he says. "Trust me."

What is it about him? He's the sort of person I habitually avoid. But he has this thing. It's an irresistible blend of danger and sweetness, and I'm drawn to it, even though I don't want to be.

And so I hear myself telling him, "Yeah, okay, sure. Eleven. Wait, maybe make it like, ten minutes later? In case we get a late rush or something?"

"I'll be here at eleven-ten on the dot," he says.

The cook calls out his order, and I turn around to get it for him. As I hand it over, my co-worker places Rex's soda on the counter.

"There's your Coke," she says.

I totally forgot about his drink.

But he just switches on the full-sweetness version of his grin and says, "See you soon, Francesca." Then he walks out the door, sipping on his Coke and carrying his bag of fish and chips.

"Is that your boyfriend?" my co-worker asks.

"Not exactly. I just met him."

She raises an eyebrow. "He looks like trouble."

She's right. But I'm excited for Rex to pick me up later, anyway.

After my shift, I rush to the bathroom to change my clothes. I try to freshen up, swabbing damp paper towels in sweaty places and putting on fresh deodorant.

True to his word, at eleven ten, Rex shows up at the door. We've already locked up, so he presses his face against the glass and moves his eyes from side to side.

Weirdo. Laughing, I hurry to the door.

"Where's your uniform?" Rex asks, once I step outside.

I tap my shoulder bag. "In here."

He pulls a dramatic frown. "I was hoping you'd have it on. You look so hot in those clothes."

I stare at him, then roll my eyes. "You are so full of shit."

He grins, then asks, "Where's your bicycle?"

"Chained up in back."

"Let's get it."

We take my bike to his big purple car, and he pops the trunk. I'm expecting it to be full of crap, including things that might be harmful to my only mode of transportation. But it's almost empty, except for a spare tire and a couple flares.

"Wow," I say. "It's so clean."

"Yeah, I have to keep it that way. Sometimes we need it for hauling band gear. Let's see if your bike fits."

It takes a little maneuvering, but we manage it.

"See, I told you," he says, satisfied. He slams the trunk shut.

All at once, I feel shy. Last time I was in his car, I was reluctantly accepting a ride home. This time, it's sort of like a date. Not exactly, but closer to a date than not.

"Up for a drive?" he asks.

"Sure. Um, where do you want to go?" I ask, as I climb into the front of his car.

"Did you ever go to that place kind of behind the high school? That big empty field?"

I know what he's talking about. It was a place kids went to party during high school. Ronnie went there sometimes. But not me.

"There shouldn't be too many people there on a Monday night," he adds.

"Unless there's a football game."

Rex shakes his head. "No game. Anyway, the moon is full. Should be amazing."

Somehow, I doubt moon-gazing is his main objective. But then he looks over at me. "We could do something else if you want. Get something to eat, or try to find a late-night movie?"

He probably doesn't have a ton of money. And neither do I. Not if I want to keep it all in the bank for college. And that's definitely what I want.

He smiles and his eyes glitter at me as he adds, "No pressure."

No pressure. That could mean anything. *No pressure to see a movie with me. No pressure to get food if you're not hungry. No pressure to have sex in my car under the full moon in the field behind the high school.*

"I could go look at the moon." Suddenly, I have a strange feeling, like I'm sealing a portion of my fate. Not all of it. But it's like I just picked a certain direction for it. I still have options. But the path I'm on just got a little less broad.

Rex starts the car. "Let's go."

CHAPTER 7

When we drive onto the field behind the high school, no one else is there. We get out of Rex's car and lean against the passenger side to look up at the moon. It's enormous, spilling beautiful eerie light over the grass. Dark trees flank the field in the distance, and all the tree-tops in the moon's pathway are bathed in its light.

"It looks full," I say. "It is, right?"

"I think the actual full moon was a couple days ago," Rex replies. "But our eyes are still seeing it like it's a full moon."

I look over at him.

"My sister's into the moon and nature cycles and stuff like that." He shrugs. "I just take her word for it."

I look back at the sky. After a while, the moon seems to be shimmering, like something ephemeral that could vanish any moment.

"Did you come out here a lot when you were in school?" Rex asks.

"No. Not ever. Ronnie did, but not me."

"I can't even remember how many times I was here," he laughs. "I feel like I'm corrupting you, or something."

"Better late than never." I wrap my arms around my shoulders and shiver.

"It's pretty cold out," he says. "Want to get warm?"

We crawl back in the car, and he starts the engine so he can run the heat. I can't believe I'm on the party field with a sort-of famous musician. Talk about out of character. Erick would be thrilled if he knew I was hanging out with Rex again.

"I feel like I should inform you my little brother is your band's biggest fan," I tell him.

"Yeah? What's your brother like?"

I ponder the question. "He's eleven. Plays air guitar in his room a lot." I decide not to reveal that Erick has been stalking him. Maybe he'd think it's funny, but maybe not. "When I told him I saw you guys play he went ballistic. He wants me to get him a fake ID so he can go to one of your shows."

Rex grins. "Does he look old for his age?"

I laugh. "Not even close."

"Maybe we could sneak him into a show sometime," he suggests.

I turn to him. "Oh, my God. If you did that, he would think I was the best sister ever for the rest of my life. Or at least for a year. Maybe even a couple years."

Rex smiles at me by crinkling his eyes. "Well, then, I'll see what I can do." He leans forward and switches on the car stereo. I don't recognize the music.

"Is this the radio?" I ask.

"Nah, it's just this tape I made of music I like. You know, stuff that's not metal?" he says, glancing sideways.

"I never heard this song before."

He lets out a sort of self-conscious chuckle. "I like a lot of weird shit."

We go quiet and listen to the song. I can still see the moonlight shining on the field, but beyond that we're surrounded by pitch dark.

The music shifts to something that's still not metal, but aggressive in its own way. Aggressive, and kind of sexual.

I notice it's getting hot in the car, and Rex must feel the same, because he cuts the engine. "I think that's enough heat," he says. But he leaves the music on. My heart starts to beat faster, almost in tempo with the song, and it's so loud I feel like Rex should be able to hear it over the music.

"Hey, Francesca?"

I turn my head. "Yeah?"

He reaches over and cups my chin in his hand.

I take a deep breath. "Yeah?" I repeat. "What?"

He scoots over on the bench seat so he's sitting just inches from me. I try to control my breathing, but I'm not doing a good job. It's getting kind of heave-y and out of sync. Rex rests one hand gently on my knee. Then he turns my face toward him, and kisses me.

The night he asked for my number, I fantasized about kissing him. Then, as the days went by and he didn't call, I tried to convince myself he'd be bad at it. Pushy. Sloppy. Too overenthusiastic with his tongue. I think I always knew I was kidding myself.

The kiss starts slow. I can feel the warmth of his hand on my knee through my whole body. When his tongue darts quick inside my mouth, it's almost delicate, the way he does it. But just that little movement makes me melt, and I feel my insides pulse in response.

Like he can sense my reaction, he tightens his grip on my knee and slides his hand up the inside of my thigh. He kisses me deeper, and I let him push my legs further apart. He places his hand against my mound and begins stroking me with his finger.

He's touching me through the fabric of my jeans, but my body doesn't seem to notice. It's reacting as if his fingers are already pushing inside me. I whimper in his mouth as he keeps rhythmically stroking between my legs.

And then a pair of headlights swings across the car, blasting us both with light. I freeze, and his fingers stop moving. The car drives past us and stops. People start climbing out of it, making noise, laughing and talking. They sound at least a little drunk.

"Good. It's not the cops," Rex breathes. He resumes stroking between my legs and kissing me, but I push him away.

"What's wrong?" he whispers.

"They can see us," I whisper back.

"Nobody cares."

But I care. I push him away again. "Stop. They're too close."

He stops his finger mid stroke, and it presses against the fabric right where my clit is.

"You sure?" he asks.

My body clearly doesn't give two shits about the people in the car. It wants Rex to keep going. But the intrusion of the headlights gave my brain a chance to catch up with the rest of me. And now, I'm not sure this is what I want. It almost feels like too much. Like if I give in to him, I could get lost in him, or something.

"Yeah," I say. "They're making me nervous."

He sighs, then sort of shudders. But he moves off me, and slides back behind the wheel of the car.

"I'm sorry. I was..." I try to find the right words. "I was having a good time."

"But then that car drove up here and gave you a chance to think twice, didn't it?" he asks. He sounds upset. But I don't think he's upset with me. His tone kind of makes me think he's down on himself.

"No," I say, feeling a need to explain. "It's just, my boyfriend and me, we went out for a long time before we ever, you know. Had sex." I'm aware my rationalization is complete bullshit, but I keep going. "I know Ronnie's my friend but we're...different. She's always been more adventurous and, like, more mature than me."

"It's okay," Rex says. "I should take you home."

He turns off the music, and we drive back to my house in silence. I start to wonder if I made a mistake, pushing him away. *He'll never want to take me out again,* I think glumly. I'm sure he's used to girls who don't freak out over something like a pair of intrusive headlights. Ronnie would have been all over him.

When he pulls up in front of my house, he says, "Don't forget, we need to get your bike out of the trunk."

"Right." I turn toward him. "I'm sorry," I repeat.

"Don't be sorry," he says. Then his eyes glitter at me. "I'm just sorry I don't have somewhere more private to take you."

I feel the intent of his words between my legs. He still wants me. I'm relieved. And horny again. It's confusing. I'm confused.

"We're playing some shows out of town starting tomorrow," he goes on. "So, I won't see you for a while."

"Oh," I say as a horrible feeling grips the pit of my stomach and I realize I'm jealous. I wonder, while he's out of town, how many girls he'll meet who would fuck him in any circumstance. Probably at least a couple. A dozen? Hell, maybe even more than that.

"Yeah," he continues. "This other local band asked us to go with them, kind of last minute? They're doing pretty well, so...." He shrugs. "It's a good thing for us."

"How long are you going to be gone?" I ask.

"About a week. C'mon, let's get your bike."

I follow him to the back of his car and wait while he wrestles my bicycle out of the trunk and onto the pavement.

I take hold of the handlebars. "Thanks."

We stand there, watching each other.

"Hang on a minute," Rex says. He goes around to the driver's side and opens the door. I hear him fiddling around with something, then he comes back to me, and hands me a cassette in a plastic case.

"What's this?" I ask, as I take it from him.

"What we were listening to in the car. Lots more weird shit on there. You can borrow it if you want."

"Oh, umm, okay. Thanks." I drop the cassette in the front pocket of my shirt.

"I'll get it back from you when we get home," he says.

I start to relax. The moon is still with us, shining down over the tops of the other houses in the neighborhood. I can feel the connection between me and Rex. It's still there. I'm sure of that much.

"See you when I get back," he says.

"See you then."

He waits in his car until I wheel my bicycle safely inside our attached garage. I'm half expecting Erick to come creeping out of the darkness, babbling with excitement about the fact that Rex Thornton of Fern on Fire is at our house again.

But he doesn't. Maybe he's asleep.

I quietly open the door between the garage and the kitchen, then take Rex's tape to my room. He's labeled it "weird-ass songs" but "*weird*" is spelled wrong. So the label actually reads "*wierd*-ass songs." I laugh. It makes me feel close to him, in a way. Yeah, he's kind of incredible. But he's also not perfect.

I slide the tape in my boombox and rewind to the first song. Then I lie down on my bed, slap on headphones, and listen. I get myself off while I do, because even though I stopped Rex back in his car, my body kept going. It still needs release.

After I come, I keep listening to Rex's mixtape. I want to see him when he gets back. But if we actually hook up, I have this feeling that somehow, in some way, I *am* going to lose myself.

CHAPTER 8

"Frankie!" Mom yells as she bursts through the front door. "Are you home?"

"In the kitchen!" I call out.

My mother enters our small kitchen. Her face, as always, is lined with stress.

It's hard to see your mother as anything but your mom. Once, Jason told me he thought she was hot, which gave me this kind of creepy feeling. But it also made me look at Mom in a different way. And I can see it now, how pretty her face is. But most of the time, all I see is the stress. Maybe because she's always trying to unload some of it on me.

Mom sets her purse down on the edge of the kitchen counter, and eyes the sandwich I've been making.

"Did you use the last package of deli meat?" she asks.

"No? There's, like, two more packages in the fridge." I lick some mayonnaise off my fingers and put the two halves of my sandwich together.

"Okay, good. Remember, we need those for Erick's lunches this week."

"Yeah, I know." I'm not sure why she's harping on me

about Erick's lunches. I'm usually the person who makes his lunch, not her.

She lets out a sigh. "I need to talk to you."

Uh oh. This doesn't sound good.

I take a bite of my sandwich, then set it down on the plate I got out earlier. "Sure. What do you want to talk about?"

"I'll just come out and say it, I guess." She fixes me with a serious look. "I need you to start paying rent."

My mind flies to my bank account. The money I plan to use for my escape. I can feel it starting to drain away, dollar by dollar.

"But you said—" I start, then stop. "I thought I was helping you out with the house, and Erick, instead of paying rent?"

"I still need you to do those things," Mom says. "But I also need you to pay rent. The price of everything is going up, and if you're going to live here, use the water and the space and eat the groceries, then I need you to pitch in a bit."

"I see. How much?"

"Fifty dollars a month."

"That's a big chunk of my paycheck," I object. "I'm saving that money for college."

"It's a lot less rent than you'd pay anywhere else," she points out.

"Yeah, but if I lived somewhere else, I wouldn't have to worry about Erick."

"I hope you'd still care about your brother, even if you didn't live here."

I feel like screaming. What would she do if I went to school in another state? Am I supposed to take care of Erick for the rest of his life? Once my brother starts junior high next year, he's going to resent anyone who tries to take care of him. Including me.

I can't say any of this out loud, though. She might blow up or start crying, and I don't want to deal with either scenario. My dad was a struggling addict, and he left the picture a long time ago. Right after Erick was born. Ever since then, Mom has kind of relied on me as a second parent. Sometimes it feels like too much to handle. But Mom gets surly and upset when she thinks I'm not doing my part to keep our family together.

I feel my shoulders slump. "When do you want me to start paying rent?"

"Next month. But if you want to find your own apartment, you could do that. Maybe you and Ronnie could get a place."

I'm not getting an apartment with Ronnie. I can just imagine how that would be. Guys like Theo and Rex coming into our space at all hours. Ronnie forgetting to pay the rent and the bills and...no thanks. I have a feeling my mom knows this.

I pick up my sandwich plate, and start out of the kitchen. "I'll give you a rent check on November first."

"Are you going to clean this up?" Mom asks, gesturing to the kitchen counter, where I left a loaf of bread and the empty deli meat container.

"I'm starving," I tell her. "I'll come back and clean up after I eat." I don't actually like to leave a mess in the kitchen, either. Even a small one. But I don't want to be around Mom right now.

I eat the sandwich sitting cross-legged on my bed. *Fifty dollars a month.* Assuming I get into college by next fall, paying that amount in rent will cut my savings by about six hundred bucks. I want to believe Mom supports my college ambitions. But I suspect she doesn't. In fact, sometimes I wonder if she's trying to sabotage me. But every time that thought crosses my mind, it seems paranoid. Mothers don't try to sabotage their children. Right?

And, to be honest, I kind of dropped the ball during my senior year. I could have applied for scholarships and I just...didn't. I'm not sure why. I graduated with a 4.0 GPA, and I got great scores on the SAT. But the deadlines for applications came, then went.

When I take my dirty plate out to the kitchen, the small mess I left behind is still waiting for me. Mom also left me a note.

Please start the dishwasher after you clean up your sandwich mess.

The note makes me angry, and I slam my plate down on the counter. I have an urge to throw it across the room, let it shatter in a zillion pieces, then refuse to clean up both messes. But that's not the kind of thing I do. Getting pissed and slamming things around in the kitchen is Erick's department, not mine. So, instead, I carefully clean up my sandwich things, then put my empty plate in the dishwasher and start it.

When I get home from work the next night, I sit down with my copy of the Princeton Review and start addressing envelopes to each college I've marked as appealing. I'm determined to apply to every scholarship I can realistically qualify for.

It's a long shot. I haven't done anything notable since I graduated from high school. But in school, I was on the newspaper staff. I excelled at it. I even won an award for one of my articles. I'm not sure if I want to be a journalist, but my high school journalism experience is the best thing I've got to leverage in my favor besides my grades and my test scores. So I figure journalism scholarships are my best bet.

I know what I truly want is to get out of this house. College has always seemed like the most logical way to make that happen. Plus, I have a hunch I'll never be able to break away from my mother unless I put a significant amount of physical distance between us.

As I carefully fill out the address labels, intrusive thoughts about Rex begin to distract me. Ronnie thinks the guys will be back home from their tour by Friday. That's in three days.

In my head, I keep seeing Rex standing in the parking lot behind the music venue in Seattle. Smoking his cigarette. Sizing me up. But the memory I return to most is the way he cupped my chin in his hand just before we started making out. There was something so possessive yet sweet about it.

I still think of him the way I would have in high school —like a stoner who means nothing but bad news for my life. *Except.* Except there's something kind of magic about him. I groan. The last thing I need is to fall under the spell of someone like Rex. I need to focus on my future.

I don't allow myself to go to bed until I've addressed every last envelope. One way or another, I'm going to make up for lost time. I *am* going to college. Whether my mother wants to help me, or not.

CHAPTER 9

Several days before Halloween, Ronnie calls to tell me the guys are back from their tour. But mostly, she wants to talk about Theo. Endlessly.

"Are you mad at me?" she asks, suddenly.

"No. Not exactly," I hedge.

She's decisive. "We need to talk. And I need to go to the mall. I'm going to come pick you up, and then we can shop and...you know. Talk."

I could say no. I want to say no. I'm still pissed at her for abandoning me with three fourths of Fern on Fire in Seattle. For not having my back. But Ronnie's been my best friend for a long time. Habit and loyalty are strong forces.

"Fine," I give in. "Come get me. But don't say anything about what I'm wearing. Comments about my wardrobe choices are off-limits."

When I get in Ronnie's car, I can tell she's biting back her response to my outfit. I'm wearing a couple layers of black shirts over my rattiest pair of jeans. But she manages to keep her opinions to herself.

"It's good to see you!" she gushes. "I'm *so* ready to shop."

When it comes to shopping money, Ronnie's lucky. She has a job in retail, though she works fewer hours than I do. However, she also receives regular infusions of cash from her dad, who divorced her mom about five years ago. His money more than makes up for Ronnie's lack of earning power. Her dad doesn't spend much time with her or her sister, but he's always giving them presents. Or rather, sending them presents. He lives in another state.

At the mall, Ronnie pops into several stores and looks at things that she calls "cute" or "gorgeous." I tag along. This part of the trip is just the prelude to her actual reason for being here. About four stores in, I'll find out what she's really here to buy.

As it turns out, she's here for lingerie. She wants to surprise Theo. I hang out with her in the fancy dressing room while she tries stuff on. It's one large room with a separate changing area behind a screen, so I don't have to ogle Ronnie while she's squeezing into each tiny piece of fabric.

"Don't you want to try anything?" she asks, from behind the screen.

"Why are you friends with me?" I laugh. Sometimes I really wonder. We aren't into the same guys. We don't have the same interests. And I've never liked lingerie. My fashion sense is more tomboyish. Sometimes I pick out a bra with a little lace on it, but that's as far as I go.

Ronnie steps out from behind the screen. "What do you think of this one?"

This one barely covers her up. It's all black, with a thong panty that leaves her ass completely bare. And the piece of the garment that covers her boobs is all mesh, so her nipples are showing.

"It's sexy?" I shrug.

"But do you think Theo will like it?"

"How the hell would I know? I'm not Theo. I have no idea what he likes or doesn't like."

Ronnie surveys herself critically in the mirror, turning around and looking at her ass, then placing her hands on her hips and staring at herself from the front.

"Too obvious," she concludes, and goes back behind the screen. "So are you going to try anything or not?" she asks again.

"It's not really my thing," I remind her.

She pokes her head around the side of the screen. "You might want to make it your thing."

"Why?"

"Rex," she says, then disappears.

"I don't even know Rex."

"That's not what I heard."

"I mean, he drove me home the night you just *left me there* in Seattle. If you want to call that *knowing* him..."

Ronnie comes back out and stands in front of the mirror. "That's not what I heard," she repeats. This time, she's wearing a bright red number. This one's less risqué. It's more cleavage and peek-a-boo butt cheeks than exposed nipples and bare ass.

But now, I'm catching on to her insinuating tone. "What did you hear?" I ask, alarmed.

She smirks. "I heard you and Rex went to the field behind the school."

And where would Ronnie hear that? Theo, probably. And where would Theo have heard it? Rex. He hasn't even been in touch since he got back in town, but apparently, the jerk told his friends about what happened between us. Of course he did. All guys are the same.

"We didn't have sex," I say. I half expect her to reply, *That's not what I heard*. If she does, I'll know Rex didn't just tell his friends about us, he also lied to them about what happened.

Instead she says, "But you guys had a good time, right?"

"Is that what you heard?" I ask, drily.

"Don't be pissed, Frankie," she says, turning away from the mirror to look at me. "I think Rex really likes you."

If I admit to her that I've been thinking about him, she'll never shut up about it. Plus, he's apparently been blabbing about me to his friends. "He's not my type."

She gets this hyper-incredulous look on her face. "Are you crazy? Then what the hell is your type?"

I shrug. "Not someone like him."

"So you prefer someone boring, like Jason?"

"Yeah, maybe," I say. "What's wrong with that?"

"Nothing," she turns back to the mirror. "If you like boring." She does the hands-on-hips pose again, then nods at herself. "This is the one. I'm done here." She goes back behind the screen to change.

After Ronnie makes her purchase at the lingerie store, we go to the mall's food court to get something to eat.

"Were you pissed off when I left you behind?" she asks, suddenly. "That first night I hooked up with Theo?"

Now that she's point blank asked me, I can't avoid it. "Yeah, I kind of was," I admit. "Actually, I was super pissed at you."

"I had a feeling something was wrong," she groans. "We need to talk, then, right?"

I shrug. "It was weeks ago."

"But I shouldn't have left you." She looks anguished. "I

mean, if the other guys had been total assholes? I left you in a bad situation."

"That's definitely it." I nod. "So, how about we just agree we won't abandon each other like that. Okay?"

She reaches out and touches my hand. "Okay. I'm sorry, Frankie."

I wave my hand, like I'm waving away her transgression. Now that she's apologized, I don't feel like holding a grudge. Besides, normally, I can count on her. Everyone slips up sometimes. "I'm actually more pissed at Rex," I confess. "I can't believe he told Theo what happened."

She practically squeals. "So something *did* happen?"

"Well, yeah," I admit. "Something happened."

Ronnie looks genuinely excited. She's happy for me, almost like I've reached some sort of important milestone.

All at once, I have a vision of her as a mom. Living in a suburban home. Telling her kids stories about her wild days, back when she used to chase after "dangerous" guys. How crazy she was back then. I bet her future kids will love that about her.

When I peer into my future, all I see is me trying to get *out* of the present moment. Somewhere far away from the life I'm currently living. I can't see anything further than that. That feels wrong, somehow. Shouldn't I want something else?

"Okay, so what happened with Rex?" Ronnie's asking. "Are you going to tell me?"

I shrug one shoulder. "We made out a little, that's all. It's not a big deal."

"Theo thinks Rex is way into you."

I shake my head. "Doubt it."

"Why?"

"Pretty sure I'm not his type, either."

Ronnie ignores me. "They're playing a show on Halloween. You should come with me."

"Maybe," I say.

"You're coming with me," she orders, with as much sternness as she can muster.

"Maybe," I repeat.

CHAPTER 10

Despite Ronnie's nagging, the day before the Halloween show, I decide to skip it. I haven't heard from Rex, and I'm not sure I even want to see him. Then, I get a phone call.

Erick yells for me from the kitchen. "Frankie! Phone!"

He's left the phone off the hook on the kitchen counter, and I pick it up, expecting Ronnie. "Hey."

"Hey, Francesca."

It's Rex. My heart starts beating faster, which annoys me.

"Hey," I say. "How is, umm... How was your tour?"

"Awesome. Better than we expected. Listen, did Ronnie tell you about the show we're playing? On Halloween?"

"Yeah, she mentioned it." Then the anger, and maybe also hurt, bubbles up to the surface. "Ronnie also told me she knows about us parking in your car in that field behind the school."

"Shit," he says, mildly. "Theo opened his big mouth. Little fucker."

61

"Actually," I point out, "aren't *you* the one who opened *your* big mouth?"

There's a pause on the other end of the line. Then Rex asks, "Are you pissed?"

"I didn't think you were going to tell everyone about it."

"I didn't tell everyone," he corrects. "Just the guys in the band."

"You told your whole band!"

"Yeah. Listen. It's not disrespect. I didn't mean it that way, anyway." Another pause. "They were all saying I didn't have a chance with you. I just wanted them to know they were wrong."

"So you used me to prove a point?"

He's quiet for a few seconds, then admits, "Kinda?"

My voice starts to raise. "Kind of? You know what? That kind of makes me feel like complete crap." Shit. I need to keep it down—I don't want Erick or Mom hearing this conversation.

"I'm sorry," Rex says.

I slump against the counter. It's not a weird thing for a guy to do. It's a very guy thing for a guy to do. Mostly, I'm pissed at myself for thinking there was something special about the evening I spent with him, or about the fact that he loaned me his mixtape of "wierd-ass songs."

Nope. It was just another case of a guy trying to score. I'm the one who's been listening to his mixtape over and over, thinking about what each song "means" to him. I'm an idiot.

"Listen," he tries again. "I wondered if you want to come to our show tomorrow?"

"The Halloween show?"

"Yeah. We'll put you on the guest list."

On a social level, this matters. Anyone with eyes and

ears knows his band is going places. But I'm still not sure I want to see Rex again.

"I'll have to think about it." I wait for him to get offended. He probably thinks I'm snubbing him. If he does, tough shit.

But he just says, "Okay. If you change your mind, you're on the list."

"Don't do that—" I start.

He rides over my words. "Talk to you later." Then he hangs up the phone. I stare at the receiver as it beeps at me, then slowly replace it in its cradle on the wall. I'm frustrated by the whole conversation. Did Rex even understand what I was trying to tell him? I doubt it, because somehow, he still thinks I'm coming to his show tomorrow night.

Erick is waiting for me in the hallway.

"Were you eavesdropping?" I ask.

"Who was on the phone?" he counters.

I push past him.. "A guy from work. He wants me to trade shifts."

"Didn't sound like a guy from work," Erick calls after me as I go in my room.

I slam my door shut, something I haven't done since my sophomore year of high school. I'm mad and restless, and confused. Mostly, I'm mad at myself. Pissed that I'm still living at home, dealing with so many things that are intrinsically disappointing. My relationship with Mom. The trajectory of my own life, which is basically going nowhere. And boys. Men. Guys. Whatever.

Something has to change. Doesn't it? Isn't it about time?

. . .

THE DAY OF HALLOWEEN, I emerge from a long shower after noon, then slowly wander out to the kitchen. There's a note for me on the counter letting me know that Ronnie called.

I dial her number, and she answers right away, sounding breathless and eager.

"Hey," I say. "What's up?"

"Frankie!" she squeals. "Are you getting excited for tonight? What are you wearing? Are you dressing up for Halloween?"

"Yeah, umm. About tonight. I'm not going."

"What? What do you mean you're not going?"

"I mean I'm not going. I don't want to go. So, you know, have fun with Theo and...everybody."

"No," she says vehemently. "That is not acceptable. Don't go anywhere. I'm coming over." She hangs up.

I don't believe her. She's pissed, but not enough to come banging on my door. Five hours later, it seems like I'm right. By early evening, there's still no sign of Ronnie. It's getting dark, and we've already had a few trick-or-treaters.

The thing is, I *could* go out. I'm not working tonight, and Mom gets super proprietary about the house on Halloween. She likes to be the person who answers the door and hands out candy, and she also likes to keep an eye on the yard in the late evening. She won't be going anywhere. Erick, meanwhile, has decided he's too old for trick-or-treating. He's already locked in his room, listening to music. Probably trying to commune with the dark side. Since, for once, my services are not required, I'm planning to curl up in my room and read something mindless.

There's the sound of someone pounding loudly on the door. Mom goes to answer it with the basket of candy bars in her hand.

"Oh, hi, Ronnie," she says, surprised. "Frankie didn't say you were coming over."

"She must have forgot to mention it. Can I come in?"

"Are you two going out tonight?" Mom asks as she stands aside.

"No," I say, just as Ronnie simultaneously calls out, "Yes!"

She pushes inside the house, carrying two large bags. Then she nods her head in the direction of my room. "I need to talk to you."

I sigh and follow her down the hall. We go into my room, and she bumps the door shut behind us with her butt. Then she sets her bags down on my bed, puts her hands on her hips, and stares at me.

"You're going with me tonight. I don't want to hear any excuses."

"I already told you I don't want to go. You don't need me. Theo will be there, right?"

"That is not the point. You know they put you on their guest list, right?"

"So have them put somebody else on it," I retort.

"Rex said you *have* to be on it. If you don't go, you're keeping somebody else from being on the list, and that's kind of shitty, Frankie."

I'm getting exasperated. "I didn't ask to be on their stupid list. Tell Theo to take me off."

"He's not going to do that," Ronnie says, speaking to me like I'm a child and she's trying to be patient with me.

I fold my arms across my chest. "I feel like I'm being manipulated."

"Frankie, for God's sake. I know you like their band. You don't even have to pay for the show! And it's Halloween.

Don't you want to have fun? Don't you want to hang out with me? What's your problem?"

The problem is Rex. The problem is I don't want to see him. But Ronnie's starting to wear me down. It *is* Halloween, and however I feel about Rex right now, I do like his band. And wouldn't it be better to go out tonight, instead of sitting at home with my mom and my brother? Isn't that kind of pathetic?

"Okay," I sigh. Ronnie wins again. "I'll go with you. But I'm not wearing a costume."

"Oh, but you are." Ronnie reaches over to the bags on the bed and lifts them both high. "That's what these are for."

An hour later, after trying on several costumes, Ronnie has coaxed me into some sort of crazy black dress. It has a long, form fitting skirt with a side slit, and spaghetti straps. The straps seem like they're more for decoration than for actually holding anything up. She's also convinced me to wear these taped on nipple-covering bra things, because one of my actual bras would look "tacky."

Finally, she adds colored mousse to my hair, so that it looks jet black, instead of its usual brown, then parts it so I have no bangs. I look different.

"What am I supposed to be?" I ask, as I stare at myself in the full-length mirror.

"Morticia Addams," she says.

I tug at the sides of the black dress. "I don't think I look scary enough to be Morticia Addams."

"You need three things." Ronnie reaches inside her bag. "Black nail polish. Eye pencil. Red lipstick."

"Where'd you get all this shit?" I ask.

"The mall. Duh. Do your own makeup, okay? I need to get into my costume."

I reach for the eye pencil, which looks thick and black, and Ronnie stops me. "Do the nail polish first, so it has time to dry."

Putting on nail polish is one of the few girly things I'm good at. For most of high school, I was into wearing eclectic colors on my nails. While I carefully paint my nails black, I watch Ronnie transform herself. When she's finished, she's wearing the piece of red lingerie she bought at the mall, but she's added a topcoat with tails, and a black top hat.

"What are you again?" I ask, blowing on my nails to dry the polish.

"A ringmaster," she says, as she checks herself out in the mirror. Then she turns around and grins at me. "Basically, your standard Halloween slut."

I retrieve the eye pencil and red lipstick and go to the mirror, nudging Ronnie aside. "Move. I need to finish my face."

"Now you're getting in the Halloween spirit," she says, sounding satisfied.

It's after eight by the time we're finally ready to leave. Erick's in the kitchen fixing himself a snack. He does a double take when Ronnie and I walk past.

"You two look amazing!" He can't seem to believe our transformation. I claw at him with one of my hands and cackle maniacally. Then I whisper to Ronnie, "Don't tell him where we're going or he'll freak out."

So of course, she does the exact opposite. "We're going to see Fern on Fire," she announces proudly to him. "Be jealous!"

I kick at her with the toe of my shoe.

"Ouch!" she cries, turning around to give me a dirty look.

"Frankie!" Erick bursts out. "You said you were going to take me—"

"I will, I'll take you, I promise! As soon as it works out." I give him a look to remind him Mom is within earshot. "But now we have to swoop away and haunt the city!" I cackle again.

Being Morticia is actually kind of fun. Or at least, being my dorky interpretation of her is fun.

"Have a good time," Mom calls out from the living room. "Drive safe."

Did she hear Ronnie say that we're going to see a band? Maybe she already knows we use fake IDs. Maybe she doesn't care. Or maybe she thinks Fern on Fire is the name of some obscure Halloween movie, but I kind of doubt it.

"Sure thing, Ms. Peterson!" Ronnie calls out. As we go outside to her car, she hisses, "What did you kick me for? That hurt!"

"I told you not to tell Erick where we're going. It's insane that he knows about them, but they're his number one favorite band. More than that. He's *obsessed* with them. You just ruined his night."

"Oh, shit, I'm sorry. Why don't you have Rex sneak him in sometime?"

I groan. Rex seems to be the bestower of all worthwhile things. Spots on the guest list. Illegal entry to his band's shows. "Wierd-ass" mixtapes.

"Let's just go," I say, nudging Ronnie in the direction of her car.

As I wait for her to unlock my door, I check my bag to be sure Rex's mixtape is there. I'm going to give it back to him tonight. Then I can get on with my life and forget about him.

CHAPTER 11

"Nobody else is dressed up," I tell Ronnie, as we approach the venue. There's no separate queue for people on the bands' guest lists, so we get in line with everybody else.

"Other people are dressed up!" Ronnie objects.

"Yeah, like maybe two other people?"

"At least four or five!"

I level a look at her.

"Theo dared me to do it," she says, finally. "I thought it would be more fun if you did it with me."

"Theo sounds like a *great* guy."

"He is a great guy. C'mon, Frankie, you were having fun before we got here. Can you just keep having fun? For once?"

Then I feel bad. It's not strange that Ronnie wants to have a good time on Halloween. I'm the one who's acting strange. "It's okay," I reassure her. "I'm glad we came out."

Ronnie tips her head. "You sure?"

"I'm sure." To prove it to her, I flap some imaginary bat wings and let out another Halloween cackle.

She wrinkles her nose at me. "Don't be weird, Frankie."

When we get to the door, Ronnie butts up against the door guy's table. "Fern on Fire's guest list."

"Name?" He sounds bored.

She gives him her name, and he crosses her off the list. Then he looks at me.

"Frankie."

He glances down at his list and frowns. "Don't see anyone named Frankie on here."

"That's messed up!" Ronnie yelps. "I know for a fact she's on it."

"Well, I know for a fact that I don't see that name on here," the guy snaps back.

"Oh wait," I say. "What about Francesca?"

He looks back down at the list and finds it. Before he crosses it off, he asks, "That's you? Francesca?"

"It's my real name," I tell him. "Frankie's just a nickname."

He crosses me off the list. "Go on in."

The opening band is just starting to play. Not only are Ronnie and I pretty much the only people in costumes, we also seem to be part of a small contingent of women attending the show. This is clearly a night for dudes.

The dudes are already moshing in the area in front of the stage, slamming into each other's bodies, lifting one another above the crowd. They look like they're having a blast, but it's not a great place for two chicks dressed up like Ronnie and me.

"Let's go backstage," she says.

"Huh?"

She takes my arm and pulls me with her, back behind the stage, which is an area I've always thought of as off limits, where the sound guys and other club employees go.

Where band members disappear after they've been out in the club having a drink or talking to people. It's a forbidden zone. I've never even considered trying to gain entrance.

But now we're going there, because I guess Ronnie is above the rules. We end up in this narrow corridor that seems to be behind the stage. There's a lot of dudes back here, some long-haired, some not. To me, they all look kind of pissed off, and I'm expecting them to chase us away any minute.

Somewhere down the hall I hear guys laughing, and I smell cigarette smoke. Ronnie seems totally in her element. She's excited and happy. But I'm not. I wish I hadn't let her talk me into this.

And then Theo pokes his head out of a door and comes over to us. He grabs Ronnie by the waist and holds her out at arms length. "You actually fucking did it."

"Told you I would."

He's all over her then, kissing her, grabbing her ass, her top hat falling off. I just stand there in my black dress and red lipstick, feeling dumb.

The floor is gross and sticky under my shoes. I eye Ronnie's hat, which landed on its side, and bend down to rescue it from the gunky floor. When I straighten up, Rex is standing in front of me. He's in all black. Black ripped jeans, black shirt, and his black leather jacket. We kind of match.

He does a double take, then grins. "Elvira?" he guesses.

I shake my head. "Morticia Addams."

Ronnie and Theo break apart. Sort of. They're still clinging to each other. To his credit, Theo seems as into Ronnie as she is into him. That's not usually how it is with the guys she chases.

I hold out her hat, and she takes it.

"It's kind of gross, it was on the floor..." I warn her. But she pops it right back on her head.

Rex and I look at each other again. I'm still pissed at him. But, dammit, he looks good.

"You girls went all out," he observes. But he's still looking at me.

"I had to force Frankie to get dressed up," Ronnie laughs. "She didn't want to do it."

"Oh, but I'm totally into it now!" I flap my imaginary bat wings, start cackling, and swoop away from all of them, through the backstage corridor, then out into the club.

Once I'm there, I'm not sure what got into me. But I felt kind of trapped. Like I was expected to behave a certain way, and I didn't feel like playing along.

I retreat to the bathroom. Since it's Halloween and I *am* in costume, I reapply my blood red lipstick in front of the bathroom mirror. Then I go out and stand at the edges of the crowd, out of range of the moshing dudes near the stage. The opening band is all right. They're good, but they don't grab me like Rex's band does.

Eventually, Ronnie finds me. "You missed out," she says. "There's extra beer in the green room."

"Oh no! No beer for me!" I cry out, singsong.

She gives me a disgusted look. "I don't get why you're acting this way. Rex really likes you. Are you trying to ruin it?"

I return her look. "I don't give a fuck what he thinks about me, so stop telling me how I should act around him."

"Yes, you do," she counters. "You definitely give a fuck, and you're blowing it."

I stare at her. Then, slowly, I start flapping my "wings" again and dash away from her to the other side of the room.

The opening band has just finished its set, and the

lights go up. Music starts blaring over the club's PA system. The Cult.

Why should I care if Rex likes me? So he almost made me come. So what? That doesn't mean I have to act like some idiot girl who's excited just because he knows my name. And why should I risk losing myself to some dude in a band who doesn't even respect me? I don't need him to feel good about myself.

Then I feel a tap on my shoulder. "Hey, Batgirl."

I turn around, and there's Rex.

"Hey," I say. Then wait.

A grin starts at the corners of his mouth, then takes over his face. "Just wanted to tell you thanks for coming out."

"Sure." I fold my arms across my chest. His eyes drop to my boobs, and I remember this dress is a little more generous with the cleavage than the clothes I usually wear. I drop my arms back to my sides, feeling silly.

His eyes glitter at me. "You look amazing." Then he starts to walk away. "Enjoy the show," he says, over his shoulder. Someone comes up to him, and he leans close to hear what they're saying.

"What did Rex want?"

It's Ronnie. I turn around and look at her. "He said thanks for coming to the show."

"I told you he likes you," she says.

"Great. But I'm not going to pretend I'm some person I'm not just because some guy *might* be into me."

"So, this Batgirl thing is who you really are?" she scoffs.

I grin at her. "Maybe you've just never seen this side of me before. *You* made me wear this stupid dress, remember? Maybe it magically turned me into my true bat self."

"You're *so* weird," Ronnie groans.

I put my arm around her and squeeze. "But you like me this way, right?"

We drift closer to the stage but stay behind the mosh pit. When the lights go down and the band comes out, I'm excited. This time, I know what to expect.

They don't disappoint.

When Rex is onstage, I can forget what I know—that he's just a guy. That he told his friends he felt me up in his car. That he probably cares more about his band than anything else, including more than any girl. Woman. Whatever.

But onstage, he's magnificent. He's doing the thing he's meant to be doing. The whole room can feel it. When he sings, you see the best of him, and it's kind of impossible not to fall in love with that. He doesn't talk to the crowd much between songs, but when he does, he's relaxed. He knows he belongs up there.

After the show, I let Ronnie drag me backstage again. It's understood, it's inevitable. We end up in the green room with the band. Todd offers me a beer, and I sip it, gingerly, while I watch the rest of the night play out.

Todd and Theo are talking about going to a Halloween party at someone's house nearby. Ronnie seems super into the idea, and I groan inwardly. Since she's my ride, I'm probably going to end up at the party, too.

"I hate to spoil the Halloween spirit," Noah cuts in, "but all of our shit has to go back to the practice space tonight."

"We'll get it there!" Theo reassures him.

"Right, well I know *I'll* get it there, because it fits in my van. It's kind of strange how the guy with the van always ends up loading the gear."

"I'll help you, man," Rex says. "Let these other idiots get wasted."

"We'll be the responsible ones." Noah lets out a dramatic sigh. "I'm always one of the responsible ones."

"Except when you're not," Theo laughs.

"Actually, I need to take Frankie home," Ronnie says. "So I have to be responsible, too."

Great. Now I'm a burden. I can tell Ronnie really wants to go to the party. But I'm not going to give. She begged me to come out with her tonight. And she promised not to abandon me again.

"I'd take her home if I had a car," Todd offers.

Noah snorts. "Well, that's helpful."

"I can take her home." Rex turns to me. "As long as you don't mind riding along to the practice space?"

Suddenly everyone's eyes are on me. It wouldn't take a psychic to figure out that Todd, Theo, and Ronnie really want Rex to take me home.

"Sure, that's fine," I sigh.

That seems to make everyone happy. Ronnie mouths "thank you." Then she flicks her eyes in Rex's direction, and winks at me.

I roll my eyes in response. But I think, when I agreed to come out tonight, I kind of knew this was how things were going to turn out.

A little later, I'm with Rex in his car, following Noah to the practice space. When we left, everyone else was on their way to the Halloween party. We haven't spoken yet. Instead, we're just driving in silence.

Suddenly, I can't help myself. I break it.

"It *is* disrespect," I say.

"Huh?" He throws a glance my way, then looks back at the road.

"When you told the guys about us making out in your car? That *was* disrespectful."

"Is that what we were doing?" he drawls. "'Making out?' I kind of thought it was going somewhere better than that."

His words make me flash back to his hand pressed between my legs. How turned on I was.

"That's not the point," I tell him.

"So what's the point?"

What is the point? Right now, I actually can't think of one. I try to explain my feelings, instead. "It's like you took something from me and then gave it to them. And that... kind of felt like shit."

Rex goes quiet. Then he says, "I don't want you to feel like shit."

Words dry up for both of us. He pulls up and parks on the street behind Noah. "You can stay in the car while we unload if you want," he tells me. "It won't take long."

I look around at the street, which seems deserted but also gives me a creepy vibe. "I'd rather not."

"Okay, Batgirl," he says. "C'mon."

I exit the car and stand out on the street, shivering in my dress. Noah opens the back of the van and starts unloading pieces of his drum kit onto the pavement. Rex helps him, then sits on the back edge of the van and lights a cigarette. He pats the spot next to him. "Have a seat."

"Aren't you helping him carry it inside?" I ask, as I sit down.

"Somebody's gotta watch everything so nothing gets stolen. Otherwise, we'd have to take stuff in a little at a time. Lock up the van each time we go in. Trust me, this is faster."

Noah props open the door of the building we're parked in front of. Then he grabs several pieces of his kit and disappears inside.

I perch on the edge of the van floor and try to suppress my shivering. Rex ashes his cigarette on the ground, then pops it back in his mouth. Without saying anything, he shrugs out of his leather jacket and drapes it over my shoulders.

I look over at him. "Thanks."

He shrugs. "I could feel the van shaking from you shivering over there."

We continue to sit in silence as Noah gets the rest of his kit inside. Rex stands up and loads the band's amps onto the sidewalk, and Noah takes those, too, in a couple trips.

When he returns, Rex says, "I think we can get the rest between the three of us." He hands me a guitar case and grins. "Here, make yourself useful. Don't drop it, though, or Todd will hunt you down and kill you."

"No pressure," I mumble.

"He's kidding," Noah assures me. "That case is so indestructible you could drop it off a bridge and it would just bounce." He locks up the van, and I follow them inside the building.

We walk through long, bare halls with doors on either side. It's dirty. The carpet is covered with a patchwork of stains, and the walls are smudged and scribbled on. The air's heavy with this sort of dank, funky odor.

Most of the rooms we pass are quiet, but I can hear a band playing behind one of the doors. Rex is carrying two guitars, and Noah's moving some large piece of equipment I'm totally unfamiliar with.

They disappear into a room at the end of the hall, and I follow them. Rex sets down the guitar cases he's carrying along one of the walls, then he motions for me to come over to him. "I'll take that," he says.

I hand him the guitar, and he stashes it with the others.

Then he looks over at Noah. "You going to set up in here tonight?"

Noah shrugs. "Might as well."

"Right on." He gestures to me. "I'm going to take her home, so see you later man."

Noah turns and gives us a wolfish smile. "Happy Halloween. Don't do anything you might regret when All Saints Day is upon us."

Rex laughs. "It's after midnight. All Saints Day is upon us already. I think we're in the clear. C'mon, Francesca, let's go."

CHAPTER 12

Once we're inside Rex's car, he says, "I need to stop by my house real quick before I drop you home, is that okay?"

"Oh, yeah. Sure."

"It'll just take a second. You don't live far from me."

I start to tell him I know that, since my little brother conducted his own suburban spy operation and figured out where Rex lives and even what car he drives. But it still sounds like a peculiar thing to say, so I keep silent.

He clears his throat. "Hey. I'm sorry about...you know. Telling the guys what happened and making you feel like shit and everything."

I look over at him, but he's concentrating on the road. "Thanks for saying that."

He just nods, and keeps driving.

To be honest, it's hard to stay angry with him. Even when he's not speaking, he exudes a kind of delicious vibe. It feels good just sitting next to him. Plus, he gave me his jacket when he saw I was shivering. That was observant. Thoughtful, too.

"Oh," I remember. "I brought your tape."

"My tape?"

"Your weird-ass songs?"

"Oh, right," he says. "I'll take it off you when we get to my house."

I don't know what to say to him after that. His jacket is still draped over my shoulders, and it feels heavy and strange. But it's also reassuring.

Then I wonder if maybe he's cold. "Do you need your jacket back?"

"You're cool," he says. "I don't need it."

There's something about wearing a guy's piece of clothing—a sweater, a jacket, a T-shirt—that makes you feel closer to him. That's how I feel now. Rex doesn't need to say anything to me. His jacket's doing the talking for him. And I'm horny again. Hormones. Dammit.

His house, when we get there, is difficult to see in the dark. But it seems like he lives in the same sort of neighborhood we do. Straight middle class, nothing fancy. Unlike ours, his house has a carport. He drives under the covered area and parks the car, where it comes to a loud, shuddering stop, then dies. He holds out his hand.

"I'll take that mixtape from you now."

"Oh, yeah, of course...." I start rummaging through my bag to find it, finally locating it at the bottom. I hand it over.

"Thanks," he says. "So, hey. Want to come in for a second?"

I study his face. In the dark, I can't get a read on what's going through his head. But I could probably guess.

Then he grins at me. "No pressure."

I keep looking at him while he waits for my answer.

"Sure," I say, finally. "I could come inside real quick."

We get out of the car, and I follow him up to the front door of his house. There's a screen door that he opens first, then the inner door. We go in, and it's dark.

"My Mom's at this prayer conference thing," he tells me. "So we don't have to keep our voices down or anything."

"What about your sister?"

"My sister?"

"I thought you said you had a sister."

"I do," he agrees, "but she's my older sister. She doesn't live here anymore."

"Oh. Okay." So, no mom. No sister. No one here except me and Rex.

I follow him through the house to his room, where he flips on a light. Instead of completely illuminating the room, it turns on several low lights placed around the perimeter. I can see, dimly, the posters on his bedroom walls. Some are girls, but most of them are bands. I don't recognize any of the bands, except for KISS. Even in the low light, they're hard to miss, with the band members in full costume and makeup.

Rex goes to his dresser and sets the cassette down on top of it. Then he opens the top drawer and slips something in his pocket.

"Okay," he says, walking over to me. "Got what I needed. I can take you home now."

"Sounds good."

He stands in front of me and gestures to his jacket. "I should probably get that back from you, too."

I start to shrug it off my shoulders, but then he stops me, and takes hold of the jacket's front edges. I look at him, surprised, as he tugs on it and pulls me closer to him.

"Don't you want this back?" I ask, stupidly.

"What do you think, Batgirl?"

He kisses me. This time, he starts slow and stays slow. It's the sweetest kiss ever, but that isn't stopping it from doing things to me. Tingles dance down my arms and my spine, and at the same time I feel an urgent sweet ache between my legs. Without thinking, I kiss him back harder, pushing my tongue inside his mouth.

I feel him laugh as he breaks the kiss. He grabs the edges of the borrowed leather coat, grips them tighter, and pulls me full against him.

"You want to stay?" he asks.

I nod.

He grins and releases the jacket, and I take it off and hand it to him. Then he hangs it over the back of a chair and leads me to his bed. "Have a seat."

I sink down on the mattress, and watch as he goes back over to his dresser, where he picks up the mixtape. "Did you listen to it?"

"Yeah, I listened to it." I'm not going to tell him I listened to it incessantly. Or that I got off several times while I did.

"What did you think?"

"I liked it," I tell him. "I mean, I liked most of it."

Rex has a proper sound system with a dual cassette deck. He pops the tape in one of the slots, and music fills his small room.

Then he comes over and sits near me on the bed. "I love this song."

"I know this song," I tell him. "I listen to Depeche Mode all the time."

He's calm. The world's most pleasant predator, biding his time until he claims his prey. Like he's certain what the outcome will be as soon as he decides to pounce. He just hasn't done it yet.

I have a sudden and intense urge to tell him about my little brother. About how Erick has been stalking him. But if I do that I might start babbling, and if I start babbling, I'll seem nervous, and I don't want to seem nervous, even though I kind of am.

And why? Because me and Rex are going to fuck. I want to, but I've never been with anyone like him before. He's a whole other level. He makes me feel things I'm not used to feeling, and I don't understand why he makes me feel them. He scares me.

It's like it was before, back in his car field. When I was afraid if I gave into him, I could lose myself. I still feel the same way. Only now, I think maybe I *want* to lose myself. That scares me even more.

"Hey, Batgirl," he says. "Chill out."

"Why do you keep calling me that?"

He reaches over and touches my hands, and I realize I've been furiously kneading the fabric of my dress between my fingers.

"We're just hanging out. Okay?"

I take a breath. "Okay."

The music shifts. I swear to God, every song on this mixtape sounds like a backdrop for sex. It's like a mix specifically for fucking. Suddenly, I wonder if Rex made the tape with that in mind.

In the same moment, he reaches over and does that thing where he frames my face with his hand. I love it when he does that. It's like he's taking a minute to actually see me.

The song feels like it's playing between us. I'm tuned

into his reaction to the music, and he's tuned into mine. I look in his eyes and sense him waiting.

"So, what do you want to do?" he asks.

"What do *you* want to do?" I counter, as if that's an intelligent rejoinder.

He doesn't answer, but I can imagine him saying, *What do you think, Batgirl?*

I decide to stop torturing myself, lean forward, and kiss him. Just as it starts to get heavy, he pulls back and gives me a level look.

"So—this is what you want to do?"

I meet his eyes. "Yeah."

"Good," he grins. "Me too." He reaches out and encircles my waist with his hand, urging me closer to him. As we kiss, I feel his hands slide up my back. He finds my zipper and tugs on it, opening the dress. I help him push it down, moving my arms out of the spaghetti straps.

His face crinkles with mirth. "Boob tape, huh?"

"Oh yeah." I fold my arms over my chest. "It was Ronnie's idea. I guess I could take it off, or something...."

"I'll do it," he says. He uncrosses my arms and tugs lightly at one of the tape edges.

"Do you know how?" I laugh, self-conscious. "I'm, like, a boob-tape virgin. I've never used it before."

He gets up. "You need lotion. I'll be right back."

Rex returns with lotion in a pink bottle, and I figure he must have snagged it from his mother's things. He squirts some on his hand and starts rubbing it over the surface of the tape and around the edges. It feels nice. I'm also kind of embarrassed.

"It's funny that you know what to do about this when I, like, have no clue."

He looks at me with that knowing light in his eyes. "You're the smart girl tomboy type, right?"

I'm kind of shocked because that *is* how I think of myself, but somehow he's making it sound like it's just this role I play. Before I can think about it too much, he sets the bottle of lotion on the floor.

"I think it's good," he says. "But tell me if this hurts."

I wince as he starts to peel off the tape. I'm sure he's going to rip it off and injure my skin. But he doesn't. He's careful, plus the lotion seems to have loosened the adhesive. It doesn't hurt, it just feels kind of weird. And intimate, which is also weird.

"There," he says, dropping the last of the tape on the floor. "You're free."

"Freedom!" I spread my arms wide, then realize I'm flapping my bare boobs in his face. I start to refold my arms over my chest, but he takes my forearms, stopping me.

"Jesus, Francesca, you're beautiful."

I feel my eyes softening, and my face flushes. "Yeah?"

Instead of answering, he urges me back on the bed and starts kissing me again. Heavy, deep kisses this time. He pushes at the dress, which is still covering my hips, and I help him move it off me. I hear a tearing sound, like fabric ripping.

"Sorry."

"It doesn't matter. It's not mine."

Now I'm almost naked. Rex stretches his body out on top of me and slips his hand beneath the waistband of my underwear. He starts to stroke me, just like he did in his car, only now he has better access. I feel him slide one finger inside me, and I clench around him.

He begins to move his finger rhythmically in and out of me. I start bucking my hips against his hand. I'm having crude thoughts. I want to beg him to fuck me, now, and I've never felt like that, ever.

I start tugging at the hem of his shirt, because I want him to be naked with me, closer to me, inside me. All of it.

He helps me get it off him and I drop it on the floor. Or did he? Maybe we did it together. I reach for the button of his jeans to undo it, and then my safe-sex training kicks in.

"Condom?"

He reaches in his jeans pocket and pulls out a condom packet. Oh, hey look, it's meant to be. He's prepared.

Rex presses the condom packet into one of my hands. Then he reaches up and takes hold of the waistband of my underwear again, and slides them down, past my hips, over my knees, and finally off.

He gets out of his jeans, then his boxers. He's excited, so he does it fast, and for the first time in months, I'm looking at an erect dick. He's kneeling at the end of the bed with his knees spread apart.

My legs start to shake. He places his hands on my knees, then slides them up my thighs, pushing my legs apart. My brain tells me I should feel shy. I don't know him that well. I don't know anything about him. But I don't feel shy at all. I want to be open to him. I want him inside me, and I want him to know I want it.

He holds out his hand, and for a second I'm confused. Then I remember the condom and hand it over, watching him open the package and roll it on as my legs continue to tremble. He stretches himself over my body again and drops a kiss on my mouth.

"You're shaking," he says.

"Uh huh."

"You ready?"

"Ready as I'll ever be."

He laughs. Then slides one hand down to my hip and pushes inside me.

I wrap my legs around him, tight, as he starts to move. It feels like he's pumping me full of this sweet, dirty energy.

"Batgirl," he says.

He's staring down at me. We lock eyes as I start to feel the first twinges of an orgasm. His eyes are intense, and kind of sweet. He looks like he's not just fucking, he's fucking *me*. Like I'm the exact person he wants to be with. All at once he thrusts hard and out of rhythm. I feel my eyes go wide as my inner muscles twitch around his dick with a life of their own. My body is into this. I'm into this. I gasp against his shoulder.

"Come for me," he says, next to my ear. And I want to. I'm trying. Every time he interrupts his own rhythm with a super hard thrust it gets me closer.

"Please, Francesca."

I don't know if it's him saying "please" or using my name, but that does it. I feel the orgasm hit me like a wave, and I'm coming. Loud. I hear him come too, echoing me, and then he slows. Stops. He stays on top of me, pressing me in to the mattress, until our breathing begins to calm down. Then he rolls off me and lazily stretches his arms back behind his head.

All at once I feel unsure. What's next? Does he want me to leave? I kind of expect him to turn into a jerk, now. So I brace myself for the brush off. I hope he'll still at least drive me home.

"I want a cigarette," he says, finally. "My mom doesn't like it when I smoke in the house." He reaches over and squeezes my bare leg. "Come with me?"

"I think my dress is ripped..."

"I'll find you something. Come on." He nudges me out of the bed. I sit up and put my feet on the floor.

I guess he doesn't want to get rid of me. It bothers me how relieved this makes me feel. But I like being with him. A lot. Maybe too much. This thing with Rex feels like it could get out of control, and I *don't* like that. But I might already be hooked.

CHAPTER 13

Rex and me are huddling close together on a tiny concrete patio as he smokes. It's cold in his small backyard, which is a simple square surrounded by a wood fence with a garden shed in one corner. I'm wearing a pair of his sweatpants and one of his T-shirts. And his jacket, again. It's strange, but the smell of his cigarette isn't bothering me. It's a part of him, so it's a part of being with him. Right now, being with him feels so good that my hatred of cigarettes is fading away as if it never existed.

He's staring across the yard, into the dark, like he's seeing something out there that I'm not aware of. He senses me looking at him and turns his head.

"You okay?" he asks.

"I'm fine."

He reaches out and places his hand on top of my head. Blows a puff of smoke out the side of his mouth. His lips quirk upwards. "Can you stay here with me?"

"Tonight?"

He raises his eyebrows and his grin grows wider as he nods.

My first thought is that Mom will freak the fuck out. But I decide I don't care. I'm eighteen. I'm old enough to pay rent or be kicked out of the house. I can stay here with Rex if I want to.

"I can stay," I tell him. "I just have to be at work tomorrow afternoon."

"I'll get you home before that." He drops his hand from my head. "Let's go inside. It's cold out here."

Back in his room, we have sex again, with me on top this time. At first I'm self conscious because Rex is looking at me, all of me, and I feel like I'm on camera. I don't know what he's thinking. But after a while, something in me clicks, and I stop stressing about how I look. Instead, I melt into him, feeling our bodies blend together, the sweet pleasure of him moving inside me, and the movement of my own hips as I ride him. He watches me while I come, and I let our eyes lock.

We fall asleep curled up together in his bed and don't wake until late the next morning. After a bit of a search, we find cereal in one of the kitchen cabinets and eat it for breakfast. I notice there isn't a lot of other food in his house.

My dress is indecent from being ripped, so Rex says I can keep wearing his sweats and T-shirt. I stuff the ruined dress in a paper bag that he finds for me. I doubt Ronnie will want the dress back, but if she does, I'll tell her it got destroyed while Rex and I were fucking. She'll love that story.

"I'm sorry it had to be my mom's house," he says once we're back in his car. "You know, for us to be alone."

"It's okay. I had a good time."

He brightens, then frowns. "Still. I wish it was different."

I shrug. "I live with my mom. And my little brother."

"Yeah, but you just graduated from high school." He sighs. "Living at home helps me put gas in the car, and we need the car. Noah's the only other one of us with a vehicle."

"I get it," I assure him. "I'm trying to save money, too."

"Yeah?" he asks. "What for?"

"College." I don't elaborate. I'm afraid he'll make fun of me. The manager at the chicken shack does, all the time. He calls me a wannabe college girl. And my own mother doesn't seem to place much value on that particular life path. I've learned not to talk about it too much.

"I could see you in college," Rex muses. "You're smart."

I laugh. "How would you even know?"

"I don't know. It's just a feeling I have about you."

Weirdly, that's the most encouragement I've got, ever, for my dream of going to college. Ronnie supports me in theory because she's my best friend. But she's never said she could actually see me doing it.

"Thanks," I say, softly.

I wonder if this is going to happen again, with Rex and me, or if it was a one-time thing. I could maybe be okay with it being a one-time thing. But I'd be lying if I pretended I don't want to see him again, because I do.

When we get to my house, he pulls up right in front of our door and stops the car. I'm nervous Erick will run out and make a scene. He's probably up by now, and I'm sure he'll see Rex's signature car out front.

He notices my nervousness. "You okay?" he laughs.

Maybe now is a good time to tell him about my little brother, the stalker.

"You know how I said my brother's your band's biggest fan?"

"I think I remember that."

"Well, it's more than that. He's kind of been stalking you."

"What?" Rex laughs.

"He like, heard you on this local radio show, and decided you were the coolest thing ever, and then he looked you up. He found out where you live. He even knows what car you drive."

"No kidding?" He doesn't seem that disturbed.

I study the front of my house, looking for movement at the windows. "I keep expecting him to run out here and start yelling at us."

Rex puts a hand on my knee. "It's okay. Don't worry about it."

I look back at him. "It doesn't creep you out?"

He grins. "Is your brother a homicidal maniac?"

"Oh, God no," I exclaim. "He just thinks you're super cool. I don't know, I guess it seemed creepy to me. I mean, he must have cased your house. That's just...weird."

"I would have done the same thing when I was a kid," Rex says, dismissively. "I was pretty obsessed with some of my heroes."

His hand is still on my knee, and just that small touch is making me react to him. If we weren't in broad daylight, in front of my house, I'd be all over him.

He crooks his finger at me, and I scoot closer. Then he puts his hand behind my head and we're kissing. So much for caring about broad daylight. I'm braless under my borrowed T-shirt, and I feel my nipples pushing against the fabric.

He pulls away, slow, brushing his thumb over one of my breasts, like he's taking note of the physical effect he has on me.

"I'll call you," he says. "Okay?"

I stuff down the urge to ask when he's going to call, because that will sound desperate. He called me once already. If he wants to call, he'll call again. If he doesn't, he won't.

"Okay," I say, trying to sound like it's no big deal.

He gives me a knowing look. "I'll call. I promise."

I surprise myself by saying, "You don't have to promise. Just do it." Then I scoot away from him, over to the passenger door, and open it.

"Bye, Francesca," he says, as I put my feet on the pavement.

I turn back around. "Bye, Rex." Then I slam the door shut and go up the walkway to our house.

Inside, my mother is waiting for me, standing just outside the kitchen with her arms folded.

"Where were you last night?" Her tone is accusatory. Like I've done something wrong. I almost fall for it. Almost.

"We were out super late, so I decided to stay with a friend." I push past her into the kitchen, where I get myself a glass of water and drink it down.

Mom follows me. "You stayed with a friend, huh? What friend was that?" She lobs a pointed look at my sweats and T-shirt, which are pretty clearly not girls' clothes.

"Just a friend," I say.

"I need to be able to count on you, Frankie." She sighs, like I'm this horrible problem she can't seem to solve. "You didn't even call last night to say you weren't coming home."

"I'm sorry. I forgot." I turn to the sink to refill my glass. I'm super thirsty.

"That's not good enough," she continues. "You need to promise me you can be responsible, or we're going to have to reevaluate things."

I take a sip of water and stare at her over the rim of the

glass. "I forgot to call, but I don't think I was being irresponsible. I didn't have to work last night. You didn't ask me to take care of Erick. It was Halloween, for God's sake."

"What if I needed you this morning?" she asks.

"If you'd told me last night that you need me this morning, I would have made sure to be here. But you didn't say anything."

She shakes her head slowly. "You know I need your help sometimes in the morning. You should have been here."

I set my water glass down on the kitchen counter with a bang. It makes us both wince.

"I have my own life," I tell her. "I'm eighteen and I'm not in school anymore. I can stay out all night sometimes. It's not the end of the world."

"If I can't count on you," she warns, "we're going to have to re-think this arrangement."

"Count on me?" I retort. "You know, at my job, they actually pay me cold hard cash to be dependable. I've been helping you with Erick for free."

She doesn't seem to have an answer for that. Yet. But I'm sure she'll come up with something.

I grab my water glass. "I need to take a shower." I start for my room, then turn around, and add, "You've always been able to count on me. And you know that."

My room is strewn with the remnants of me and Ronnie getting dressed up for Halloween. I set my water glass on the nightstand and start to clean up the mess.

As I clean, my heart pounds hard in my chest. I can't believe I just managed to make my mother speechless. It won't last, but still. I did it. It's funny. I was so scared if I slept with Rex I would lose myself, or that he'd sap my power like some kind of sexual kryptonite. But instead, I feel good. Maybe even strong.

I get my room finished in record time. Then I hear a knock at the door. Mom's probably thought up some new way to give me grief.

"Yeah?" I call out.

"Hey, it's me," Erick says. He sounds upset, so I go over and open the door.

"Can I come in?" he asks, in his husky voice.

I'm honestly not in the mood to talk to Erick. I want to take a shower and process my night with Rex. But one look at my brother's face tells me he needs to talk to me, so I let him in.

Erick doesn't sit down this time. He paces. "Mom said I have to pick a sport next year in junior high. She said I spend too much time in my room listening to music."

"She's just trying to feel in control."

"She said she's going to sign me up if I don't do it myself." He stops pacing and looks at me. "I don't want to play sports. I want to be in a band."

I decide not to point out that he doesn't play an instrument. "Junior high's almost a year away," I remind him. "Maybe we can change her mind before then. Anyway, I don't think she can force you. You don't have to play sports if you don't want to."

"Yeah, but if I don't do it, life will suck. Will you talk to her?" Erick asks.

"Sure," I say, automatically. However, I wonder how much sway I still have with Mom. We seem to be moving into a different phase of our relationship, where both of us are drawing lines in the sand. But there's no point trying to explain this to Erick.

"I don't know why she gets on my case all the time," my brother grouses. "I try to stay out of her way."

"Stop thinking about it," I tell him. "You don't even know where Mom's head will be at in six months."

"Yeah, maybe." Erick admits, grudgingly. Suddenly his demeanor shifts, and he gives me a sly look. "I saw you getting out of Rex Thornton's car again."

I keep my voice level. "He drove me home."

"You going out with him?"

I pretend to think about it. In reality, I know Rex and I aren't "going out." Having sex with a girl and telling her "I'll call you" is hardly a declaration of exclusivity.

"I think we're more hanging out," I say, finally.

"Well, if you're lucky, you won't be one of those girls he just uses and throws away."

I stare at my little brother. Where does he get this shit?

"You should enjoy it while you can," Erick goes on, with the air of someone who knows about such things. "Cuz someday he'll be famous, and he'll have lots of girls. And he won't have any time for you."

I don't know how to respond, so I say, "Do you have anything else you need to talk to me about?"

"No."

"Okay." I point at the door. "Then you need to leave now. I have to take a shower."

I follow him to the door, to make sure he goes. On the threshold he turns around and says, "You're still gonna take me to one of Fern on Fire's shows, right?"

"If it works out," I agree. I figure I shouldn't get his hopes up about sneaking him into a twenty-one and over show, because that depends on Rex. And I'm not sure where we stand, or if I can count on him to go through with his offer to get Erick into a show.

"I really need to see them," my brother pleads. And I think he does. He needs it on a soul level or something.

"I'll see what I can do," I promise him.

Erick steps closer to the door, and whispers, "Maybe if you give Rex a blow job? Maybe he'll do something about it then?"

"Oh, my God!" I yell, then point away from the door. "Not okay. Not an okay conversation topic. Go away, now!"

Erick holds up his hands, then turns and walks back down the hall to his own room.

Seriously, where is my brother getting the information he puts in his brain? Did I know about guys using girls for sex when I was eleven? Did I know about blow jobs?

I'm not sure whether I did. But I probably *was* aware of those things by the time I was thirteen. And Erick is a guy. He's also the younger sibling, the one who's trying to catch up. Plus, he marinates his brain in heavy metal music and culture. He's probably absorbing his sex education through that.

Still. I never thought I'd hear my brother say I should give someone a blow job just so he can go see his favorite band. That one was completely off my radar.

CHAPTER 14

Ronnie calls me a couple days after Halloween.

"So," she giggles into the phone. "How'd it go with Rex?"

"I don't know." I'm wary. "What did you hear?"

"I haven't heard anything."

"Right."

"I'm serious! Theo won't tell me anything. I think Rex told him to keep his mouth shut. Or maybe Rex didn't tell him anything, either."

"Sure," I scoff.

"Frankie! I mean it, I have no idea what happened. Are you gonna tell me, or not?"

I twirl the phone cord around my fingers, and peer into every corner of the house that I can see from the kitchen counter. I don't spot my mom or Erick anywhere. So I turn around, and tell Ronnie, "Okay, fine. We did it."

"You did it!" she shrieks. "You and Rex had sex?"

"Yes, geez. Don't scream in my ear."

"I knew it!" she screams.

I hold the phone away from me.

"When are you seeing him again?"

I shrug. "I don't know. He said he'd call, but he hasn't called yet."

"He'll call," Ronnie says, with certainty. "He likes you."

I have an early afternoon shift, so after I get off the phone with Ronnie, I ride my bike to the chicken shack and start work.

I kind of like earlier shifts, because I start out by making batches of coleslaw in the kitchen. I get to hang out with the cooks, and I don't have to deal with customers. The one drawback is it can get hot in the kitchen. It was especially heinous over the summer. But now that it's November, it's all right. Once I finish making and packaging the coleslaw, I'll help out front with the dinner rush.

I'm scooping the freshly made coleslaw into takeout containers when LuAnn, one of my co-workers, comes back to the kitchen and taps my shoulder.

"Hey, LuAnn, what's up?"

"There's someone here to see you."

I'm puzzled, but I follow her out to the front counter. Rex is there.

He grins at me. "Hey."

I'm wearing a baker's apron over my uniform to keep it from getting dirty. I'm embarrassed that he's seeing me like this. The apron has little pieces of shredded cabbage and carrots all over it. Probably some of the coleslaw dressing, too.

"Hi," I say.

"Do you have a couple minutes?"

I shake my head. "I don't get off until seven."

"So...do you get a break?"

"Go ahead, Frankie," LuAnn urges. "Take your break. We've got another hour before the rush hits."

"Hang on," I tell Rex. I go in back, take off the apron, and set it on the bottom shelf of the table where I've been dishing up coleslaw. Next, I wheel the pre-packaged containers to our walk-in cooler, then roll the industrial sized mixing bowl with the remaining batch of coleslaw to the walk-in, too.

When I go out to the dining room, Rex is sitting at one of the tables. He's holding a disposable drink container with the restaurant's logo on it. I have a hunch LuAnn gave him a drink for free.

He stands up when he sees me. "Let's go outside."

As we head out the door, he puts his hand on my back.

I look over my shoulder at him. "Do you have some-thing against using the phone?"

His eyes glitter at me, but he doesn't answer.

I spot his car in the parking lot, and he ushers me over to the passenger side, where he opens the door for me.

It's a sunny but chilly day. Most of the fall-colored leaves are still clinging to the trees because we haven't yet had a big storm to blow them away. It's a bit cold in the car.

Rex gets in the driver's side, and we're alone together.

"I'm all gross," I say. "I've been working in the kitchen."

"I told you I love that uniform on you."

I give him a look, and he laughs. "Sorry I didn't call. But I wanted to see you, so I thought, you know. It would be better to come here."

He wanted to see me. It takes a few moments for that to sink in, but once it does, I feel kind of warm inside, despite the chilliness of the day.

"How come?" I ask.

"How come what?"

"Why'd you want to see me?"

Now he gives me a look. "You know why," he says, reaching for my waist. He urges me closer. Kisses me.

I'm sure anyone eating in the restaurant and looking out the windows can see us. But I don't care. I'm this strange new person who will sit in a parking lot in broad daylight and make out with a guy. Because the guy is Rex, and for some reason, there's something magic about Rex.

HE PICKS me up later that night. He wanted to come by when I got off work, but I insisted on going home and showering first.

We drive out to this park that feels more secluded than the field behind the school, then have sex in his car because his mom is back at his house. By now, I'd probably have sex with him in the field behind the school. I almost fucked him in his car in front of the restaurant earlier today.

I also understand Ronnie better. How she gets all excited and crazy when she's into some guy. Because I'm starting to feel that way about Rex.

I'm not sure I like how I feel. But it's as if a new part of me has taken over my body, my brain, and my decisions. All he has to do is touch me a little, or look at me a certain way, and I want him.

He brought a blanket tonight. I recognize it from his bed. We're huddling under it, side by side, in the front seat.

"You cold?" he asks.

"Nope."

Our legs are twined together under the blanket, and he's playing with my hair, or petting it, like I'm some sort of creature. It feels good, though.

"Whatcha thinkin', Batgirl?"

"Why do you keep calling me that?"

He laughs. "It was Theo, on Halloween? You did that thing where you flapped your wings and flew away, and Theo started calling you Batgirl. Then we all did. It fits you."

I pound on his shoulder in protest as he laughs harder. Then I sigh. "I guess I brought it on myself by acting weird."

"You're not weird," he says.

"I'm pretty weird sometimes."

"Okay, fine, you're weird."

"Thank you. Oh, God. You know what's actually weird? My little brother said I should give you a blow job to get you to play an all-ages show. I mean, my *brother* is trying to dictate my sex life. *That's* weird."

"Yeah, an all-ages show is not gonna happen," Rex says. "The scene won't support it. Sneaking him in is the only way."

"Right."

"I'll take a blow job, though."

I turn my head and stare at him. "I'm not gonna do that for my *brother*. That's fucked up."

He grins. "Don't do it for your brother. Do it for me."

I give him a look, and he laughs, then twines his fingers in my hair. "There's this holiday thing we're doing the week before Christmas. Should be pretty loose. I bet we can sneak your brother into that show, but don't tell him yet. Let me talk to the guys first."

"That would be awesome," I say. "Especially if it makes him shut up about it."

I hope Rex has given up on the idea of a blow job. At least for tonight. I'm still grossed out by the fact that Erick suggested it. I don't want to be thinking about my little brother while I'm doing something sexual.

We both go quiet. I feel comfortable. Safe. Right now, if

you asked me what my favorite place in the world is, I'd say it was here. In this car.

"Wish my old man was as excited about my shows as your brother is," Rex says.

He's never mentioned his dad. I've always assumed his parents are divorced, like mine. And that maybe he doesn't like his dad, since he never talks about him.

"Where's your dad live?" I ask.

Rex kind of grunts. "Seattle. But he might as well live in another country. He got a whole new life after he and my mom split up."

"I'm sorry."

"Nothin' for you to be sorry about," he says. "He's the one who acts like me and my sister don't exist." He moves his fingers through my hair. "What about your old man? What's he like?"

I feel my body go rigid. I'm not used to talking about my dad. It's sort of an unspoken rule in our house that nobody talks about him. Especially not me and Erick. "We don't know where he is," I say, finally. "He—he's kind of got addiction issues."

Rex lets out his breath, slowly. "Now I'm sorry. That's rough."

He pulls me closer to him, and I lean my head on his shoulder. Even though we just had a sort of sad conversation, I feel so alive and close to him.

"There's this other show we have," he says, presently. "In a couple weeks. Our manager said there's supposed to be some A&R people there."

I think I know what he means, but I'm not sure. "Is that, like, people from record companies or something?"

"Yeah. They're kind of like talent scouts. So...we're screwed," he jokes.

"But they could get you a record contract? Or whatever it's called?"

"They could get us signed," Rex agrees. "This show could be a big deal."

"Sounds like it."

He moves his fingers through my hair. "It would be cool if you'd be there."

"Yeah?"

"Yeah. Will you?"

"I'll be there," I promise.

I always laugh at Ronnie for this kind of thing, though not to her face. She gets so excited when some guy in a band asks her to a show or when she's included in something important that this band or that band is doing. She always acts like she's achieved some massive feat, and I've always assumed it means her self esteem is dependent on others' opinions of her.

But now that Rex has told me he wants me to be at this important show, I have a glimmer of where Ronnie is coming from.

I feel chosen.

I could probably make fun of myself for that. But I like being chosen. Something about it feels powerful. So I cut myself some slack.

CHAPTER 15

Mom is stressed about Thanksgiving this year. She stresses about it every year, but this year she's extra stressed because her younger sister, Carrie, is coming to our place for dinner. It'll be me, Erick, Mom, plus Carrie, her husband, and their two kids.

I think Mom feels like she's in competition with her sister. Whatever the heart of that competition is, I've gathered Carrie is usually the winner—maybe because she has a husband who makes good money and Mom's a single mom. It seems ridiculous to me, but that's my best guess. Then again, it could be something I'm not even aware of.

Whatever the actual reason is, Mom's driving me crazy. She keeps shopping for little things to make our Thanksgiving table more complete. So far, she's bought festive holiday napkins, table centerpieces, plus candles and holders. None of this stuff is anything we typically use. We never even eat at our table. I figure Mom's already spent all the money I paid for November rent on cheesy Thanksgiving decor.

I want to say something about it, but keep my mouth shut. I need to choose my battles.

To distract myself from Mom's pre-Thanksgiving freak out, I've been indulging Ronnie's whims. A lot. That means tons of shopping trips.

She's beyond excited about the band's big show before Thanksgiving and thrilled Rex asked me to be there. I think she's planning a life where we both follow the band around and then eventually marry into it, like it's a big family or the mafia or something.

I'm pretty sure my brother's take on things is more realistic—one day, Fern on Fire will be famous, with unlimited access to women, and Rex will no longer have time for me.

But that's the future. This is now. For now, I'm at loose ends while I figure out how I'm going to get to college. For now, Rex is into me. I'm into him, too. He's like a drug, and I'm developing a habit.

I let Ronnie take me shopping for something to wear to the show. I'm not comfortable in the kind of clothes she usually wears, but she does convince me to get a pair of tight black jeans and a skintight blue shirt. The outfit makes me look good without making me feel like I'm trying too hard.

Or as Ronnie puts it, "See? Classy, not slutty."

She calls me the night before the show. "I'll see you tomorrow. At seven," she says. "Be ready, okay?"

I promise her I will be. She wants to be sure we're at the venue as soon as the band loads in, for "moral support." I can't help but wonder if they'd prefer not to have us underfoot before the show, but Ronnie's determined, and she's my ride. So, early arrival it is.

As I hang up, my mom walks into the kitchen and opens the fridge.

"Was that Ronnie on the phone?" she asks, in a conversational tone.

"Yep," I confirm.

"Do you two have plans?"

Mom's carefully calm demeanor is making me nervous. "Sure, yeah, we've usually got plans to do something."

She takes a diet soda out of the fridge and shuts the door. Then she smiles at me, but her smile isn't quite friendly. "Well, I hope you don't have plans tomorrow night, because I need you to stay with Erick."

"What?"

"I have to take a safety class for my job," she says, nodding. "It's required, so I need you to be here with your brother."

"Erick's old enough to stay home by himself," I reply, automatically. "He's home after school by himself all the time."

I was nine when Mom started letting me carry my own house key. I stayed alone in the house when I was younger than Erick. Sometimes even at night. Erick had tons of ear infections when he was little, and there were lots of late night trips to the hospital, when Mom would take him and leave me here.

Now, she gives me a pitying look. "He's not responsible like you were at his age. Somebody needs to be here with him, and it can't be me because I'll be at my class. Is this going to be a problem, Frankie? Did you have plans with Ronnie tomorrow?"

I have a feeling she knows I did. Or at least, she suspected I did.

"Yeah, we have plans."

"Maybe she can come over here while you look after Erick," Mom suggests.

That, of course, is not going to happen. Tomorrow night's show is a big deal. There's no way Ronnie's going to miss this show. And I don't want to miss it, either. I promised Rex I'd be there. I don't want to break my promise.

"Can't you find him a sitter?" I ask.

Mom says, in a magnanimous tone, "You're welcome to find him a sitter and pay for it if you want to, as long as it's someone I approve of."

I feel a surge of fury in my gut. She wants me to take care of Erick for free. Again. I know what she's doing. I've been standing up to her lately, so she's testing the waters, to make sure I'll still drop my own plans to help her out whenever she asks.

I want to tell her I won't do it. Then see how she responds. But I know from experience it could go in a number of directions—likely none of them pleasant. She might blow up. It's been a while since Mom had one of her big blowups—almost a couple years—but if I tell her I won't help, that could happen. Or she might come up with a way to get back at me, like asking me to pay even more rent, which would likely force me to move out and get my own apartment.

I don't want to risk either of these outcomes. Especially one of her blow ups. Last time that happened, I had a stomach ache for a week, and it was hard to even be in our house. Maybe it's the coward's way out, but I decide that this time, subterfuge is the best solution. I'll give her what she wants. Then I'll figure out some way to still go to the show tomorrow night.

"Okay," I sigh. "I'll stay with Erick." I try to inject a note of defeat in my voice, to let Mom know she's won this round.

"Thanks, Frankie. I really appreciate it." She kind of flounces out of the kitchen.

I watch her until I'm sure she's out of earshot. Then I call Ronnie back and ask if I can come over to her house before my chicken shack shift. When she asks why, I tell her I can't talk about it while I'm still at home.

That piques Ronnie's interest, and she tells me to come right over. I'm not trying to be dramatic for her benefit. I don't want to risk Mom hearing anything, because there is no way I'm missing Rex's show tomorrow night. I'm going to keep my promise.

I'm WAITING for Mom to go out the door for her class. She's taking forever. She keeps going back in her room and changing her clothes, and I'm starting to wonder if she's actually taking a class, or if maybe she has a date instead. Either way, it's already after seven. Ronnie's going to be so pissed at me.

Once Mom does go, I'll leave her a note saying that Ronnie dropped me and Erick at the movies. But what we'll actually do is leave Erick at the cineplex, then drive down to Seattle for Fern on Fire's show.

In order to make this work, Ronnie had to agree to go to the show later than she planned, and she'll also have to leave sooner than she wants, so we can pick Erick up from the mall. Right now, she's lurking a block away in her car, waiting to see when Mom leaves the house.

To get Erick on board, I had to tell him about Rex's idea to sneak him into a show. I warned him that if he squeals to Mom about any of this, all bets are off. I won't take him to see Rex's band. Once I played that card, he was all in.

When Mom finally leaves, it's already seven-thirty. She

gives me a breezy, "Thank you so much for helping out, Frankie," as she goes out the door. I don't even have time to feel pissed. I rush back to my room to change my clothes.

Erick stops me in the hall. "When's Ronnie gonna get here?"

"Any second," I say, pushing past him. "I told her to wait a couple minutes, but if she gets here, let her in, okay?"

My brother nods, all serious, like I've just given him a direct order. If I weren't so nervous about pulling this off, I'd probably laugh.

I go to my room and change my clothes. On a whim, I dab some of the blood red lipstick from Halloween on my lips. Then I grab the note I've already written for Mom, the one telling her we've gone to the movies.

Just as I'm leaving the note on the kitchen counter, there's a knock at the door. Erick runs for it.

"Hey, Ronnie."

"Are we ready to go?" she asks, sounding anxious.

"Are you ready?" I ask my brother.

"I'm not the one taking forever to do my makeup," he retorts.

I grab my coat and my crossbody bag that's not really a purse. "Let's go."

When we get close to the mall, I make sure Erick understands the plan. "You have to stay at the movie theater. You got that, right?"

"Yeah, I got it," he says.

"Don't go anywhere else. You need to be here when we get back, because if you get in trouble or you get yourself killed or something, then you can't go see Rex's band with us."

"I'm not going to get myself killed," he mutters.

"Or in trouble," I repeat. "If you get in trouble, Mom will

find out, and then she'll be watching you like a hawk, and I won't be able to sneak you into anybody's show."

"Okay, okay!"

"You've got your money?"

Erick pats his coat pocket. "Right here."

We drop him off in front of the cineplex, and as he starts to go in, I roll down the window and yell at him, "We'll be back at midnight!"

He nods, waves, and goes inside.

"Oh, God," I groan. "If my mom knew about this, she'd kill me."

"She's not going to find out," Ronnie assures me. "I hope we make it there in time."

I turn to her. "Thanks for doing this. You could have gone without me."

"It's okay." She giggles. "I like you this way. All scheming and devious."

"It's not devious," I protest. "I'm just doing what needs to be done."

She throws me a sidelong glance.

"Okay," I admit. "I guess it's a little bit devious."

CHAPTER 16

When we get to the club where the band is playing, Ronnie goes straight for the backstage area, and I start to follow her. But then I see Rex.

He's inside the main room, leaning against a wall. But he's not alone. There's a girl talking to him. She's this short, compact creature with dyed black hair. She wears it in a bob, with impossibly thick bangs. Now, she's looking up at Rex, and he's laughing at whatever she's saying. I feel an unpleasant pull in my gut.

Ronnie gives me a nudge. "Don't just stand there, go get rid of that bitch."

A jumble of thoughts run through my head. I truly don't know Rex. We've barely talked to each other. I don't even know how to classify us—if we're just screwing or sort of together or kind of something else. So why am I feeling so possessive and jealous? Because that's exactly how I feel. Possessive. Jealous.

I'm done thinking about it. I go up to Rex and the girl and stand between them. The girl seems annoyed, but Rex gives me an amiable smile.

"Hey, Francesca."

I want to say something witty. Something subtle, but definite, that will let this cute little button of a girl know she doesn't have a chance. He asked me to be here. Me. Not her.

Or what if he asked both of us?

"Hey," I say to Rex. "Did you drive here?"

He looks a little bewildered. "Yeah?"

"Good. Because I have something for you, but I can't give it to you here."

He studies me for a second, and I swear, if he doesn't come with me, I'm going to be insanely pissed. I lied to my mom and left my brother alone at the mall so I could be here. If he doesn't appreciate me being here, I am going to feel so...stupid.

But Rex grins, and says, "Ok, let's go."

As we leave, he turns around and tells the girl, over his shoulder, "Nice meeting you."

"Yeah, you too." She sounds angry.

Fine. Let her be angry. It's not my problem. At least not right this second. Right this second, my problem is following through with my intention, which is to give Rex a blow job in the backseat of his car.

I follow him out to the car, which is parked behind the venue. There're several people hanging around back there, talking and smoking. Great. I wasn't counting on a potential audience. I'll just have to deal with it.

Rex opens the passenger door and gestures for me to get in.

"No," I say. "Backseat."

"You sure?"

I wave him forward, and he crawls in the backseat. I go in after him, and struggle to get the door shut.

"Need some help?" he asks, just as I manage to shut it.

I sit back on the seat next to Rex. The first thing I notice is there's not as much room back here as I thought there would be. The way I planned this isn't going to work. Maybe this is why Rex always initiates sex in the front seat of his car.

I start to feel a bit panicked. Not only are the logistics of this situation messed up, but this is out of character for me. I'm not sure I can do it.

"So what did you have for me?" he asks. He has that knowing look on his face, which makes me feel even more ridiculous.

I look up at him. "A blow job?"

He grins again. "Yeah?"

"Yeah. Except I thought there would be more room back here...." My voice trails off.

Rex laughs and takes my hand. He pulls me forward and, at the same time, lays back on the seat. A little more maneuvering, and I'm kneeling between his legs.

His eyes glitter at me. "Have enough room?"

"Yeah," I say. "I think this is doable."

Don't think, just do it.

I reach for the button of his jeans and unfasten it, then pull down the zipper. He's already hard, which is gratifying. Unless the girl in the club was responsible for that?

I can't go there.

I pull at the edges of his jeans to give me better access, then free his dick from his boxers and curl my hand around the base of it. Then I take the head of his cock inside my mouth and start licking.

I'm licking and sucking and pumping him with my hand, hoping he likes it. That I'm making him happy. Then I feel his hand on my head. Not pushing me down, just touching me, twining his fingers in my hair. It makes me feel connected to him.

I stop worrying about the other people hanging around behind the club, and I stop caring whether they can see us. I just focus on getting him off. I feel his hips move upward and I adjust, then keep licking, sucking, pumping...licking, sucking, pumping...

"Oh God..." he says.

I sense he's getting close and pick up the pace, then suck hard on the end of his dick.

"Jesus..."

And then he's coming, and I swallow his cum as it spurts in my mouth.

He reaches for my hand again and pulls me forward, so I sprawl on top of him. He reaches up and pushes my hair away from my face. "Thanks, Batgirl."

"Was that okay?"

"More than okay." He plants a quick kiss on my mouth, then takes hold of my hips, and maneuvers me off him so he can sit up. He refastens his jeans.

"You're not going to be late for your set?"

He looks over at me and shakes his head. Then he studies my face, and says, "You've kind of got lipstick all over...." He gestures to his own face.

"Oh, crap." I swipe at my mouth and feel the lipstick residue on my skin.

"Here," he says, and lifts the bottom of his T-shirt up to my face. He scrubs at the lipstick. Then he sits back and examines me again. "I think I got it, but you should check it out inside."

"Right." My words dry up. I feel fragile, but also close to him.

He nudges me. "I should go back in."

"Oh, yeah, of course." I wrestle with the door again and get it open. We both clamber out of the backseat, and Rex slams the door shut and locks it.

We walk toward the venue together, and he opens the door for me. Once we're inside, he snakes an arm around me and pulls me against him.

I haven't told him Ronnie and I need to leave early to get my brother. I figure now isn't the best time to mention it. Hopefully I'll have time to tell him before we leave.

"I'll see you after," he says.

"Yeah, see you then." I don't wish him good luck, in case music performance is anything like theater.

He squeezes my waist and kisses the top of my head. Then he lets go of me and walks down the corridor to the green room.

After I re-do my lipstick in the bathroom, I spot Ronnie out in the main area of the club and go over to her.

"And where have *you* been?" she asks.

"With Rex."

"Mm-hmm. Doing what?"

I turn to her and smile wide. "Blowing him?"

She holds her hand up for a high five, and I slap it. Then I look around the club. It's a somewhat different crowd tonight. There's the usual collection of dudes, but there are more girls here. And it just feels different. There's an intense air of excitement and anticipation.

"Kinda crazy in here," I say.

"There's a ton of local rock press at this show," she tells me. "The guys were saying they don't usually get this much attention."

"From local rock press?"

"Right."

"And the A&R people are here?"

"Yep," Ronnie nods. "Definitely here."

I have an odd moment where I feel like I'm outside myself, observing my own behavior. Is this me? Blowing a guy in a band in the backseat of his car. Being interested in the buzz around that band. Even the lipstick I'm wearing. All of it seems to belong to this other person. Some character I'm playing.

But being here is real. The excitement in the room is making me excited, too. I feel like I'm part of something. The fact that I got Rex off makes me feel kind of dirty and proud at the same time. And whatever. I even like the dumb lipstick.

When the band comes out, the crowd is cheering before they even start to play. Rex goes to the mic and jokingly tells everyone to "simmer down." But of course nobody does. Everyone just laughs, and the excitement level in the room goes up.

The minute they start to play, it's clear they're going to rise to the occasion. They're high energy, synced with each other, but also loose. Even kind of playful. I get actual chills listening to Rex sing.

When the crowd brings them back for an encore, Ronnie yells in my ear, "If that doesn't get them signed, those A&R guys are idiots!"

"Totally!" I yell back.

They blow through two more songs, happy and confident, knowing they killed it.

Ronnie and I both yell and scream when they leave the stage for the second time. She turns to me and pulls me into an exuberant hug.

"That was so amazing!" she yells. "I'm so glad you're here!"

I'm touched. And then I remember: Erick. I glance at my

watch, but it's not digital, and I can't see it. Then the lights go up in the club, and the face of the watch becomes visible. It's exactly eleven.

"We have to go get my brother!"

"What time is it?" Ronnie asks, unconcerned.

"Eleven."

"We've got tons of time. Let's go find the guys."

I always marvel at Ronnie's ability to push past the big, burly, pissed-off dudes who monitor the backstage area. She either charms them or doesn't give a fuck or both. They always give way for her.

The green room is wall-to-wall people and it's hard to maneuver. Still, Ronnie manages to attach herself to Theo's side, and he puts an arm around her, like she belongs there. I spot Rex talking to someone else across the room. I can't imagine going over to him, leaning into him, standing with him while he holds court. It doesn't feel natural.

I wonder if this is some sort of insecurity on my part. Or maybe it's because I don't want to be on Rex's arm while he talks to other people? I want him to talk to *me*.

I stand with Ronnie and Theo and try to look like I belong there. Todd comes over and joins us.

"You guys," Ronnie says, giving him an appraising look. "You fucking killed it."

"Thanks," Todd looks pleased. He nudges me. "You talk to Rex yet?"

"I talked to him...earlier," I say.

Todd grins, and I wonder if everyone here knows about me blowing Rex in the parking lot. Probably. I decide I don't care.

"We have to go pick up my brother," I tell Todd. I'm starting to have horrible visions of Erick getting beat up in the parking lot at the mall or doing drugs with some new "friends" out behind the movie theater.

"Where's your brother?"

"At the movies. At the mall near where we live. I was supposed to be watching him tonight."

"Uh oh," Todd smiles at me, then nudges my shoulder again. "I'll be back in a minute."

"Don't worry, Frankie," Ronnie says to me. "We'll get your brother. We can hang out for a few more minutes. He'll be fine."

"Fine, yeah, okay." I fold my arms over my chest and try to not look worried. But by the glares Ronnie shoots in my direction, I can tell I'm not succeeding.

Suddenly, I feel someone grab my waist from behind. It's Rex. I know it's him, because I already know how his hands feel on my body.

He drapes an arm over my shoulder. And there it is again. That chosen feeling. A part of me hates that it means so much to me. But it means a lot.

"I heard these two are gonna bail on us," Rex tells Theo.

Theo shakes his head with mock disapproval. At least, I think it's mock disapproval. "Gonna miss a hell of a party," he says.

"I'm coming back," Ronnie informs him.

Rex nudges me. "You should come with her."

"I'll try. It depends on...a few things." If Mom's not home, I won't leave Erick in the house alone. If she's there —I'll think about that when I get to the house. I look up at Rex. "Your show was so good. I mean, really great."

"Thanks," he smiles at me. I can tell he's happy I said it.

"What did the A&R people say?" Ronnie asks.

Rex and Theo exchange glances.

"Things are...moving," Rex says.

"They're *in process*," Theo adds.

Rex nods, gravely. "A lot of processes and processing. And tons of movement."

Ronnie looks pouty. "Okay, so you're not going to tell us anything."

"There's not much to tell when things are *in process*." Theo looks at Rex, and they both crack up.

"Oh Jesus," Ronnie groans. "Forget it."

"Why don't you take Francesca to pick up her brother," Rex tells her. "Do something useful."

She rolls her eyes at him, then sighs. "Okay, Frankie, let's go."

"Do you have the address where we're gonna be at later?" Theo asks her.

Ronnie gets the address from him, and we leave. As we do, I see the girl Rex was talking to earlier. The girl with the bangs. She's heading back to the green room area.

Ronnie bristles. "Her again." She gives me a pointed look. "You better be sure you come back down here with me. You need to be at that party."

I hate the nervous feeling in the pit of my stomach. I hate that I know Ronnie is right.

"Let's go get my brother." I force myself to walk all the way out of the club, leaving Rex with *her*.

CHAPTER 17

I'm nervous all the way back to the mall. My imagination keeps conjuring up increasingly dire scenarios. By the time we get there, I'm certain Erick's either been murdered by thugs, or that he's been initiated into a band of them.

But it's pretty anticlimactic when we finally pull up in front of the cineplex. He's right there in front, waiting for us. I unlock the back passenger door for him, and he gets in the car.

"Took you guys long enough," he complains, as he settles in the back seat.

"We're only fifteen minutes late," Ronnie points out.

I turn around in my seat to look at him. "How were the movies?"

"Okay," he says. "I had to watch the same one twice. The rest of them were dumb."

I smile at him. "Thanks. I owe you."

"Are you going to take me to see Fern on Fire?"

"We were just talking to the guys about that tonight,"

Ronnie tells Erick. Unless she talked to Theo about it, which I doubt, she's lying. But my little brother eats it up.

"Yeah?" he asks. "What'd they say?"

"They think they can definitely get you in." She catches his eye in the rearview mirror. "So, you're not gonna rat on Frankie about tonight, are you?"

"No." He's sulky. "I already said I wouldn't."

"Just checking." Ronnie glances over at me, and says, low, "Are you going to come back with me after we drop him off?"

I match her tone. "I don't know. It depends if Mom's home."

"What are you two whispering about?" my brother asks.

Ronnie is cheerful. "None of your business."

"Did you have any money left?" I ask him.

Erick sounds indignant. "You said I could get popcorn and stuff."

"Just checking." He probably spent it all. Or he's pretending he did. Either way, it's all right. It looks like we pulled this off. Even if he's hanging on to some of my money, I'm grateful to him. I made it to Rex's show. I kept my promise. And then some.

Back at our house, Mom's car is in the driveway.

"Looks like your mom's home," Ronnie observes. "I'll wait for you."

Erick and I start for the front door.

"What do we say to Mom?" he asks.

"If she wants to know, just tell her we went to the movies. She should know that anyway, I left her a note."

We go inside, and Mom is there, waiting in the kitchen. "How were the movies?"

"They were great!" Erick gushes.

I cringe. I hope he doesn't arouse her suspicion by over-doing it.

"It was fun," I add.

"Glad you guys had fun. What movie did you see?"

Fuck. Why didn't I anticipate this question? I look over at my brother, trying to signal with my eyes that he should let me answer. But he forges ahead on his own.

"We saw *Steel Magnolias*. Twice. It was good, but Frankie cried, like, both times." Erick sounds genuinely disgusted, as if this is something that actually happened. Thank God he mentioned a movie I've already seen.

"It's so sad when she dies, though," I sigh. "I *had* to cry."

He rolls his eyes.

Shit, the kid is actually good at this.

Mom's tone is tolerant. "At least you got out of the house."

She seems to be buying our story, which is good, because I have a feeling she was all set to call bullshit on us. I mean, she's essentially been lying in wait, hanging out in the kitchen after midnight and drinking diet soda like some kind of suburban inquisitor.

Mom drinks a ton of diet soda. Another thing, in my opinion, that we could save money on if she'd dial it back. Though, to be fair, she always buys the store brand kind.

Erick and I start down the hallway to our rooms, and he whispers, "I saw *Drugstore Cowboy*. It was awesome. Thanks, Frankie."

"No problem," I tell him, bewildered. When we picked him up, he seemed pissed we abandoned him at the cine-plex all night. But now it sounds like he actually had a good time.

It isn't until we both go into our respective rooms that I remember *Drugstore Cowboy* is rated R. Erick is too young to see *Drugstore Cowboy*. How the hell did he get in? Twice, no less?

I don't have time to worry about it. I comb my hair, freshen up my lipstick, and head for the front of the house.

"Where are you going?" Mom asks, as I open the door.

I turn and look her in the eye. "Out with Ronnie. We'll be in Seattle. You don't need to wait up for me."

Without waiting for her answer, I go down the walkway and get back in Ronnie's car.

"How'd it go with your mom?" she asks, as she pulls away from the curb.

"Handled it," I say. "For now."

The party is at a rental house in the University District. Apparently, a couple guys who are friends of the band live there. Ronnie finds a place to park a few blocks away, and we walk to the house.

I can hear the party as we approach—loud music, laughter, guys yelling. The door is open and we go inside. It takes me a few seconds, but I spot Rex. He's hanging out with a group of people, imitating somebody, and making everyone laugh. He seems a little drunk.

Near the edges of the group I see the cute girl with the bangs, waiting in the proverbial wings. Biding her time. For once, Ronnie doesn't have to nudge me. I head right for Rex.

I have no idea what I'm going to do. Maybe go up to him and hang on his arm, the way Ronnie does with Theo. Or plant myself where he can't miss me and stand my ground. But I need him to know I'm here.

I also need to know if he cares that I'm here. Because if he doesn't, then I have to let this thing with him go. For my own pride, if nothing else. I'm not going to chase him or beg him to pay attention to me. That does not strike me as a fun way to spend the next several months.

So I sort of insert myself in the circle of people he's with. After a couple moments, he sees me, and I raise my eyebrows at him.

His face breaks into a full smile. Then he comes straight over and gives me a hug. He's less controlled than he usually is, which is probably because he's drunk. But this is good.

"You're here," he says in my ear. "I'm so glad you're here." He breaks off from me and asks, "Did you get a drink?"

"Not yet."

"Go get a drink and come back here. You're my good luck charm."

He gives me another quick squeeze, then lets me go and returns to entertaining his friends without missing a beat.

If I needed validation, I just got it.

I go in search of alcohol, even though I don't really drink. I hardly ever drank in high school. My fake ID is for getting into shows, not for drinking. But I'm here, and everyone else is getting drunk. When in Rome, and all that. I'm tired of going against the grain.

CHAPTER 18

I wake curled against Rex in an unfamiliar bed. My head is throbbing, and I want to brush my teeth and take a shower. I don't remember how much I drank last night. I lost count after the first couple drinks.

I blink my eyes a few times and look around me. We seem to be in someone's bedroom. There's another couple on the floor under a blanket. They might be naked. It's hard to tell for sure. Rex and I aren't, though. We're still wearing all our clothes.

I try to stretch without disturbing him, but then I feel his arms tighten around me.

"Going somewhere?"

"No, I'm stretching."

He nudges me with his knee from behind. "I'm starving. Let's go find food."

We carefully step around the couple on the floor, then I close the bedroom door behind us.

Out in the main area of the house, there are people sleeping everywhere, on the floor, on furniture. Rex goes over to Todd, who's sprawled on one of two couches in the living room. I hear him talking, quiet, and Todd replying in a groggy, unintelligible voice.

Rex comes back over to me. "Let's go."

It's pitch dark outside as we walk to his car, and the air is chilly.

"Why is it so early?" I ask. "Does Ronnie know we're leaving?"

He laughs softly. "She and Theo are long gone. They left last night. You were pretty out of it."

So Ronnie abandoned me again. It doesn't piss me off as much this time. But I'm still pissed. Because we talked about this. About not abandoning each other. Then, I wonder just how out of it I was that I didn't even notice she left without me.

Rex goes to the interstate and starts driving north, so I figure he's taking me home.

"Did I umm...did I do anything stupid last night?" I venture.

"Not too stupid," he says. "But everyone really enjoyed your stripper routine. You made a lot of new friends."

I look over at him in horror. "I took off my clothes? In front of people?"

His face crinkles in a grin. "Just kidding. What happened was you were laughing really hard, and then you just passed out, mid-laugh. Stuart—he lives there—he said we could use his room."

"Oh. Okay." I'm still embarrassed. I'm not in the habit of drinking until I pass out. In fact, this is the first time I've ever done it.

"Sorry if I was a major pain in the ass," I say. "I don't remember much about last night. Did I piss anyone off?"

"Francesca, chill out. It happens."

It's probably because I'm hung over, but his words strike a compassionate note. Like it's okay for me to fuck up and get drunk, sometimes. He won't judge me. Suddenly I'm afraid I might cry. So I start talking instead.

"I need to brush my teeth," I groan. "I feel like I have a monster in my mouth."

"Interesting image."

I look over at him, and we both crack up.

He surprises me by stopping at the Food Mart.

"Why are we here?"

"Breakfast."

I start digging in my shoulder bag. "Let me give you some money."

"You don't have to do that."

I hand him a five. "Take it. Okay? It's just five bucks."

"All right," he gives in, and takes the money. "I'll be right back."

It's still dark. I glance at my watch and see that it's just after six-thirty. We're the only car at the Food Mart, and it feels strangely peaceful, just chilling in the parking lot.

Rex comes back carrying a plastic sack in one hand and balancing two paper cups with lids in the other.

I scramble across the seat to open the door for him.

"Here, take these," he says.

"Take what? The bag?"

"Anything, hurry up before I drop it all," he laughs.

I take the cups from him. They're warm. I scoot back across the seat with one of them in each hand, being careful not to spill.

"What's in these?" I ask, as Rex gets back behind the wheel. He slams the door shut and puts the plastic bag between us.

"Really bad coffee," he says. "But drink it. You'll feel better."

I pass one of the cups back over to him, then take a sip from the other one. The minute I taste it, I want to spit it out. Rex sees my reaction, and laughs.

"Told you it was bad." Then he says, mock serious, "Be a good girl and drink all of it, now."

I take another sip of the coffee and try not to gag. "What's in the bag?"

He pulls out some pastries wrapped in plastic. I've secretly always liked the sad-looking pastries they sell at the Food Mart, but right now I can't stand the thought of eating anything. I put up my hand.

"Can't eat yet?" he asks.

I nod.

"Stick with the coffee then."

He starts in on one of the pastries while I nurse the cup of coffee. After a few minutes, I do start to feel a bit better and even eat a few bites of a pastry before wrapping it back up.

We're just sitting in the stupid parking lot at the Food Mart. It's hardly a glamorous setting. But I'm ridiculously happy. I feel like Rex is taking care of me. It's unexpected, but it feels amazing.

He reaches in the plastic bag again and pulls out a bottle.

"What's that?"

"Mouthwash. Better than nothing, right?"

I grab the bottle eagerly. I can't wait to get the sour, fuzzy feeling off my tongue. I pour a capful and swish it around in my mouth. Then I realize I don't know where to spit, and look over at Rex, panicked.

He's amused. "Open the door and spit it on the ground."

I do as he says and spit the mouthful of blue liquid on the asphalt, where it drenches a smattering of old cigarette butts. Something about that makes me want to laugh my ass off, but right now I forget why. I hit the bottle of mouthwash again, then swish and spit it.

"Better?" Rex asks, as I slam the car door shut.

"Much."

"Well don't hog it all," he says. "Hand that bottle over here."

He tucks the mouthwash back in the plastic bag when he's done with it, then asks if I'm ready to go.

I nod. The sky is just starting to be tinged with light. The sun will come up soon.

Rex starts the car. When he leaves the parking lot, instead of turning right to go up the hill to my house, he turns left.

"Where are you going?" I ask. "I thought you were taking me home."

"If it's okay with you," he says, glancing over at me, "I thought we could go up to the field behind the school? It's not just great for looking at the moon. The sunrise looks super cool from there, too."

I laugh. "You really want to fuck me in that field, don't you?"

"Is that a bad thing?" he asks, grinning.

"No. Let's go."

The field is empty when we get there, but I wouldn't care if it was full of cars. The caffeine from the coffee is starting to hit me hard, and I'm excited to be with him. Fucking while the sun comes up sounds glorious.

He pushes all the stuff from the Food Mart over to his

side of the car, scoots over, and maneuvers me on top of him on the passenger side. For a while we're a mess of pushing and pulling at the clothing that's keeping us separate. It's too cold to get any kind of naked, so once we're unclothed enough for fucking, I get close to him so he can push inside me.

I'm grinding my hips against him in this slow, rhythmic way, loving the feeling of control it gives me, when all at once I see cold, late autumn sunlight splashing over the seat all around him. The light makes it seem like he's golden, and glowing.

"Your hair is on fire," he says, and I realize he's seeing the sun light me from behind. He twines his fingers in my hair and pulls my head closer so he can kiss me.

When I come, I know that from now on, every time I see autumn light like this, I'm going to think about this moment. And Rex.

We finish as the rising sun floods the entire car with hazy beams of light. I get off Rex and settle next to him. After a few minutes he reaches across the seat for the plastic sack from the Food Mart. "Hungry?"

We share the rest of the pastry I didn't finish, then sit still, bathed in chilly sunshine. He's playing with my hair again and it feels good.

"Did I miss anything else last night?" I ask. "You know, after I passed out?"

He half laughs, half snorts. "You missed everyone doing lines."

I freeze. "Lines? Like, you mean coke? Cocaine?"

"Yeah. So you didn't miss much. I don't do that shit. Too fucking expensive. Plus it's just...it's not my thing."

I believe him. I heard the disgust in his voice when he said people at the party were doing lines. I can't expect every place we go to be drug free. The important thing is that he isn't doing them. He keeps running his fingers through my hair, and I relax again.

Suddenly, Rex says, "I feel like I should have known you sooner."

It's a strange thing to say. But I kind of know what he means.

"I feel the same way," I tell him. Then yawn.

"Tired?"

"Yeah. Aren't you? We left so early."

"I've been running on pure adrenaline since last night. Hey." All at once there's an urgent note in his voice.

"Yeah?"

He turns to me, then reaches out and puts his fingers under my chin. His eyes are glittery and warm, and I start feeling the same way inside.

"Are you my girl?" he asks.

As I look in his eyes, I know whatever this is between us, it's changing me. It scares me. But I don't want to stop it.

"Yeah," I say. "I am."

His face breaks into the sweetest smile. How did I not see the person he is sooner? At first, all I saw was the clothes, the car, the cigarettes. He's all of that, too. But he's a lot more.

He kisses me again in a small explosion of happy energy, making me laugh. Then he puts his arm around me, and we just sit there, staring out over the sunlit field.

"I'll take you home in a minute," he says. "But I kind of like it here."

"I'm not in a rush," I tell him.

We sit and absorb the sunshine for a while, then he slides behind the wheel and drives the car back to the road.

In front of my house, he asks, "You got a pen?"

I produce a pen from my bag, and he takes it from me. Then he reaches out for my arm and starts to write on it.

"This is the number at my mom's house," he says. "I'm not there a lot, but it's one place you can find me. She'll take a message if she answers the phone." A grin tugs at the corners of his mouth. "You might want to write that down somewhere else, like, before you take a shower or something."

"Or I'll have to track you down where you work, right?" I laugh. Then I wonder if he has a job. He's never talked about having one.

"I work," he says, as if he just read my mind. "I work for this electrician friend of my mom's. I know she hopes I'll give up on the band and do that instead, but...."

"But your band might get signed any day," I remind him.

His face lights up again, then he smirks. "That's right. Things are 'in process.' We can't give up now. We'll fuck up the process."

I can tell he's making fun of himself. "Do you want to give up?" I ask him. When he doesn't answer right away, I wonder if it was a dumb question, and I start to feel squirmy.

But then he says, "No. I don't want to give up."

"So don't."

He grins. "Okay, Batgirl. Thanks for the pep talk. Now go take a shower."

"*You* go take a shower," I retort, automatically. Then I grin back at him. "Thanks for the ride."

"Thanks for the sunrise." He leans forward and kisses me quickly. "I'll see you soon, okay?"

I get out of the car and wave at him through the window as he drives away.

I'm in way deeper than I ever planned to be. On some level I know this thing with Rex is doomed. If either or both of us gets what we want, our lives will go in completely different directions.

But it doesn't matter. I don't want to stop seeing him. I want to be his "girl." Whatever that means, I'm all in.

CHAPTER 19

On Thanksgiving Day, Mom gets up before five am and starts cooking. She never said she wanted me to get up early, too, or that she needed my help. But by the way she's banging around in the kitchen now, I have a hunch she does want me to help her.

I'm exhausted. I worked a late shift on Wednesday night. But there's no way I'm going to be able to sleep with Mom making so much noise.

So I get up and go to the kitchen, where I find her standing at the sink. I fold my arms over my chest. "Need some help?"

She turns around and gives me this relieved look. "Can you finish peeling the potatoes? It takes forever, and I want to start cleaning the house."

"Sure," I sigh. "I'll take over."

She leaves the kitchen and goes to the hall closet for the vacuum, while I pick up the potato peeler and start to work on a sink-full of russets.

By early afternoon, between the two of us, we've managed to stuff the turkey and prepare several sides, including the mashed potatoes, green bean casserole, and homemade cranberry sauce. Both the potatoes and green bean casserole are waiting in the fridge. We're going to reheat them closer to dinner time. Carrie, Mom's sister, is bringing the pies, so we don't have to worry about those.

We've thoroughly cleaned the house. Every surface has been dusted, polished, or vacuumed. We also put the extra leaves in the table, then added a tablecloth, and candles. I have to admit, it looks classy.

Erick has been in his room all day, hiding from us. Part of me thinks it's pathetic Mom didn't make him help us get the house ready for Thanksgiving. Then again, if he had helped, he and Mom would've been sparring all day, which would have sucked.

Around three, a minivan pulls in our driveway behind Mom's car.

"They're here!" She's trying to sound cheerful, but I can tell she's about to start climbing the walls.

I walk toward the front door. "I'll get it," I tell her.

When I swing the door open, Carrie is there, holding a pie. Just behind her is her husband, Jared.

I take the pie from Carrie. "C'mon in."

"Good to see you, Frankie," she says with a smile. "You're so grown up! Jared, can you get the other pie from the car, and...everything else?"

"Sure hon." Uncle Jared goes back to the minivan, and I let Carrie inside.

Mom goes over to her sister, and they exchange a somewhat stiff embrace.

"Where are Jared and the kids?" Mom asks. "Still in the car?"

Carrie serves up another smile. "Jared's bringing in a couple more things."

I get this strange feeling she's trying a little too hard.

"Erick can't wait to see his cousins," Mom says. "It's been a long time."

Carrie's smile goes a bit stale. "About that. The kids' grandma—Jared's mom, you've met her, right?—she really wanted to see the kids this Thanksgiving. So we dropped them at her house on the way over."

Mom stares. "They're not coming? I made dinner for seven people."

"I'm sorry, Kat. But Jared's mother is getting up there, and we just didn't want to deprive her of a chance to be with her grandchildren—"

Mom cuts across Carrie's words. "Fine. Then I guess we'll just have too much food for five people." She turns to me. "Frankie, go take two of the place settings off the table."

"Okay." I look at Carrie, and gesture to the pie. "Does this pie...?"

She nods at me. "Yes, just put it in the fridge."

I take the pie to the kitchen, and after some maneuvering, I find space for it in the refrigerator. Then I go to the dining room table and dismantle two of the place settings.

As I'm putting the unused plates back in the cupboard, Mom comes in the kitchen. "Put the sides in the oven, will you?"

"Sure." I open the fridge again and pull out the green bean casserole and the large, round baking dish with the already mashed potatoes. I spot a cheese plate on the bottom shelf of the fridge and turn around to look at Mom. "Should we do the hors d'oeuvres now?'

"I don't care," she mutters.

"Now's probably the best time?" I venture.

She puts out her hand. "Fine. Give it to me. Let's get this Thanksgiving thing over with."

I hand her the cheese plate, and she rips off the plastic, then pops a piece of cheese in her mouth. She carries the plate out to the living room, yelling, "Cheese plate, everybody! Cheese plate coming through."

I stare after her for a few seconds. Once she gets in a mood like this, it's hard to get her out of it. There's a fifty-fifty chance dinner is going to be an ordeal. I entertain a wild fantasy about leaving and riding my bike to Ronnie's house. Or Rex's. Or anywhere I could be free of the tension in our house.

Then I snap out of it and gather some plates and serving utensils for the cheese tray. After depositing them in the living room, I go back to the kitchen and put the sides in the oven. Then I arrange some crackers on a plate, and take those out to the living room, too.

"Well look at that," Mom says, as I set the plate down on our coffee table. "All fancy and pretty. It's just like a *real* Thanksgiving!"

"Thanks, Frankie," Jared grins at me. I can tell he's amused by Mom's behavior. If he's lucky, he'll still feel that way by the time we've all had pumpkin pie.

"Anyone need anything else?" I ask.

"Why don't you sit down and relax with us?" Carrie suggests.

I try to smile at her, then give a slight shake of my head. "Thanks, uh, I think I'm going to check on Erick. I'll be right back."

I go straight to my brother's room and pound on the door.

"Come in!" he yells.

When I walk in, he pulls off his headphones. I can hear

metal music still pulsing through them. I shut his door and lean against it.

"What's it like out there?" he asks.

"Jared Jr. and Cynthia aren't here," I inform him. "They're at their grandma's for dinner tonight."

"I figured. They didn't come say hi, so…" he shrugs. "Is Mom pissed?"

I nod. "She's in a mood."

Erick grimaces. "You can stay in here if you want."

"Maybe just for a few minutes." I slide down to the floor as Erick puts his headphones back on and resumes listening to music.

The tinny sound of heavy metal bleeding from his headphones is strangely comforting. It kind of reminds me of Rex.

After a few minutes I get up and go back out to the kitchen.

By the time we all sit down to dinner, Mom is a bit tipsy. Carrie and Jared brought a couple bottles of wine with them. They broke open the first bottle with the cheese tray, then opened the second one with dinner.

The food is actually pretty good. I was worried about the potatoes being too dry, but we made them a touch runny, so reheated, they're kind of perfect. And I spent most of the afternoon basting the turkey, so it turned out juicy and tender.

The table looks odd with the leaves still in. It's too big for the number of people sitting at it. Mom is at one end, and Jared's at the other. Erick and I are sitting next to each other, and Carrie is across from us, with one whole long side of the table to herself.

Mom downs the rest of her glass of wine, and Jared gets up to silently refill it for her.

"The turkey is wonderful," Carrie says.

Mom casts a glance over at me. "Frankie gave me a lot of help."

Just as I'm feeling gratitude toward her for giving me some credit, she goes on speaking.

"She's had quite a few changes in her life lately. Haven't you, Frankie?" Her eyes flash at me, and I don't like the look in them.

"Yeah," I let out a self-conscious laugh. "I mean, everything's been kind of a blur since I graduated."

"We're so proud of you, Frankie," Jared tells me. For the past half hour or so, he's been catching on to the family dynamic. He's significantly less amused than he was during the hors d'oeuvres portion of the evening.

"Yep, Frankie graduated. And she's got a new boyfriend, too." Mom's tone is cheerful, but for me, it rings false.

"Oh really?" Carrie beams at me. "What's he like?"

"He's a deadbeat," Mom cuts in, before I can answer. "He drives this terrible old car." She takes another sip of wine and laughs. "Whenever he drops her off it stinks up the whole block. Total loser."

"No, he's not," Erick mutters. "He's a super cool dude."

Jared forces a cheerful tone. "So, what have you been up to, Erick?"

"Yeah, how's school for you this year?" Carrie chimes in. "You're in junior high next year, aren't you?"

My brother nods, grimly. I can tell he's still worried about Mom pushing him into playing sports.

"Well, enjoy the sixth grade while you can!" Jared's voice is artificially hearty. He sounds ridiculous, but I know he's trying to keep the conversation light. I feel kind of bad for him.

"Frankie wants to go to college," Mom announces. As

far as she's concerned, there's been no subject change. We're still discussing my post high-school life.

"Great!" Carrie enthuses. "Where are you going to apply?"

Before I can answer her, Mom goes on. "She's trying to save up money. Working at a chicken restaurant? She's working at a greasy fast-food place, dating a deadbeat loser, and she thinks she's going to college. I mean, have you ever heard of anything more stupid?"

"Well," Jared says, struggling to maintain his jovial tone, "With a lot of hard work, anything is possible—"

Mom looks straight at me. "I don't think I've ever heard of anything more stupid in my life."

I've had enough. I stand up. "At least I'm not the drunk bitch who's ruining Thanksgiving!"

She explodes, then, and starts yelling at me, nonstop.

"Don't you talk to me that way, young lady! I can have wine with my Thanksgiving dinner, and I can have an opinion about your boyfriend, or any of the other things you're doing to screw up your life! You're going to end up pregnant and stuck with a goddamn deadbeat asshole. If you think the way you're living is going to get you into college, you've got your head so far up your ass your brain has stopped working. You're stupid, stupid, stupid!"

She bangs her wineglass on the table with each "stupid." Wine sloshes over the sides of the glass and on to the tablecloth.

"I'm not stupid! Stop saying that. Stop it!"

"Stupid," she repeats, glowering at me.

Her eyes are snapping with an unpleasant emotion I can't identify. Whatever it is, I don't want to look at her any longer. I push my chair aside and run for the front door.

It's cold outside. The golden autumn weather we've

been enjoying for most of October and November is gone. The sky is dark and cloudy, and the clouds are spitting rain. There's a bit of wind too, rattling the leaves and loosening them from the trees.

I don't care, though. It feels better to be in the rain and wind than inside at the dinner table. It even feels good to be shivering.

The front door opens, and I turn my head. In the porch light, I see Carrie's slight frame. She's wearing her coat, but her arms are wrapped tightly around her body, like the coat isn't enough.

She comes over to me. "How are you doing?"

"Not so great."

"Kat went to bed early. She said she's not feeling well."

It always freaks me out to hear someone call my mother by her actual name. Her first name is Katherine, but her family has always called her Kat.

"Why don't you come inside and have some pie with us?" Carrie urges.

Mom's sister is a kind person. I want to make her happy, but right now, the thought of going back inside is impossible. I shake my head at her, and she touches my arm.

"I think it's great that you want to go to college, Frankie. That's a good goal to have. I'm sure you can do it."

To my horror, I feel tears start to spill out of my eyes. I wipe them away, quickly.

"Your mom probably isn't helping much, is she?" Carrie guesses.

"She isn't helping at all." The words come out in a sob, and I stop talking to get myself under control. When I can speak again, I say, "I don't think she wants me to go. Although God knows why she wants me to stay here. She doesn't even like me." I swipe a few more tears away from my eyes.

"She doesn't like herself," my aunt corrects, gently. "You know it's not okay that she said those things to you, right? That's not how she should talk to you."

"I shouldn't have said what I said, either." I'm already feeling guilty for calling Mom a bitch.

Carrie smiles at me. "It wasn't your finest moment. But she baited you into it. And she's the adult here."

"She's not usually like that," I defend. "I think it was the wine. She never drinks wine. She drinks diet soda. Like, all the time. Gallons of it."

Carrie frowns. "We shouldn't have brought wine tonight. I knew it was going to be—uncomfortable—and Jared thought wine would help us loosen up. But it just made everything worse."

"It's not your fault," I tell her. "It's just that when Mom drinks, she tells you what she's actually thinking."

Carrie gives me a searching look.

"I promise, Mom doesn't have a drinking problem." And I don't think she does. I've only seen her drink a handful of times, including tonight. But she sure gets ugly when she does drink.

"I'll take your word for it," Carrie relents. She takes a deep breath. "Don't let her stop you from going to college, Frankie."

I stare at her, shocked. I know *I've* been thinking Mom wants to stop me from going to college, but it sounds crazy whenever I attempt to say it out loud. Why would a parent not support her kid trying to get ahead in life? It doesn't seem real.

"I bet you feel lots of responsibility for her, and for

Erick, too," Carrie goes on. "But she's the mother. Erick is her son, not yours. You need to go live your life."

I feel a fresh urge to cry. "What if she doesn't take care of him? What's going to happen to him?"

"Right now, she's putting a lot on you because you're here. If you leave, she'll have to adjust." She smiles at me, but there's an edge of seriousness to her smile. "Nobody's going to look out for you as well as you can. Figure out what you want and go for it. If that's college, go for that. And don't ever look back."

Her words make me feel overwhelmed with emotion. I'm afraid if I speak it will all spill over, so I keep my mouth shut.

"Ready for some pie?" Carrie asks.

I nod at her.

"Good, then let's go inside. It's freezing out here!"

We go in. Mom is conspicuously absent from the table, and there are some wet paper towels on the tablecloth where she spilled her wine. I help Carrie serve up pumpkin pie for everybody. As soon as Erick finishes his slice, he slips back to his room.

"We need to get the kids from their grandma's house," Carrie tells me, "but I'll help you clean the kitchen first."

I pack up several containers of leftovers to send home with my aunt and uncle. As they're leaving, Carrie turns to me. "Stay in touch. We're just a phone call away."

"Okay," I nod.

"I mean it. And tell me when you get into college."

The phone rings as Carrie and Jared are driving away, and I pick it up, quickly, so it doesn't wake Mom.

"Peterson residence."

"Uh...is, uh, Francesca there?"

"Hi, Rex. It's me."

"Hey, you. You sound different."

My nose is stuffed up from crying, but I don't tell him that. "How was your Thanksgiving?" I ask.

"It's over," he laughs.

"Yeah, same."

We're both quiet. We sit there for a couple minutes, being with each other on the phone. I can hear the TV at his house and the sound of guys yelling in the background.

"Watching the game?" I ask.

"My uncles are. I should probably go watch with them." He hesitates a second, then says, "Just wanted to hear your voice."

"I'm...I'm really glad you called." I feel close to him, but also confused. I agreed to be "his girl" and I know it means something. But I'm still not sure what status that gives me in his life.

"You working tomorrow?" he asks.

"Not until, like, early afternoon."

"Wanna get breakfast?"

"What time?"

"Nine?"

"I'll see you then," I tell him.

WHEN HE PICKS me up in the morning, we get more bad coffee and pastries from the Food Mart, then head straight for the field behind the school. This time, it's grey and wet outside. The gloomy weather gives sex with him a different flavor.

"You okay?" Rex asks, as he plays with my hair.

I love how he's obsessed with my hair. "Yeah, I'm fine," I say, automatically.

"Liar," he laughs.

I sigh. "It's just my mom. She got kinda ugly at dinner last night. She was giving me shit about college. And about you. Whatever. I'm used to it."

"I hope she gave you shit about me," he laughs again. "I'm every mother's worst nightmare."

I pound his shoulder. "I don't care what she thinks about you."

"So don't care what she thinks about anything," he responds. "Including college. If you want to go, she can't stop you."

His words are an echo of my aunt's. It's heartening to realize I have two people on my side. Carrie and Rex. Maybe that's enough.

I snuggle closer to him, feeling safe. In fact, I feel more safe in Rex's loud, purple, foul-smelling GTO than I've ever felt anywhere in my entire life.

When he drops me back home just before eleven, I notice Mom's car is gone from the driveway. Inside, there's a piece of paper with her writing on it, sitting on the kitchen counter.

I pick it up, and read it.

I shouldn't drink. Sorry I ruined Thanksgiving. -Mom

I stare at the note for several seconds before I crumple it up and toss it in the trash underneath the sink. Then I go to my room to start working on scholarship applications.

CHAPTER 20

To sneak Erick in to see Rex's band, I have to make up a reason for me and Ronnie to take him to the city. I tell Mom we're treating him to a Laser Floyd light show at the Pacific Science Center in Seattle. To make sure she doesn't get suspicious of us doing something so spontaneously nice, I say it's my early Christmas present for Erick, but we have to go before the holiday. After that, the show is moving on from Pink Floyd to a different type of music. Music that Erick won't enjoy.

The night of the show we're hanging out in the kitchen, waiting for Ronnie to pick us up. Erick is wearing another metal band T-shirt, but jeans instead of his usual sweats. I'm back to my practical layers look, which is what I would wear if we were actually going to Laser Floyd at the Science Center.

Erick is beyond excited. He's drumming on the kitchen counters with his fingers and singing songs under his breath. Fern on Fire's songs, from their demo tape.

If my mom had any familiarity with their music, I'd be worried about her catching on to our plan. But since they're not on mainstream radio, and since she doesn't like rock music, we're safe. So far, she hasn't even come out to bother us with last-minute suggestions for the evening.

"Try to calm down," I mutter to Erick. "You're way too excited for a laser light show."

"Maybe laser light shows make me really excited," he retorts.

I look at my watch. Ronnie should be here any minute.

Just then Mom makes her appearance in the kitchen. In fact, she looks like she's dressed to go out herself.

"Ronnie's not here yet?" She's using this conversational tone that always makes me nervous she's about to ruin something.

"She should be here any minute," I reply, keeping my eyes on the front door.

"I was thinking maybe I could go with you," Mom says.

Both Erick and I whirl around and stare at her. Praying that he keeps his cool, I kind of laugh, like I think the idea is absurd. "I didn't know you were a Pink Floyd fan."

"I don't know, it sounds interesting. Maybe it would be a nice thing to do as a family."

It takes everything in me not to look at Erick. If the two of us exchange any kind of freak out energy, she's going to be on to us in a heartbeat.

"I don't know, Mom," I say. "I think it's more of a thing for hardcore Pink Floyd fans than, you know, a family activity?"

There's a knock at the door then, and Erick leaps up to answer it. "Hey, Ronnie."

She comes in and sees Mom standing with me in the kitchen. "You guys ready for Laser Floyd?" she asks, looking from Erick to me.

"Yeah, we're ready." I give Ronnie a look I hope she'll

understand. "Mom was just saying she wants to come with us."

"Oh!" Ronnie sounds shocked. Then she recovers and laughs. "I mean, sure Ms. Peterson, you can come with us, but I don't know if you'd have a good time."

"Why not? It sounds like fun."

Ronnie chews her lip, like she's trying to decide how much she should say. "Well, okay. I don't want to gross you out, but for a thing like Laser Floyd, you know, a lot of guys go to it? They can be kind of gross. Sometimes they do, like, a lot of farting during the show."

Mom lifts an eyebrow. "Farting?"

"You know how guys are," Ronnie nods. "I mean, I'm sure it won't bother Erick. He's probably used to hardcore public flatulence."

"Me and my friends fart all the time!" Erick crows.

Mom sounds suspicious. "How do you know about this —farting—thing?"

Ronnie's reply is prompt. "I went to see Laser Floyd a couple weeks ago with my boyfriend. It was pretty bad." Then she shrugs. "But if you want to come with us, hey, the more the merrier. We kind of need to go now, though, or we're going to miss it."

She turns around and starts to head for the door.

"Oh, never mind," Mom says. "I just thought it might be fun. I'll think of something else we can do as a family."

It kills me to prolong this any further, but I look at Mom and ask, "Are you sure you don't want to come with us?"

She gives a passive aggressive shrug, which is her way of saying she's not coming. I don't think Ronnie's fart story is what changed her mind. I have a hunch Mom caught on that Erick doesn't want her to be there. That he wants to have this experience without her. And even though we're on the way to a completely different experience than she thinks we are, it's true in essence.

I nudge Erick. "C'mon, let's go."

We're both silent as we follow Ronnie out to her car and get in, Erick in the back, me in the front. As soon as all the doors are shut, I turn to Ronnie. "'Hardcore public flatulence?'"

She shrugs. "It's something I heard Theo say once."

"You could have just said the show was sold out, or something."

Ronnie rolls her eyes at me. "She's *your* mother. You could have told her that before I got here."

"Oh my God! Oh my God!" Erick yells. "I thought she was going with us. I was so sure she was going to come with us!"

"But I saved your asses," Ronnie glances over at me, then at Erick in the rearview mirror. "You both owe me."

"We loooove you, Ronnie," I croon, singsong.

Erick starts his own song from the backseat. "Ronnie is awesome, Ronnie is so awesome, Ronnie is the awesomest EVER!"

She groans. "Okay, both of you shut up. God. The two of you at the same time is unbearable."

At the venue, we park in back. Theo told Ronnie it was okay. This way, we can easily sneak Erick in the back door from the parking lot. He's donned a hooded sweatshirt with the hood pulled over his head. He could arguably pass for a skinny girl.

On the way to the show, he insisted on using my eyeliner, which surprised me. I didn't know he was into makeup. But he must be, because once he got hold of the eyeliner, he put it on like he knew what he was doing.

The effect is dramatic. It makes him look older, though

nowhere near twenty-one. But he definitely looks less like my little brother than he did a few hours ago.

We go up to the back door, and Ronnie tells us to wait while she slips inside to find one of the guys. The plan is to smuggle Erick in just as the band's going onstage. Everyone will be focused on the show, and no one will notice my brother or question whether he should be there.

Erick and I stand just off to the side of the back door, so we're out of range of the dim light shining above it.

"You excited?" I ask.

"Duh," he says.

"I hope you know a lot of people are working to make this happen for you."

He rolls his eyes so hard I can see it in the low light. "Yeah, yeah, I should be eternally grateful. I owe you for the rest of my life. I get it."

"I'm kind of not kidding," I say.

His face goes serious. "I get it, okay? I'm just afraid somebody's going to catch us before we get in."

I shake my head. "Not gonna happen." I don't know why I'm so sure. But I am. I can hear the band sound-checking inside. Noah pounding on his drum kit. Theo and Todd testing the sound of their instruments. Rex speaking, then singing into the mic. Jingle Bells. This is a holiday show, after all.

The back door to the club opens, and both Erick and I jump. But it's just Todd. I nudge my brother.

Todd smiles at us. "You guys ready?"

"Absolutely," I tell him. "Thanks for doing this."

He shrugs and opens the door, then gives my brother a nod. "Welcome to our world."

I can hear the self-mockery in Todd's tone, but Erick takes him one hundred percent seriously. As far as my brother's concerned, he's just been formally invited to step across the threshold of the realm of rock n' roll.

Todd points us down a corridor. "Go that way. We're gonna start as soon as I'm back onstage."

I nod at him, and we head down the passageway. Before we even get out to the main room, I hear the band begin to play. Erick's hands ball into excited fists as we enter the room.

The club is more packed than usual. I figure it's because there are a ton of bands on the bill tonight. Well, not a ton, but there are five, which is more than usual. Every band is playing a shorter set.

I turn to Erick and yell, "Want to get close to the front?"

He nods eagerly.

"Stick by me!"

I start weaving my way through the crowd. Erick puts his hand on my shoulder, so we don't get separated. We manage to get sort of close on the right side of the stage, which is where Todd stands.

Erick points at him, and yells in my ear. "Is that the guy who let us in?"

"Yeah!"

And from that moment, he's mesmerized. In fact, I spend most of the show watching my brother.

He's fascinated with every move each band member makes. When Rex interacts with the crowd and locks his grip with some of the audience members' outstretched hands, Erick stretches out his own hand, as if Rex could reach it. He laughs his ass off when Noah jokes around and plays a disco beat as a false start to one of their songs. But the person who catches his attention most is Todd. Almost every time I look over at Erick, he's watching Todd, like he's trying to memorize everything he does.

For the first time, I realize this is more to Erick than just goofing around playing air guitar in his room. It's about more than the posters of heavy metal bands that plaster his bedroom walls or the band shirts he wears like some kind of uniform. This is my brother's dream.

I've always been worried he'll get in with the wrong crowd once he starts junior high. I don't want him acting tough, getting high, and ultimately going nowhere. But what if he actually has a talent for music? What if he could be somebody like Todd? It might not be the safest option for him, but playing guitar and being good at it would give him a chance to be *somebody*. And when you're a kid trying to find yourself, that's worth a lot.

The band ends with a glam-metal cover of "Up on the Housetop." Rex hams it up, doing stereotypical rock star poses all over the stage, bending over backwards and screaming out the chorus. He gets the audience singing it with him. Erick belts out every word while he pumps his fist in the air.

By the time they get to the end of their set, my brother is glowing. As they exit the stage, Erick turns to me and gushes, "Oh, my God, that was so fucking amazing!"

"We need to get you out of here," I remind him, and to my relief, he doesn't fight me. I propel him back down the corridor where we came in, and we head out the door to the parking lot. I'm hoping the guys will come out and talk to him, but I know they might not.

Suddenly, I realize I don't see Ronnie's car where she parked it. Did she go somewhere? She couldn't have left with Theo already, since he just got off stage. Could she? If she's abandoned me *and* Erick, I'll kill her.

Before I have time to get more worked up, Rex sticks his head out the door.

"Hey!" He motions us to come over to him. "You got to see the show, right?"

"Yeah, we saw it," I assure him. I look over at my brother, who seems to have gone speechless. If he sees Todd as a musical hero, I have a feeling he thinks Rex is some kind of god. I give Erick a nudge.

"Hey, man," he squeaks. "You guys were so amazing, man. So amazing."

Rex smiles at him. "Thanks, man. Appreciate it." He looks at me. "Why don't you come inside for a few minutes?"

I roll my eyes in Erick's direction.

"It's fine," Rex assures me. "It's total mayhem backstage. Security's got better things to worry about than your brother."

"Want to go in?" I ask.

Erick nods vigorously, and I follow Rex inside to the green room. Like the club, it's packed. Everyone's drinking and smoking. A guy walks by us with a case of beers, handing them out to anyone who asks. He spots my brother.

"Hey, kid, want a beer?"

"Yeah!" Erick says enthusiastically, and the guy starts to hand one over.

I grab the beer from the guy's hand. "No, he doesn't want a beer. He's eleven."

I know it's likely Erick will be drinking beers underneath the bleachers at the junior high as soon as next fall. But he's not going to do it on my watch.

"Sorry, kid," the guy laughs. "I guess she wants your beer."

I glare at him and toss the beer back in the case, where it clanks against the other cans. Despite the fact that I've loosened my own standards around alcohol, I figure it's probably not good if Erick sees me drinking.

"Where's Ronnie?" I ask Rex.

He shrugs. "I haven't seen her. Just chill out for a while. If I see her, I'll let her know you're here." Then he sneaks his arm around my waist and gives me a quick squeeze before he disappears in the crowd.

"So, is he your boyfriend now?" Erick asks.

I still don't know the answer to that question. It was so much easier in high school to define someone as your boyfriend. I agreed to be Rex's "girl," but does he belong to me in the same way?

"It's complicated," I tell my brother.

He looks nonplussed, but I figure that's because I stopped him from having a beer.

"Hey!" Ronnie's suddenly at my side. She looks flushed, and happy. "Rex said you were looking for me, so here I am! How'd you guys like the show?"

"It was amazing," Erick gushes. He still sounds starstruck.

"Yeah, it was great," I agree. "Did you go somewhere for awhile?"

Ronnie laughs. "Huh? No? What are you talking about?"

"We went outside, and I didn't see your car. So I wondered if maybe you went somewhere?"

"No, I didn't go anywhere...." All of a sudden, her face goes white. "Oh *shit*!" she says. "Shit. I don't think I locked my car when we got here!" She starts pushing out of the green room. Erick and I follow her.

She's in a state of panic already, but when she gets to the place where her car was parked, she starts losing her shit.

"Somebody stole my car!" she screams. "My fucking car is gone!"

She goes on screaming, swearing, and freaking out. I want to tell her she should find a way to call the police, but she's so worked up I don't even feel like I can get near her.

"That sucks," Erick says. Then, "How are we going to get home?"

"I don't know," I tell him. "But if we're late, we'll just tell Mom that Ronnie's car got stolen. I mean, it's the truth, right?"

The back door bursts open, and a bunch of people come out in the parking lot, including Rex and Theo.

Rex comes over to me. "What the hell's going on? It sounds like someone's getting murdered out here."

Theo's with Ronnie, and he's holding her while she starts to sob on his shoulder.

"Someone stole Ronnie's car," I tell Rex.

"Shit, that sucks," he says. "How are you going to get home?"

"Exactly," my brother agrees, solemnly.

CHAPTER 21

Rex ends up taking us home. For Erick, that's just icing on top of an already perfect night.

As we drive north on I-5, he peppers Rex with questions. When did he start playing in bands? Was he always a singer? Is Fern on Fire trying to get signed? Are they touring soon? Rex answers them all. He's being really nice to my brother, which I appreciate.

And then, Erick asks a question that shocks me.

"So are you my sister's boyfriend or what?" There's a different edge to his voice. He sounds almost...protective? Of me? Can that be possible?

There's an uncomfortable silence. Then Rex drawls, slowly, "Yeah, I'm her boyfriend." He looks at my brother in the rearview mirror and cracks a grin. "You got a problem with that?"

"No," Erick says, his tone frank, and serious. "I just wanted to be sure you're not using her."

I choke down a fit of laughter.

Rex glances in the rearview mirror again. "I really dig

your sister, okay?" he says. "Nobody's using anybody. I promise."

"Okay." My brother seems satisfied. Like they've settled it, man to man.

After we pull up in front of the house, Rex turns around so he can talk to Erick in the backseat.

"So," he says, sounding almost stern, "since I know you want the best for your sister, if your mom asks why I brought you home, tell her Ronnie's car got stolen. Frankie found a pay phone and called me for a ride. You don't need to tell her anything else."

I turn around in my seat, too, and add, "Except that Laser Floyd was awesome."

Erick nods earnestly.

"Tell me what you're going to tell your mom," Rex says.

"Ronnie's car got stolen. Frankie called you for a ride." My brother thinks for a second. "And Laser Floyd was awesome."

"You've got it," Rex nods. "I need to talk to your sister for minute, so she'll follow you inside in a bit, okay?"

I get out of the car so Erick can crawl out from the backseat. On the curb, he calls out to Rex, "Thank you for..." I see him visibly stopping himself from talking about the show. "Thank you for everything."

"No problem, man." Rex waves a hand at him. "I'll see you around."

I get back in the car and watch Erick let himself inside the house. Then I turn to Rex. "You know you just made his year, right? The whole show—that's the happiest I've ever seen him. He was like a different kid."

"Glad he had a good time." Rex chuckles. "He's a *serious* kid. All those questions."

I hesitate. "Did you mean what you told him?"

"About what?"

"About being my boyfriend."

He gives me a patient look. "Didn't I already ask you to be my girl?"

"Yeah, but I mean, does that go two ways?"

"Two ways?"

I take a deep breath. I'm nervous, but this is important to me. "Yeah. If I'm your girl, does that mean you're my... guy?" It sounds silly when I say it out loud. I hope he knows what I mean. If I'm "his girl," if I belong to him in some way, then I want him to belong to me, too.

He reaches out and puts his finger under my chin. "Yeah," he says. "It goes two ways." He pulls me toward him, and we kiss. If Mom is watching, she's getting an eyeful.

We pull apart just before we start sliding down the slope to X-rated territory. Rex grins. "Does this mean we're 'going steady?'"

"It means we're both in it," I explain. "Like, the same amount."

He kisses me one more time. "Okay, Batgirl," he says. "I should get back down there and see if anyone else needs a ride."

"Oh, yeah, right. I bet Ronnie will need a ride up here."

"That's what I was thinking."

I scoot over to the passenger side door and pop it open.

Rex looks over at me, and his eyes are alive with humor. "Have a good night, *girlfriend*."

"Take care of yourself, *boyfriend*," I shoot back.

"I'll call you soon." He grins again. "Or show up at the chicken shack. One or the other."

"See you at the chicken shack." I slam the door shut. As he drives away, I feel good. Rex and I are officially a thing. My brother thinks I'm cool. And yesterday, I mailed out a batch of scholarship applications. It feels like things are shifting for the better. Like the universe is finally making room for me.

In the house, there's a light on in the living room. Mom is there, reading. I start to go straight to my own room.

"Erick said you had a good time at the laser show."

I change course and go toward the living room, standing just at the edge. Mom has her finger in her book, marking her place. The book's facedown in her lap, so I can't see what she's reading, but she's been into self help books lately, so I assume it's one of those.

"Yeah," I say. "The laser show was a lot of fun."

She looks up at me. "It was nice of Rex to bring you home. What's Ronnie going to do about her car?"

I sigh. "I don't know. I'll give her a call tomorrow. Look, Mom, I'm really tired, so I'm going to bed, okay?"

Mom flips her book over and puts her eyes back on its pages. "Thanks for looking after your brother."

"I always do." I turn around and start for my room. Maybe her thanks are genuine. Maybe they aren't.

I wish she was easier to read. But I'm not going to let her bother me tonight. Not when I know I just pulled off sneaking my brother in to see Fern on Fire. Not when I know, for sure, that Rex and me are a thing. A real, two-way thing. And not when I'm so certain that it's time for my life to start getting good.

When I go in my room, there's a sheet of folded over notepaper slid under my door. I pick up the note, shut the door behind me, and unfold the paper. It's written in Erick's scrawl, and it's short.

Thanks for the best night ever. You rule.

Nope. There is no way I'm going to let anyone or anything ruin this moment.

NEW YORK CITY
1995

CHAPTER 22

I leave *Rags to Bitches* with the Fern on Fire CD in my bag and my mission in mind—to interview the band. But first, I have to go to my shift at the coffee shop, where I find it extraordinarily difficult to concentrate on the correct configuration of espresso shots, flavored syrups, and foamed milk.

It doesn't seem real that I'm going to see the guys again: Theo, Todd, Noah. And maybe Rex. Then again, it's possible most of them will skip out on the interview. It's not like *Rags to Bitches* is a big deal. We're not *SPIN*. We're not *Rolling Stone*. We're not even the next tier down. I'm just as surprised as Tom that they agreed to let us interview them.

I'm torn between hoping Rex will show up and hoping that he won't. Six years after I first met him, I'm right back where I started—ambivalent about seeing him—though I'm not sure why.

Ever since Fern on Fire hit the mainstream several years ago, I've tried to ignore them. The life I was living when I knew those guys feels like a different time. A time I'm no longer connected to.

I've heard rumors about Rex's struggles with addiction. Maybe it's heartless, but I've tried to ignore that, too. Addiction is such a common story in the rock and roll world.

Thankfully Tom never pushes me to dig for that kind of information when I interview musicians, and I never do. I've never thought it's any of my business. Plus, I hate how stories of addiction and recovery can be sensationalized in music publications. I have a hard time reading articles on the subject.

This summer, a "tell-all" piece about Fern on Fire appeared in a mid-tier magazine. Because Rex's band was featured, that particular issue sold more copies than usual. Everyone who cared about music read it. For once, I read it, too.

Most of the article was about the band's new album, but they also devoted a significant amount of ink to Rex's addiction issues and his time in rehab. The journalist put him in a favorable light, noting how healthy he looked. Editorializing that sobriety seemed to agree with him. That he presented like an older, wiser version of his former self.

The article fucked with my head. It dredged up old feelings, and I don't believe it's good to wallow in the past. There's nothing you can do to change it.

But here and now, at the coffee shop, the past seems to keep intruding. I make tons of mistakes with drink orders and spend most of my shift apologizing to customers. I'm too distracted to think about crafting anyone's perfect cup of coffee. Eventually my boss asks me if I'm feeling sick, and since I can tell he wants it to be true, I say that I am. He tells me to leave early and go home.

Instead of taking the subway, I walk the twelve blocks back to my apartment, hoping the exercise will clear my head. When I get there, my roommate, Mark, is sitting at our tiny kitchen table, in our even tinier kitchen, building a tower of pennies.

"Productive day?" I ask.

He gives me a dirty look. "You know it's my day off."

"Yeah, I know." I peer in the fridge, which is also small. Everything is small in New York. It has to be. There are so many people to cram into a limited space. I find some left-over Chinese food and sit down at the table with it.

"And what have you been up to?" Mark asks. "Being a model citizen all day? Up at the crack of dawn, serving coffee? Making the world a better place?"

Mark and I used to be a couple. We met near the end of my sophomore year at NYU, then broke up just before I graduated. Now, I can't imagine why we were ever together. He annoys the shit out of me. But he's a stable person and he pays the rent on time. He likes that about me, too. So now we're roommates, because living in New York is expensive.

I look at him directly. "I'm interviewing Fern on Fire tonight. For *Rags to Bitches*?"

He blinks. "Shit," he says, finally. "That's a big deal."

"Yeah, I keep waiting for Tom to call and say they backed out."

"I bet they won't," Mark says. "This could be your chance."

"My chance?"

"For a better job? This is a high-profile interview. Exponentially increases the value of your portfolio."

I stare at him. Of course, he's right. But for some reason, that hasn't occurred to me all day. All I've been thinking about is whether I'm going to see Rex again.

But now that Mark's brought it up, it's obvious. This is a big opportunity for me. It could be *the* big opportunity, the one that gets me to the next level. And that feels like a problem.

Even though I've been trying to ignore the band, a few things have slipped through the cracks. One thing I've noticed is they're infamous for giving rock journalists a hard time. I have a feeling if I try to work the situation to further my career, the guys in the band will be merciless. Their relatively cooperative interview this summer was a rare departure from how Fern on Fire usually deals with the press.

I stab my fork into the container of Chinese food. "I doubt I could top that tell-all piece from July."

"You never know," Mark says. "If you ask the right questions, you might get some juicy new tidbit."

"Like what?" I ask, sarcastic. I don't know why Mark is bothering me so much right now, but I'm beyond my usual level of irritation with him. He's still stacking pennies. The tower's starting to look precarious, but it hasn't fallen yet.

Mark looks up from the tower and smiles at me, showing his dimples. I used to be a sucker for those dimples. I'll never forget the day I looked at him and knew I didn't want him anymore.

We were talking about taking a trip together after graduation, and in the middle of our conversation, I realized I didn't want to take a trip with Mark. Or have a future with him. Or even fuck him. His dimples had lost their power over me. It was like a switch flipped inside. When it happened, I wondered if that was normal, or if it meant I just sucked at being someone's girlfriend. A counselor I saw for several months told me it was possible I struggled to form deep and meaningful emotional connections with romantic partners. To which my silent response was "Well, duh, lady. That's why I'm seeing a counselor."

Now, Mark goes on, oblivious to my angst. "Like what?" he repeats. "I don't know. Relapses? Romances? Rumors? You've always been good at ferreting out information. I have faith in you. You've got that killer instinct."

Even though he's ostensibly giving me a compliment, somehow, it sounds like a putdown.

I stand up. "I have to get ready."

As I leave the table, Mark's tower of pennies topples.

"Dammit, Frankie!" he says. "You ruined it."

I'm unsympathetic. "It was going to collapse under its own weight anyway." I take the Chinese food container to my closet of a bedroom and shut the door. Then I sit cross legged on my bed, eating and staring straight ahead.

If I see Rex tonight, I don't want him to think I'm using this interview as a stepping stone for my career. I'm not sure I even want a career in rock journalism. But I always act like I do, because when you live in New York City, you're supposed to be ambitious for something. At parties, I play the role of the girl who writes for the underground rock music magazine. Who knows her own worth, even if the rest of the world doesn't yet.

But the truth is, when it comes to my career, I don't know what I want. Sometimes, being involved in rock journalism grosses me out—even at my current low level. I love live music, and I love that my job at *Rags to Bitches* takes me into live music spaces. But I don't love reading rock journalism. Even—and sometimes especially—my own.

And yet, despite my ambivalence, I'm going to interview international superstars, Fern on Fire, in just a few hours. I need to prepare. Fast.

What a fucking terrible time to have an existential crisis.

CHAPTER 23

I'm staring at my blank notebook so hard I'm starting to feel hypnotized. I can't think of any good questions to ask the members of Fern on Fire. I'm screwed.

There are questions I want to ask, but they're personal. I could try to rephrase them so they sound like legitimate rock journalist questions. But if I do that, if I sneak in my personal questions under the guise of "journalism," I think I'll hate myself.

Maybe this is why I still work for *Rags to Bitches* instead of a publication that could pay me a real salary.

What am I going to ask them? Even focusing on their new album is problematic because I've heard the album in its entirety just once. And that was at a party when I was only half paying attention. I *have* heard the new singles from the record. A ton. You can't miss them, they're always on the radio.

I need to listen to their record, the CD Tom gave me, so it's fresh in my mind. But the truth is I'm scared. Scared to actually listen to it. From what I've gathered, the new album is dark.

If that's true, it's a testament to the band's genius that they've made dark music so marketable. But the idea of delving into their world—into Rex's world—makes me uncomfortable.

All the questions I truly want to ask are about Rex. How is he really doing? Are his addiction struggles behind him or is that just a story the band sold to the press? Why did Rex decide it was a good idea to share such personal information, especially since they're notorious for evading questions about their personal lives and struggles? Have they ever thought of taking an indefinite break, so their singer can hyper-focus on addiction recovery?

These questions are selfish because they're things I personally want to know. But even if I had the guts to ask them, even if the band would actually answer them, I know I wouldn't want to share their answers. And the whole point of an interview is to share that interview with the public.

I am so, so screwed.

I throw my notebook and pen down on the bed and go to the bathroom to take a shower.

When I get back to my room, I pull the CD Tom gave me out of my bag and pop it in my CD player. Then I sit back down on the bed with my notebook and pen. I'm going to listen to this, all the way through, and jot down any notes or questions that come naturally. That will leave me just enough time to get dressed and take the subway to the venue.

The first notes of the opening track split the air in the room. It's just drums and bass, setting up a foreboding, driving beat. Then the guitar. Then the vocal.

It's definitely Rex. His voice is impossible to mistake for anyone else.

I slip into a zone where I don't force myself to write or even think. I'm just absorbing. Whatever I glean from this listening session will form the foundation for tonight's interview. For better or for worse.

By the end of the album, I've abandoned my notebook. I'm lying on my bed and staring up at the ceiling. Fern on Fire's new album is an experience. Not every record is like that. Tons of records are singles plus filler. The better ones are a mood throughout the entire thing. But the rare album is like taking a ride on some magical machine that transports you to another reality. This record is like that.

I sit up and look at my notebook. My notes are pretty short. I've written:

sorta dirge-y

soul-scraping

Japanese koto or guitar effect? ask Todd?

mind kinda blown this hurts

Yep. I'm screwed.

There's a knock at my door, and I'm so dislocated from the present that for a second I think it's my brother. But no, Erick is back home, still living with Mom. It's his senior year of high school. He's over six feet tall now, and he plays guitar in a band with some other kids from his school.

I go to the door and open it. It's Mark, of course. His eyes drop to the opening of my robe, and I instinctively pull it shut. "What do you want?"

He leans against the door frame. "I was just wondering if you need some moral support tonight. It's got to be pretty intimidating, interviewing a band as big as Fern on Fire."

I smirk. "The magazine didn't give me a plus one. I can't get you in. Sorry."

"Well can I get a ticket?" Mark asks. "I mean, I'll buy a ticket if you need the support."

I shake my head. "It's invite only. Tell you what. If anyone offers me a ticket to their show at the Garden, I'll ask for a plus one, okay?"

"Oh, you don't have to do that," Mark says. "I mean, I did get you in to Jane's Addiction that one time, but it's not like you owe me for that or anything—"

"I do owe you," I tell him. "Okay? If I can get you a ticket, I will. Now fuck off, I have to get dressed."

"Thanks so much, Frankie. You're a sweetheart."

I make a face at him and shut the door. Then I go over to my closet. If Rex does show up tonight, I want to wear something that will catch his attention. But I have no idea what that would be.

If I wear something that doesn't feel like me, I won't be comfortable. So, finally, I decide to dress the way I would for any other band interview, in something relaxed that still makes me feel kind of hot.

About a half hour later I'm ready to go. I'm wearing fine wale cords that make my ass look good and a form-fitting blue sweater. I top it off with a denim jacket and a knit hat, because it's chilly out. The hat will flatten my hair, but I'll just have to deal. I'm not going to freeze to death for Rex Thornton.

I put on a little makeup, too. Just a touch. Eyeliner. A subdued lipstick I've been fond of this fall. A bit of powder, to soak up oil, because God forbid I should have a shiny nose.

I smile, then grimace at myself in the mirror. I'm still not satisfied. But if I take any longer, I'm going to be late. I grab my purse, which is a newer version of the cloth cross-body bag I used to carry in high school. Only now it sort of fits current fashion trends.

When I go out through the kitchen, Mark is still at the table, presiding over a new tower of pennies.

"Don't come near it!" he yells.

I roll my eyes. "Don't worry, I won't."

As I go for the door, he calls out, "Break a leg!"

I turn around. He actually looks sincere.

"Thanks," I say, gratefully. Then I go out.

CHAPTER 24

I walk to my subway stop, acutely aware of the autumn aura in the air. Even in New York City, where it's difficult to find trees outside of Central Park, you can sense that autumnal vibe.

A couple years ago, when Mark and I were still a couple, he drove me to New Hampshire so we could look at the changing leaves. I'd always heard the East Coast has the most spectacular fall colors, and it was true. It was certainly more spectacular than where I grew up. Seattle is colorful in the fall, but there are so many evergreen trees everywhere that it mutes the experience.

But it doesn't matter whether I'm on the West Coast or the East Coast. The fall always reminds me of Rex. The string of golden, chilly days when we were first getting to know each other. I can still picture the hazy sunlight bursting through the windows of his purple car when we had sex in the field behind the school.

Even when Mark drove me to see the leaves that day—when the two of us were supposedly in love—all the color and glory and beauty in New Hampshire made me think of

Rex. Of course, I didn't tell Mark that. And who knows. Maybe Mark had someone else on his mind, too.

When I get on the subway, it's crowded and there's nowhere to sit, so I have to stand and hold on to one of the straps. As I struggle to keep my balance, I think about possible questions for the band. Since I'm supposed to interview them before the show, I need to be ready to get a conversation started the minute I walk in the door. But of course, there's more on my mind than my lack of preparation for the most consequential interview I've done to date.

If Rex does show up, I'm wondering if it will give me some kind of closure. Maybe seeing him as he is now—successful, scarred, and famous—will finally erase my memory of the radiant, ambitious kid I knew six years ago. Because he has to have changed. He can't be the same person. It's inevitable.

I've changed since then, too. I'm no longer as willing to subject my life to the whims of beautiful, selfish young men. I want to follow my own whims. I just wish I was better at figuring out exactly what those are.

Sometimes I cringe when I remember how desperate I used to feel around Rex. Almost every blow job I ever gave him was initiated by that sense of desperation. And then there's the way I felt when I saw him around other girls. The constant urge to stake my claim to him.

On the flip side is the guilty, nagging feeling that I abandoned him to his addiction. I saw the start of it. But I did nothing to help him. I protected myself and left him behind. I don't feel good about that.

When I get to the venue, I'm surprised it isn't mobbed by fans. The band's management must have done a good job keeping the location secret. I'm supposed to pick up my ticket at will call, flash my press pass, and get access to the venue to interview the band.

I go up to the ticket window.

The guy in the booth looks bored. "Can I help you?"

"Yeah, thanks." I pull out my press card and show it to him. "I'm Frankie Peterson. I'm here to interview the band for *Rags to Bitches*. I think I have a ticket waiting?"

He consults a list, and nods. "I have a wristband for you." Then he leads me inside the venue, where he secures a bright pink band on my wrist. "You can wait here," he says. "I'll get their tour manager."

There's no seating, so I stand around to wait. The stage is small. It's amazing I get to see Fern on Fire here, in a venue like this. It's the same size venue I always used to see them in. But it's been impossible to find them booked in this kind of small club setting for years.

In moments, I'm going to be face to face with at least one of the guys from the band. My heart is already starting to pound, and my stomach is a mess of nervous flutters.

From somewhere in the depths of the club, a guy with a shaved head comes over to me. He's wearing black jeans and a T-shirt, and he has this efficient, no-nonsense energy.

"Hi, are you from *Rags to Bitches*?"

"Yep, that's me."

He puts out a hand. "I'm Jeff, the band's tour manager."

"Frankie," I say, as I shake his hand.

He gives me a direct look. "So, there's been a change of plans. We aren't going to be able to do the interview before the show. It'll have to happen right after it's over. Will that work for you?"

Like I have a choice. "Yeah, I guess. I can make that work."

"I'm so sorry for the inconvenience," he says in this

smooth, practiced way that tells me he's used to delivering unwelcome news.

I wonder why the interview's been postponed. I suspect it's because some other magazine has shown up to do an interview. Some magazine that has more clout than *Bitches*.

"It's no problem," I tell him, even though I'm kind of annoyed. Then I remind myself it's nothing short of miraculous that *Rags to Bitches* is getting to interview the band at all. Plus, now I have more time to come up with questions. "Should I come back later?"

Jeff shrugs. "You can, but people are already starting to line up." He gestures to my wristband. "That'll get you back in, but you'll have to stand in line. If I were you, I'd just hang out here. The bartender will be in soon. Free drinks with the pink wristband."

"Where do I go after the show?" I ask. "For the interview?"

"Just be sure to stick around, and I'll come find you," he promises. Then he slaps his hands together. "You good?"

I point in the direction of the bar. "I'm going to wait for the bartender. Thanks for your help, Jeff."

"My pleasure. Enjoy the show."

He disappears into the bowels of the club, and I'm alone. I go over to the bar and lean against the counter.

Despite the extra prep time, it's a letdown to have to wait until after the show for the interview. I was getting myself psyched up to do it, so now I have a ton of energy and nowhere to put it. I need a drink.

As soon as the bartender shows up, I order one and sip it slowly. I don't want to get drunk. Just calm my nerves. I wonder if the band is even in the building. Or if they'll remember me when I see them. It's possible they won't. It's been a long time, and as far as they're concerned, I'm just some girl Rex used to go out with.

Presently, the venue's doors open, and the crowd outside starts to filter in. It looks like everybody is wearing a wristband, but there are different colors. Some are bright blue, and some are lime green. I only see one other person with a pink wristband, like mine.

People start to make their way to the bar. I'm not in the mood to chat with anyone, so I finish my drink and move back into the club space. The room is buzzing with excitement and a certain kind of VIP energy that I don't like. But since this show is by invitation only, I suppose the VIP vibe is inevitable.

Roadies start arranging equipment on the stage. That's different. The last time I saw Fern on Fire play in a venue this size, they were still setting up their own equipment.

Suddenly, I have a strong urge to run away. I don't want to do the interview. I'm not even sure I want to see the show. I should have told Tom I was the wrong person for this assignment. Rex isn't just some guy in a band that I used to know. He's the guy who broke my heart.

I become aware of the song playing in the background of the club. "Ordinary World." Duran Duran. It feels like it's playing through my chest.

This is how I used to experience songs when I was with Rex, listening to music in his car. I have an urge to start crying, and I don't completely understand why. When the guitar solo near the end of the song starts blaring through the speakers, I get a huge lump in my throat. Just as I think I'm going to totally lose it, the music fades.

The crowd starts cheering and moving closer to the stage. I'm moved with them, and I'm grateful for the unthinking, non-individualistic quality of crowds. The mob swallows up my emotion, burying it in collective anticipation.

They start chanting. "F-O-F! F-O-F! F-O-F!" It takes me a second to figure out they're calling out the initials of the band's name. Almost everyone in the room is doing it.

Whatever happens next, I won't be experiencing it alone. I'll be sharing it with the crowd.

I hold on to that thought as the members of the band start to walk onstage. Everyone cheers louder, and I cheer with them, because right now, there's nothing I want more than to be a part of something louder, stronger, and bigger than myself.

CHAPTER 25

The crowd applauds each band member as they take the stage. Noah and Theo appear first. They both have short hair now. Then Todd walks on. He looks exactly the same. Same long mane of hair, same understated swagger. From the audience at least, he doesn't look any older.

Rex takes the stage last, and the small crowd goes nuts.

He's different. His hair isn't as short as Noah's or Theo's, but the unruly long hair I remember is gone. Now, it's just a little too long to be "respectable." He has it slicked back so you can see the shape of his face, his cheekbones, the length of his jaw. He's thinner than I remember.

Sporting jeans and a more elegant, expensive leather jacket than the one he used to wear, he projects an air of understated nonchalance. He always looked like he belonged on stage. But now, he knows he's earned the right to be the center of everyone's attention.

The band starts an intro to one of their new songs, and it reminds me of the first time I saw them play. I watch as Rex listens into the song, getting the vibe of it, and I realize

I'm scared for him to sing. Even though I've tried to ignore anything related to the band, it's impossible to shut out everything. I've heard the rumors. That Rex's drug addiction has rendered him a shell of his former self. That his voice doesn't hit as hard as it used to. I don't want the rumors to be true, and I'm afraid they will be.

But the minute he opens his mouth and starts singing, all my fear evaporates. The focus and power are still there. In fact, his focus is more intense than it used to be. He's a pro, now.

His voice *is* different, though. It's hard to pinpoint exactly what it is that's changed. There's something haunted in his eyes, something that was never there before. I catch glimpses of it when he looks out over the crowd. Sometimes, the look in his eyes bleeds into his singing, giving it a new, eerie quality. Maybe that's what people mean when they say his voice isn't what it used to be. Anyway, as my little brother would say, all the rumor mongers can "go pound sand." Rex still has it.

I wonder if he can see me or anyone else in the crowd. Or if all he sees are the lights and a shapeless mass of people. I never used to care about that before. I guess that's because back when we were together, he always knew when I was there, watching him. I realize I'm hoping that he knows I'm here now.

The band blows through six songs before he stops to talk to the audience.

"How are you all doing?" he asks, and everyone goes crazy, like he's just delivered a prophetic word.

"We wanted to say thank you for sticking with us all this time, so we hope you're enjoying the free show…"

The crowd breaks into more loud cheering.

"...and thanks for being here tonight."

"Thanks for letting us say thanks," Todd adds, from the side of the stage. Then he starts a new riff, and they launch into the next song.

They don't do much more talking to the audience. It's a tight, explosive beast of a set, and they play for almost two hours. By the end of it, I'm sorry I spent the last six years avoiding them. Maybe I have an uncomfortable history with Rex, but a great band is a great band. And they are definitely at that level.

The crowd calls them back for two encores, and that's when they play some of the old songs I remember. Songs from the time when Ronnie was going to ride off into the sunset with the entire band, and I believed Rex and me would figure things out.

Now Ronnie's married to someone else. And I'm living in New York City, pretending I want to be a rock journalist. Suddenly, I can say that—that I'm pretending. Because now, in this exact moment, I know it's true. After watching Fern on Fire play a blistering, two-hour set, I see my life more clearly.

I came to New York to escape from my mother and my life at home. Nothing more, nothing less. I got a chance, I took it, and I never looked back. But tonight, with such a visceral reminder of the past in front of me, I'm looking back. A journalism scholarship got me here, but I didn't come here to be a journalist. I came here for independence.

When I started working for *Rags to Bitches* it was so I could get into shows for free. I wasn't thinking of it as a steppingstone for building any sort of career. Then, over time, I let the job become my default reason for staying in New York.

But now, I'm caught up in the myth of this city. Nobody moves here to simply exist. If landing in New York City is going to mean something, I have to become *someone* while I'm here. And the thing in my life that has the most momentum is this job for *Rags to Bitches*, doing work I know I'm not truly passionate about. At its best, rock journalism can be clever and insightful. But it's not going to change anyone's life. Not the way a good song can.

If I stay in New York, who am I going to be? Because I don't want to be someone who writes about people like Rex. I want to actually *be* like Rex. I want to be a person who finds a way to move other people. To give them something meaningful. Or, at the very least, something that makes their lives a little more bearable.

After the last encore, the band again thanks everyone for coming, then they exit the stage. Once they're gone, I'm jolted out of existential crisis mode and back to my fundamental questions. Am I going to see Rex again? Do I want to?

Someone taps me on the shoulder. It's Jeff, their tour manager. Without saying anything, he beckons me to follow him, so I do. He takes me beyond the stage, to that forbidden zone Ronnie used to conquer, night after night, to be close to her muses.

The walls in the back corridors of the club are painted black and covered with graffiti. I wish I could stop and read everything, but Jeff is moving at a brisk clip. He stops in front of a nondescript looking door and knocks. Then he glances over his shoulder at me and says, "They should be in here."

After waiting a few minutes, he knocks again. And then I hear someone inside call out, "C'mon in!"

"All right, you're up," Jeff says and actually gives me a

genuine smile. His sudden friendliness makes me inexplicably nervous.

He opens the door. I'm seconds away from interviewing Fern on Fire, and I have no questions prepared. I'm about to walk into a disaster of my own making. I take a deep breath and follow Jeff inside.

PACIFIC NORTHWEST
1989-1990

CHAPTER 26

The day after the Christmas show, I'm still reveling in the fact that we pulled it off. Erick's been going around the house singing Fern on Fire's songs, nonstop. He knows them amazingly well. It gives me an idea, something I need to talk to Rex about. I decide to call him. But first, I call Ronnie to find out if the police have any news about her car.

"Nothing," she reports mournfully. "They think it's gone for good."

Not only has she lost her car, but apparently Rex asked her for ten bucks in gas money when he drove her home, so she's not in the best mood.

"I give *you* gas money all the time," I remind her. "And he did make two trips between here and Seattle. That's a lot of gas."

"He should have waited and taken us all together," she retorts. "I bet he didn't ask you for gas money."

"Well, no—"

"Oh, whatever, you're fucking him—of course he didn't ask you for gas money. Theo needs to get a car."

I stay on the phone with Ronnie until she's calmed down a bit. She's got a legitimate reason to be upset, but I have a feeling a new car will show up in her life soon, courtesy of her father.

After I hang up, I take a deep breath and call the number Rex gave me for his mom's house. I've never actually tried to call him there before.

It rings four times, and I'm about to hang up, when I hear a click on the other end of the line, then a well-modulated female voice.

"Hello? Thornton residence."

"Um, hi," I say. "Is, uh...is Rex home?"

"Just a minute." I hear her set the phone down, and call out, "Rex! Rex, one of your little girlfriends is on the phone."

One of his little girlfriends? Does he have a collection?

I hear him pick up. Then he says "Hello?" in a sleepy sounding voice.

"Hi. It's Frankie. You know, one of your little girlfriends?"

He kind of groans. "Don't freak out. That's just how she talks. What's up?"

I lower my voice. "I want to get my brother a guitar for Christmas. Do you know where I could get one, like, kind of cheap?"

"Huh." He goes quiet, like he's thinking. "No," he says, finally. "But I bet Todd does. You want me to ask him?"

"Could you?"

I can hear the shit-eating grin in his voice as he says, "Anything for one of my little girlfriends."

"Shut up. It kind of needs to be soon because it's almost Christmas—"

"Yeah, I know, next week. I'll ask him when I see him today."

"Do you guys have another show?"

"No." He gives a tired laugh. "We're meeting with the A&R guy. Again."

"Things are still in process?" I guess.

"You know it. You working tonight?"

"Until seven."

"Pick you up at eight?"

"See you then."

We hang up. "Pick you up at eight" means we'll go somewhere and have sex in his car. Maybe it should bother me that Rex assumes I'll be available for sex whenever he asks. But I like being with him. Plus, it's more than sex. It's a way to get out of my house. And when I'm with him, in his car, it's one of the only ways I feel free.

So, yeah. If he wants to pick me up at eight, I'm available. Whenever he wants.

HE CALLS me three days before Christmas and asks me to go for a drive with him. He says he has good news, and he wants to tell me about it in person. I hope that means Todd found a guitar for Erick. Rex said he thought Todd could find something basic for about fifty bucks, and I've decided to part with that much money from my savings account.

After he picks me up, he drives to this little waterfront town that's just west of where we live, and parks at the beach.

Rex surveys the view for a while, then says, "I should come here more often." He glances over at me. "It's pretty, huh?"

"Yeah, it is," I agree. "What's your good news?" For some reason, I feel on edge. When he picked me up, I thought he was going to tell me Todd found a guitar for Erick. Now, I'm not sure what he's going to say.

He looks at me, and his pale green eyes are glowing. "We got signed."

For a second, I'm not sure I heard him right. "You mean, like, an actual record deal?"

"Yep," he nods. "An actual record deal."

I want to be happy for him. I *am* happy for him. But now, everything feels one hundred percent more uncertain than it did ten minutes ago.

"That's...amazing!" I say, finally. "Congratulations." I know I sound less than enthusiastic.

"Hey." He smiles at me. "Don't stress, Batgirl. We'll figure it out."

"I guess a lot of things are going to change, right?"

"Nothing's changing yet. We're recording an album in January, so that'll be different. But we'll be around. Same as always."

In my gut, I know it won't be the same. How can it be? Instead of local guys in a local band, they'll be professional musicians, with new and different pressures on them. New opportunities. And new temptations.

"What about your college thing?" he asks.

"What about it?"

"You still want to go, don't you?"

"Yeah." There's a seagull on the beach in front of Rex's car, and I watch it strut across the sand. When seagulls cry in flight, they give me this powerful and sad feeling inside. But when they're walking on a beach, they're kind of comical. I turn back to Rex. "I just sent out a bunch of scholarship applications, but I haven't heard anything back yet."

"You'll get one," he says, decisively.

"I'm really glad about your record deal. I mean it. I am."

He flashes another smile at me. "That's not the only good news. We got an advance with the deal, and we bought some new gear. Todd's donating his old Yamaha electric to Erick. It's in the trunk."

"Are you kidding?" I yell.

"Don't get too excited," Rex cautions. "It's not a fancy guitar. But if he wants to learn how to play, it's just what he needs."

"It sounds perfect. How much does Todd want for it?"

Rex's grin grows bigger. "Even more good news. Nothing."

"I have to give him something," I object.

"If you have to, give him twenty bucks. He threw in a new quarter-inch cable and some picks. Twenty bucks would cover that and buy him a couple beers."

I resolve to slip Todd the money the next time I see him.

"One more thing," Rex says, reaching behind him. He pulls out a thick plastic bag, and hands it to me.

"What's this?"

"Your Christmas present."

"Crap, I didn't bring yours, I have it back at the house...."

"Just give it to me when we get back." He nods at the sack and grins. "You gonna open it?"

He's made the effort to tape the bag shut, so I have to rip that off first. Then I reach inside and pull out what looks like a mask with large, pointy ears. I start laughing. "Seriously, what is this?"

"It's a bat mask. Why don't you put it on?"

Rex scoots forward and helps me. It fits over my head, with large holes for my eyes. He grins with satisfaction. "Now you look like a real bat girl."

I can tell by the gleam in his eyes that he'll probably

want to fuck me while I'm wearing it. The idea appeals to me, too, and I wonder when I got so weird.

"I should probably get back home," I tell him. "There's some stuff I need to do before work."

He hesitates. "Hey, Francesca?"

"Yeah?"

"I love you."

Everything in me melts. I'm an instant puddle of emotional goo and desire. My voice is so quiet it's almost a whisper. "I love you, too."

He kisses me, bat mask and all, until we both start laughing. But inside, I'm a swirling mass of conflicting emotions. Exhilaration. Adoration. Confusion. Fear.

The first thing Rex told me, that his band got signed, is the thing that's going to rule his life, and mine, from this moment forward. In the realm of the real world, it's the most consequential thing.

But in the realm of here and now—and in my heart— I'm in love. Rex bought me a bat mask, and he loves me, and I love him back. Here and now, nothing else matters.

CHAPTER 27

Erick goes crazy over the guitar when I give it to him on Christmas morning. He immediately starts trying to play it, making plinking noises on the strings.

"It might need to be tuned, or something," I tell him.

"Yeah, yeah, I know." He keeps playing, anyway.

Mom gives me a suspicious look. "I thought the laser show was his Christmas present?"

I tell her how Rex's friend had an extra guitar, so it didn't cost me anything. It's a bonus present.

"Well, isn't your boyfriend nice, helping your brother get his own guitar." I know she doesn't mean it. I'm pretty sure she thinks it's a bad direction for Erick's life, and to be honest, six months ago, I would have agreed with her.

But she didn't see him light up in the presence of a real live band or how mesmerized he was when he watched Todd shredding his guitar on stage. Of course, I can't tell her about that, so instead I spit out something pathetic about how it's good for kids to have hobbies. Like I'm some expert on what's good for kids.

Ronnie gets a new car for Christmas from her dad. She

comes by the next day to show it off. He bought her another Honda, but this time it's an Accord, not a Civic, and a coupe, not a hatchback. It also has leather seats and power windows. She takes both Erick and me for a ride, and he goes crazy over her sound system, which is, I have to admit, one of the best ones I've ever heard in a car.

Then she makes Erick get out and go back to our house, so we can go somewhere for breakfast.

Over pancakes, Ronnie announces, "I'm going to start working for Fern on Fire. As their publicist."

"Okay," I say. "What does that mean, exactly?"

"It means I'm gonna help them get more media attention." She gives me a pointed look. "It also means they might need me to travel with them sometimes. You should work with me."

"Work with you?" I laugh. "Doing what? Being your co-publicist?"

"Doing whatever. Then if I go on tour with them, you can go, too."

"How much would they pay us?"

Ronnie sort of tosses her head, as if she finds the mention of money offensive. "I'm donating my services. For now. Until they catch on and start making some real money. Then I'll renegotiate."

"In other words, they're not paying you." I feel like we're back in high school, and I'm trying to make her see how she's being used by the guy she's dating. Back then, it happened a lot, but I thought things were changing for her. I've been assuming Theo is different because of the way he is when he's with her. He's *into* her. But this free publicist thing? It seems a lot like the old days.

"It's not about the money." She sounds impatient. "I don't want to stay at home for months while Theo's on tour. This is a way for me to be with him." She gives me a probing look. "How about you?"

"What about me?"

"Are you cool with Rex being gone for months? It's a long time to be apart."

I try to keep my voice calm. "We're gonna figure it out." But I'm agitated. When Rex told me his band got signed, I knew it meant changes were coming. Maybe Ronnie's smarter than me. Maybe she's just confronting those changes head on. But I still can't shake the feeling that she's being used by the entire band.

"Let me know if you change your mind about helping me," she says. I can tell she thinks I'm making a huge mistake.

"Not gonna happen."

"C'mon Frankie. You don't want to work at the chicken shack for the rest of your life, do you?"

"At least I get paid to work at the chicken shack," I retort. "I need an actual paycheck to save for college. Whose idea was this, anyway? Did you *ask* to be their publicist for free, or did Theo get you into this?"

She gives me a strange look. "It was Rex's idea. And I thought it was a good one, so I said I'd do it."

Great. So the person who's using Ronnie is Rex. Now I'm pissed, because this means I'm going to have to say something to him about it.

Ronnie and I meet the guys in Seattle for a New Years Eve party. Once we're there, it's clear it's not a good time to ask Rex about anything serious. Everyone's drinking and reveling, including me. This time, the party's in a huge, open-concept apartment on the top floor of some old warehouse, where the top level of the building has been converted into a number of living spaces.

Before I get too drunk, I find Todd and slip him a twenty-dollar bill.

"What's this for?" he asks, mystified.

"For my brother's guitar."

"I didn't want money for that."

"Just keep it," I tell him.

He shrugs and pockets the twenty bucks. "How does your brother like the Yamaha? Is he playing it?"

"All the time," I nod. "He has your demo tape and he's trying to learn every single one of your guitar parts."

Todd flicks his long hair back over his shoulder and grins. "Sorry about that."

I grin back at him. "You're his hero."

"Well, tell him I said to keep it up." He beckons with his hand and intones, in this half evil, half dorky voice, "C'mon, Francesca. Help me claim your brother for the dark side."

"I think he's already chosen the dark side. But I'll tell him."

I go to find Rex, but before I get to him, I spot something that stops me in my tracks: lines of white powder on the coffee table in the living area. A couple people are kneeling next to the table, and I watch as they bend over the lines of powder and inhale.

I know it's coke, but I'm having trouble processing the fact that I'm watching actual people do illegal drugs. I'm not used to seeing scenes like this.

"Idiots," Rex says in my ear.

I look up at him. "They're snorting coke, right?" I feel dumb asking him, but I still can't believe what I'm seeing.

"Yeah," he affirms. "That's what they're doing, because they're idiots. Just ignore them."

He spins me around, playfully, and pretends to hide my face against his chest, like he's protecting me from being corrupted. Then I feel his attention shift. He pushes away and looks down at me.

"I need to go talk to somebody, are you going to be okay?"

I wave my hands at him. "I'm fine. Go mingle."

"Find me before midnight," he says, with a quick kiss. Then he shakes a mock serious finger at me. "Don't do drugs."

"I wouldn't dare."

He laughs, then leaves me and goes over to a guy I recognize from another local band.

For the rest of the night, I force myself to stay away from Rex. To talk to other people. I don't want to cling to him, but it's hard. It seems like every time we're out in public, the buzz around the band has grown louder and stronger. They still appeal mostly to dudes. They play loud, hard, heavy rock music. But now that they're signed, they're "going places." And that seems to attract more and different people. More media. More fans. More women.

I spend most of the night sneaking glances over at Rex, trying not to care when I see some girl fawning all over him. To pretend I'm having a good time on my own. And I am, kind of. I'm getting better at socializing, and that's something.

But I'm also stressing over when I should muscle in and plant myself at his side. I make my move just before midnight. Rex is talking to a couple of guys, and I insert myself into their circle. When he puts his arm around me, I get the adrenaline hit I do each time I feel like he's choosing me.

We're together when the countdown to midnight

starts, and share a drunken kiss at the New Year. He holds on to me for a long time afterwards, almost like he's afraid to let me go.

Someone comes over to wish him a happy new year, then starts congratulating him on the record deal. The guy is drunk, like we are, and he keeps repeating himself. Rex slips his arm around my waist as he talks to the guy, answering the same questions over and over.

In the morning I wake up curled around him on a futon mattress on the floor. I don't remember how we got there. When I start to stretch my limbs, I feel his arms tighten around me. I'm hungover. My head is throbbing, and I'm thirsty, but I'm happy where I am. I don't want to move.

The room is quiet, but I hear low voices here and there. I have to pee. Bad. I start to disentangle myself from Rex but he stops me.

"Where are you going? Don't go. Stay here." His voice is sleepy.

"I'll be right back."

As I wiggle out of his arms, he makes a little moaning noise that strikes me as kind of adorable. On my way to the bathroom, I see Ronnie sprawled on one of the couches, asleep. Theo isn't with her. I wonder where he is or if he was with her earlier.

She looks vulnerable, alone and asleep on the couch.

I DON'T GET to talk to Rex about Ronnie until the weekend after New Year's. He picks me up from work, and we go to his house because his mom is gone again for another religious thing. I'm starting to suspect one of the reasons she's so religious is because it gives her a reason to get out of town.

All week, I've been trying to talk myself out of asking Rex about Ronnie's publicity gig. She's thrilled about her new "job." It seems kind of dumb to defend her against being used when she's not even a little bit upset about the arrangement. But I can't get rid of the feeling that I should speak up.

Once we get to Rex's house, I risk it. We're in the kitchen, and he's peering into his mother's fridge, looking for something to eat.

"Hey, um," I venture. "I need to talk to you about something."

He pokes his head back around the refrigerator door. "Yeah?" His voice is wary.

"It's about Ronnie."

"Okay." He looks inside the fridge again, and comes out with a bowl of something, which he sets down on the small kitchen island.

"What's that?" I ask.

"Butterscotch pudding. I think. Want some?"

I shake my head. He gets a smaller bowl out of a cupboard and starts spooning the pudding into it. It looks kind of lumpy. He grins and points to his bowl. "Sure you don't want any? This is gourmet cuisine, right here."

"I'm not hungry. I ate at work already."

He takes a spoonful of pudding and tastes it. "Still good! No food poisoning!" Then he gives me that knowing look he gets sometimes. "What do you want to know about Ronnie?"

I take a deep breath. "She said you asked her to be the band's publicist."

"I did."

"And she said you're not paying her."

Rex takes another spoonful of pudding. "Is she pissed about that?"

"No," I say slowly. "I'm pissed about that."

He smiles at me, but there's a glint in his eyes I'm not sure I like. "No offense, but what does it have to do with you?"

"Ronnie's my best friend," I remind him. "I don't want her to get ripped off."

He shrugs. "We can't afford to pay her. Until the record's released, promotion for anything we do around town still comes out of our own pocket, and we haven't even started working on the record."

"So are you going to keep Ronnie as your publicist when the record's released? Or are you going to hire someone more professional?"

His eyes flash, and I can tell he's getting irritated. "I don't know. That's almost a year away. Why are you so freaked out about this?"

"Ronnie thinks I should help her do publicity for you guys."

"Do you want to do that?"

I stare at him. "I can't work for free."

Rex grins. "So don't work for free."

"Ronnie shouldn't be working for free, either."

"That's her decision, not yours." When he sees I'm not pacified, he sighs. "Look, if she wants to be a publicist, if that's her lifelong dream, then this gets her foot in the door, right? And if she wants to hang out with Theo, then she's still getting something out of it."

I give him my own version of his knowing look. "You know she's just doing it to be with Theo."

"So?" He shrugs again. "What's wrong with that?"

"You're taking advantage of that. That's what's wrong with it."

He groans. "But it's what she *wants*. She gets what she wants, we get a publicist. I don't see how there's anything wrong with that."

"Because she should have a real job! She needs to earn her own money. We're not in high school anymore."

Rex laughs. "Have you seen the car she's driving? If Ronnie ever needs money, her old man's going to bail her out." He gives me an earnest look. "She's not like you."

"Huh?"

"*You* need to earn your own money. You work your ass off. You're trying to get somewhere. I respect that."

Does he? I want so much to accept that Rex believes in me. He just admitted he's taking advantage of Ronnie's desperation, but even so, I want to believe him when he tells me I'm different. I need to believe he won't take advantage of me, too.

"I'm not getting anywhere yet," I mutter.

"You will." He reaches across the kitchen island and laces his fingers with mine. Then he smiles at me in this way that makes me sure he means it. He truly does think I'm going to get somewhere. Or at least, that's what I decide to believe. Because it's what I want, and it's what I need.

CHAPTER 28

"What do you think?" Erick asks. "Does it sound like them?"

I'm in his room, and he's playing me his rendition of "Renegade," which is the opening track on the six-song, self-produced demo Fern on Fire released a year ago, before they got signed. I know specifics like this now, because these are the kinds of things Rex Thornton's girlfriend should know.

For the first few days after Christmas, Erick played Todd's old Yamaha without amplification. But then he went out and found an equally old stereo amplifier and speakers. He got them for free, then begged me to enlist Ronnie to haul them to our house. She wouldn't do it until we promised to put down sheets to protect her leather seats.

So now Erick has a way to play his guitar semi-amplified. He doesn't do it when Mom's home, but he knows I don't care if he plays. It's loud, but nowhere near as loud as a real guitar amp would be.

"You're getting good," I tell him. And I mean it. He practices every day. He puts as much time into learning to play the actual guitar as he used to put into playing air guitar.

"But does it sound like them?" he repeats. "I want it to sound like them."

"Don't you want to develop your own style? Part of the reason Todd's playing is so awesome is because he does his own thing."

"I know that." Erick sounds impatient. "But I want to figure out how to play exactly the way other guys play. Then I'll be smart enough to make my own style."

Sometimes, I don't give my brother enough credit. "Why don't you play it for me again?"

He starts it again, and I listen until he finishes the song.

"So?" he asks.

"I think you've got it," I say. "It sounds like the song to me."

He gives me a serious look. "Be honest."

"I'm not a musician," I warn, "so this might be way off. But I think Todd plays it more...laid back...or something?"

"Yeah," Erick slumps. "I'm doing it too fast."

"You *just* started learning guitar," I reassure him. "Todd's been playing for years."

My brother strums a few chords. Even if he hasn't mastered Todd's guitar style, he already seems like a natural with the instrument. "Mom's been on my case about the sports thing again," he says. "You know, for next year?"

"She can't make you do it," I remind him.

"Yeah, but she won't stop bugging me about it. Did you talk to her?"

"I haven't yet, but I will," I promise. "You know she's just trying to mess with you."

"Yeah." Erick looks up at me, and his eyes are troubled. "Why does she do that?"

"Why does she try to mess with you?"

"She does it to you, too. Not just me."

I have a hard time answering him. Finally, I answer with the truth. "I don't know. But I don't think she likes her life much."

"I don't want to hate my life," Erick says.

I poke a finger at his guitar. "Then keep doing things you like."

He plays another sequence of chords. "You don't have to stay here."

"Huh?" I say.

Erick looks at me. "You know, if you want to move out or something. You don't have to stay here."

I often think of my brother as this clueless but lovable little shit who buries himself in his room and his music. I assume he's just a kid who misses a lot of what goes on in our house. But as it turns out, he's actually a perceptive little shit.

"I'll talk to Mom about the sports thing as soon as I can," I tell him.

The opportunity comes sooner than I expected. I have an early shift that afternoon, and when I get home around eight, Mom is in the kitchen, heating up a frozen meal. I'm tired and sweaty from my bike ride home and don't really feel like talking to her, but I promised Erick that I would, and it feels important. Like I should do it now.

"Hey, Mom. How was your day?" I ask as I approach.

She shrugs. "Just a typical day, I guess." The microwave beeps, and she takes out her meal. It's some kind of pasta thing, maybe with Alfredo sauce. It's very white and bland looking.

She gets a fork out of a drawer and starts eating the pasta right out of the cardboard container. I lean against the counter, across from her.

"Are you going out with your boyfriend?" she asks.

"Not tonight." The band is starting the recording sessions for their album tomorrow. Rex said they were going to rehearse, but I have a feeling they'll actually spend the night partying and raising hell. Male bonding rituals or musician bonding rituals, or whatever they do to get in sync with each other.

"How'd you even meet someone like him?" Mom asks. For once, I can't hear any hidden malice in her voice. She sounds genuinely curious.

But I don't trust her, and I don't want to open up just so she can make another dig at Rex. "I met him through Ronnie. Listen, Mom, there's something I need to talk to you about."

"I'm not changing my mind about you paying rent," she says.

"It's not about the rent. It's about Erick."

Mom takes a large bite of pasta, chews, and swallows. "What about him?"

"I don't think he wants to play sports when he goes to junior high next year."

"He has to get involved in something," she says. "If he doesn't, he'll end up with the wrong crowd."

"I agree with you, but it doesn't have to be sports. He's actually really good at music."

Mom rolls her eyes. "You're just saying that because you got him that guitar for Christmas."

"But he's *good* at it," I insist. "Maybe it would be better for him to focus on music activities, you know, since he likes it and he's got talent for it?"

She narrows her eyes. "Why did you get him that guitar, anyway? Were you trying to impress your boyfriend?"

I stare at her. "Have you seen Erick's room? It's wallpapered with musicians. He's obsessed with music. He's been obsessed with it for literally years."

Mom scrapes the last of the pasta out of the cardboard container. The sound hits me like nails on a chalkboard, and I cringe. She sets the empty container on the counter and fixes me with an enigmatic look. "Did you know that when you were born, your father didn't want me to name you Francesca? He said it was dumb, because our last name is Peterson, and neither of us were Italian."

"Um, okay...."

"You want to know why I named you that?" Mom asks.

This is not the conversation I was expecting. I'm not sure how to handle it. I don't know if she's about to say something nasty or interesting.

"Why'd you name me that?" I ask, wearily.

"Because of what it means. You want to know what it means?" She looks at me intently, and then, without waiting for my answer, she says, "It means *free*. So, I hope you're feeling free, Frankie."

She moves past me and chucks her empty frozen meal container in the trash. Then she leaves the kitchen, saying over her shoulder, "There's some mail for you. Looks like stuff from a college or something."

And with that, she leaves me alone in the kitchen. I saw the mail when I came in and didn't pay attention to it. Now I walk over to the pile of envelopes and start sifting through it until I find the letter. It's from one of the two Seattle schools where I applied for a scholarship. I also applied to two more schools in state, but outside the city. The rest were out of state.

I open it carefully and lift out the letter. It's on good paper, and it has the school's logo on the top. I let my eyes drift past the date, to the first paragraph.

We regret to inform you that we are unable to offer you a scholarship for our Journalism program for the 1990-1991 academic year....

I skim the rest of the letter. There isn't much to it. It says there were many qualified candidates and, unfortunately, this time, I was not chosen. It encourages me to try again.

It's only one rejection. I sent out over a dozen scholarship applications. One of them has to come back with good news, but this rejection narrows my chances of staying close to home.

Ever since Rex told me his band got signed, I've been thinking it would be good to go to school in the city. Maybe I could get an apartment near campus and be in town whenever Rex is home from touring. But now there's only one more chance for that. If the second school in Seattle rejects my scholarship application, I'll have to move out of the area for college.

I tell myself there's no reason to panic. That it's going to work out. But it's hard to shake the feeling that this rejection is some kind of bad sign.

CHAPTER 29

The band starts work on their album, and Ronnie and I immediately see less of the guys. I expected that, but it's kind of a bummer.

I didn't realize how much I've been counting on Rex to smooth out the rough edges of my life. He's been adding fun. Color. Excitement. When I don't spend time with him, all the mundane and frustrating things in my world seem to grow more powerful. It's like Rex is some kind of magic charm who keeps those things from overwhelming me.

Ronnie finds tons of excuses to get down to the studio to see the band, but I don't go with her. I don't want Rex to think I'm a pest. But then, one day in late January, she asks me to go to the studio in her place. She promised to bring them cookies, of all the ridiculous things. But her mom cut her finger slicing an onion, and it was bad enough to need stitches, so Ronnie had to drive her to the emergency room. She called before she left to say she'd be driving her mom's car and could I *please* take hers to deliver the cookies she'd made?

It's important to Ronnie, so I agree to do it, even though

the whole thing seems silly. It's not like the guys are going to die without the cookies. Plus, I'm not in the best mood, because last night, I received two more scholarship rejections in the mail. I try to shake the irritation off, and bike over to Ronnie's house where I find the keys to her car under a potted plant, like she said they would be.

When I unlock the car, I spot the Tupperware container of chocolate chip cookies in the front passenger seat. It's stuff like this that makes me certain Ronnie will eventually become a suburban mom.

Even though the Tupperware container is shut tight, I can smell the cookies as I drive to the studio. I've never been there before, and I'm afraid I'm going to get lost. Ronnie left directions for me. Her handwriting is neat, so the directions are legible, but they're also written in a kind of free associative style that's hard to understand.

While I'm waiting at a traffic light, I give in to temptation and open a wide corner of the Tupperware container to snag a cookie. As I'm trying to get one out, the light changes, and I put my foot on the gas. I'm not used to Ronnie's car, and it lurches forward. The cookie container flies off the seat and lands on the floor.

Shit.

I have to drive. I still need to figure out where the studio is. The cookies will have to wait.

I finally find the place. It's a surprisingly nondescript building in one of Seattle's urban neighborhoods. Next, I have to hunt down a parking spot, which takes me several trips of driving around the block. As soon as I'm parked, I go around to the passenger side and inspect the cookie damage.

It could be worse. About seven of the cookies have escaped from the Tupperware container and are languishing on the floor of the car, but the rest are still in there, all jumbled up. I salvage the cookies that didn't fall out and arrange them in rows, the way Ronnie had them. I'll take care of the ones on the floor later.

I lock up the car and walk to the studio. It's tucked in between a few businesses and homes, and it's nothing like I imagined it would be. There's a locked door off the street with the building number above it. I lodge the container of cookies under my arm and knock.

It's dead quiet. I can't even hear any music coming from inside the building. Just as I'm wondering if maybe Ronnie gave me the wrong address, the door swings open. It's Noah.

"Hey," he says. "What are you doing here?"

I hold out the container of cookies. "Ronnie wanted me to bring these."

"Then why didn't Ronnie bring them?"

"She had to take her mom to the emergency room so... I'm here instead."

Noah just stares at me, and for a second I think he's going to snatch the cookies out of my hands and slam the door in my face. He has that vibe.

But then he swings the door wide, and says, "So bring 'em in."

"Thanks." I step inside the building. There's a tiny lobby with a small couch and a chair facing each other, and closed doors to the right and just ahead of me. Now that I'm inside the building, I can hear muffled music coming from somewhere.

"Did you want to talk to Rex?" Noah asks.

"Not really," I say, uncertainly. "I'm just here to deliver Ronnie's cookies."

He takes pity on me, and opens the door to my right, motioning for me to go in.

The guys are all in there, listening to music. There's something that looks like a big control panel that spans one side of the room. Above the control panel is a window where you can see into a different room, where it looks like the band's instruments are set up.

Theo spots me first. "What's she doing here?" he asks.

I'm instantly annoyed. Who would have thought bringing some stupid cookies to the studio would be such an ordeal? They're all giving off a slightly hostile vibe, as if I've interrupted something holy. Like I should have had a secret password to be allowed entrance to their sacred space.

I hold up the Tupperware container. "I have cookies."

"Aww, isn't that sweet," says this guy I don't recognize. "She made cookies."

I feel a need to clarify. "Actually Ronnie made them. She had to drive her mom to the hospital, so she asked me to do this for her."

Todd catches my eye. "Hey. Francesca's not a groupie and she doesn't make cookies. Right?"

I nod at him.

Rex comes over, and takes the Tupperware container from me, then hands it over to one of the guys. "Can we take a break?" he asks.

"A break?" Theo repeats. "How long do you need? Three minutes?"

They all start laughing, then the guy I don't recognize says, "I could use a sandwich. Let's take an hour." He points at Rex. "But be sure you're back here in an hour." I figure he must be somebody from the record label. Or maybe he's the person in charge of making their record.

"I'll be here," Rex promises. He takes my arm. "C'mon, let's go."

The "in charge" guy calls out, "Thanks for the cookies, sweetheart!" For some reason they all find that even more hilarious. They're still laughing as Rex and I exit the building.

"Sorry about that," he says, once we're outside. "It's been a fucked up vibe in there all day."

I shrug. "I was just doing a favor for Ronnie."

He nudges me. "Well, I'm glad you're here. You want to go somewhere?"

I glance up at him, and recognize the look in his eyes. He's horny. As far as he's concerned, I showed up with his lunchtime sex delivery. And I want to give it to him. We're in love. I love him. I want to make him happy.

When we get to Ronnie's car, he notices the cookies on the floor of the passenger side.

"Oh crap," I groan. "I forgot about those."

"What happened?" he laughs.

"There was a...mishap on the way over."

"Ronnie will kill us if we mess up her car." He kneels down, carefully scoops the cookies off the floor from the passenger side and tosses them on the sidewalk. "That's not littering," he grins at me. "That's food for the local pigeons."

He directs me to a nearby park, telling me what lane to get in, then where to turn. We pull into a wooded parking lot. We're not the only people parked there, but it has a deserted feeling, anyway.

"You drive Ronnie's car better than she does," Rex laughs. "Todd and me caught a ride with her a couple days ago and I thought we were gonna die."

We crawl in the backseat and I give him a blowjob,

because I don't feel comfortable having sex in Ronnie's car in broad daylight. After I get him off, he pulls me back against him and puts his arms around me. Kisses the top of my head. And I feel loved.

"Do you need to get back?" I ask.

"We've got time."

I relax against him, and for a while I revel in being close to him, in the warmth of his body mingling with mine. Every time I'm around him, I feel like I'm merging with this vibrant, radiant presence. He's a person who's doing exactly what he wants to do with his life. I want to absorb as much of his energy as I can. To make it my own.

"I think I'm going to move in with Todd while we finish the record," he says.

Involuntarily, I tense up. "Oh, yeah?"

"Yeah. They expect us to get there early most of the time, and it sucks having to come all the way down to Seattle every morning. It'll be easier if I'm already here."

I'm quiet. If he stays in Seattle, that means I won't see him as much. And he won't have any reason to drive up north, where I live.

He kisses the top of my head again. "Don't freak. We'll figure it out."

I want to believe him. But so many things are shifting, and it seems like 'figuring out' how to be together is slowly moving out of the realm of what's possible.

I know he won't love it if I start grousing about how hard it's going to be to find time to see each other. I also think I should be able to bring it up. It bothers me that I'm struggling with whether to tell him how I feel.

"I guess I should get back," he says.

"Okay," I start to move away from him. "Let's go back."

Rex tugs at my arm, and I turn around. He plants a kiss on me. "Thanks for the cookies."

"You're welcome."

When I drop him off at the studio, he knocks at the door, then disappears inside. I drive away, trying to shake the feeling that this thing with Rex is barreling toward its expiration date.

But maybe he's right. Maybe we'll figure it out.

CHAPTER 30

Rex moves in with Todd in February, and I see him even less. He's making a record, I have my job. He's in Seattle, I'm not. I have to help out at home, and I don't have a car.

Sometimes he remembers to call me from Todd's place, and sometimes he forgets. I cave and start going with Ronnie down to the studio under the pretense of bringing something they "need," like more food or cigarettes. Or weed. That's Ronnie's department. I don't know where she gets the weed, and I don't ask her.

Whenever I'm down there, Rex and me try to find a way to be together. We steal moments for sex and blowjobs in his car or sometimes at Todd's apartment. Every time I'm with him, I feel like I'm fighting to hold on to the connection between us. To keep it alive.

He's always happy to see me, and he never makes me feel like I'm bothering him. But I can tell I'm just a pleasant distraction, because he's focused on making their album. Right now, that's the most important thing in his life.

By the end of February, I get several scholarship rejections, which makes me progressively more nervous. Two of them are for schools on the East Coast, which were a long shot anyway. But the other one is for the University of Washington, which was my last hope to stay near Seattle for school. So now I know for sure that if I go to school in the fall, I'll be moving somewhere else.

I don't say anything to my family or Ronnie or Rex about the scholarship rejections. I plan on telling them if I actually get one, but I don't see the point in sharing my disappointments. I can't bear for Mom to gloat over my failures. And both Rex and Ronnie are wrapped up in planning the future of his band. I don't want to be a downer.

They finally finish the album in early March. To celebrate, one of the band's friends throws a huge party. It starts out okay, but after a couple hours it gets uncomfortable for me.

There are tons of people, and the two-story rental house where it's happening is packed from wall to wall. It's not a gathering of friends. It has the feeling of being the party that everyone *in the know* knows they're supposed to be at. I lose track of Rex in the first fifteen minutes we're there. Which is okay. By now, I'm used to fending for myself when I'm out with him.

But tonight, instead of finding someone interesting to talk to, I keep getting approached by guys who want to know if I'm Rex's girlfriend. Sometimes they don't even say his name, they just say, "Hey, are you Fern on Fire's girlfriend?" It happens enough times that I start to feel like I'm not here as me, but as an extension of the band. A few of the guys are in bands themselves, and they have that vibe of trying to get an "in" with Rex. Some of them hit on me in this understated way. They want to fuck me, but not because they want to fuck *me*. They want to fuck me because Rex already is.

Besides that, there's something going on in a back room of the house that seems shady. Every once in a while, someone goes in, then comes back out several minutes later. I don't find out what's going on until Ronnie tracks me down. I've hidden myself in a corner in an attempt to avoid being identified as "Fern on Fire's girlfriend," and I'm nursing a plastic cup filled with straight whiskey over ice. I'm growing slowly, blissfully intoxicated.

"Insane party, right?" Ronnie says, as she wedges herself next to me.

"The most insane yet." From where we are, I can see the people coming and going from the back room of the house. It's not a ton of people, and it's not a constant thing. But it's definitely a thing.

I jerk my head in the direction of the room. "What's going on back there? A secret poker game?"

Ronnie gives me a strange look. "Chasing the dragon."

"What?"

"They're shooting up, Frankie." Her tone is exasperated. Like she thinks I should have known.

But I didn't know. I'm shocked.

"Don't freak out," she says. "Nobody we know is into that shit."

I'm assuming she means the band. "Are you sure?"

She rolls her eyes. "All those idiots care about is getting plastered and fucking shit up."

I have a feeling Ronnie sees more of the real lives of the guys in the band than I do. My experience of them is kind of curated by Rex. But Ronnie, by the simple virtue of having her own car, is able to be around them more often. She sees what they're up to when they're not on stage.

"So like," I venture, "you've never seen one of them do, I don't know, like a line of coke?"

Ronnie shakes her head. "No, never. They're not into that shit. Why? Have you seen one of them doing coke?" She lowers her voice. "Rex?"

"No, never!" I echo her. "I was just wondering, since you see them more than I do, maybe you've noticed—"

Suddenly, from the upstairs of the house, there's noise and yelling.

I look at Ronnie. "What the hell?"

"That sounds like Theo," she says, and starts running for the stairs. I follow her. When we get there, several people have already started drifting upstairs to investigate. Ronnie pushes through them, trying to get to the top of the stairway.

Before she does, two guys stumble out a door onto the landing. It does look like Theo. And Todd.

"I am not fucking paying for that, man!" Theo yells.

"Nobody's fucking paying for it!" Todd howls. He sounds like a different person. Usually, he's mild mannered —except when he's on stage. He's an aggressive guitar player, and I've always assumed he gets out any violent urges he has in music. But maybe not.

"You're fucking crazy man," Theo says. "I am not fucking, not fucking... Fuck." I hear the sound of retching.

Ronnie breaks through the people on the stairs and goes over to Theo. "Leave him the fuck alone," she yells at Todd.

Todd holds up his hands, then starts laughing like an idiot. He's crazy drunk.

Then Theo starts laughing, too. "Oh, shit, I puked. All over the carpet." He and Todd stare at each other for a few seconds, then begin laughing hysterically together.

Ronnie urges Theo in the bathroom, and Todd follows

them, mimicking her. "Hey, leave him the fuck alone, Ronnie. Stop it."

People are chuckling and drifting back down the stairs. I reclaim my secluded corner and return to nursing my own drink. I'm not going to get raging drunk, like Todd and Theo, I tell myself. I'm just trying to make it through this party.

Not long after, Ronnie rejoins me.

"How's Theo?" I ask.

"Fuck if I know. Someone ripped the shower head out of the wall in the bathroom. Theo says it was Todd. Todd says it was Theo."

I try to picture how that could have happened, but my imagination fails me. "So are they...okay?"

"They're fine. They think it's hilarious."

Rex joins us then. He slips an arm around my waist and I relax into him, relieved that he's finally near me.

"There are some real assholes at this party." He looks at Ronnie. "Like your boyfriend."

"And like your guitar player," she shoots back. "Do you think the label will pay for the damage?"

"Don't worry about it. It's not your problem."

"It will be if they're fighting like this when we're out on the road."

"You don't have to come with us," Rex points out.

A frustrated look crosses Ronnie's face. There's a weird dynamic between her and Rex. It almost feels like a power struggle. I have a sense Rex has already won, but Ronnie hasn't figured that out, yet.

"I'm gonna go find Theo," she says, and starts to walk away from us.

"When you do," Rex calls after her, "tell him what an asshole he is."

She spins around and flips him off. Then she leaves.

"Theo started the fight," Rex explains, then grins. "But I'm pretty sure Todd's the one who destroyed the shower."

My head feels like it's spinning. What am I doing here, with people shooting up heroin in the house and stupid fights and episodes of intentional property damage? Why are things so weird between Rex and my best friend? Who am I? How drunk am I?

Then he maneuvers me so my back is against the wall, and puts his hands on either side of my head. "How's your night?"

"Great. I've had tons of guys ask me if I'm 'Fern on Fire's girlfriend.'"

He starts laughing. "That's fucking hilarious."

"If you say so."

He presses up against me, so I'm pinned against the wall. Then he kisses me.

Maybe it's dumb, but I love it when he chooses me in front of other people. Still. If anyone's watching us now, they'll know for sure that I'm "Fern on Fire's girlfriend." And that's how they'll think of me from now on. I love Rex, but it feels strange, being defined in relation to someone else. Especially when I still haven't figured out how to define myself.

CHAPTER 31

Rex surprises me when he calls my house, late at night, in mid-March.

I haven't seen him much since the party where Todd tore the shower head out of the bathroom wall. Technically, Rex and me are still together. But I'm starting to have doubts.

After the band finished the record, he kept living at Todd's place in Seattle. He said it would be easier, since they're starting rehearsals for a month-long tour in late March. They're going out with a different local band that's doing well, hoping to build some buzz before the record release this summer.

Ever since they finished their record, I've been feeling like Rex is starting to drift in a different direction. Like I'm fading into the background of his life.

So I'm not expecting his call.

"Peterson's," I say, as I pick up the receiver.

"Francesca?"

"Yeah, it's me."

"Are you going to be around for a while?" He sounds

terrible, which is puzzling. He's been so happy lately. Cocky, even. On top of the world. Now, all the confidence has drained from his voice.

"Yeah, I just got home from work. I'll be here. What's going on?"

There's a strange sound on the other end of the line, almost like a sob. "I can't tell you on the phone," he says. "Can I come up there and see you?"

"Of course. I'll be here," I tell him.

I hang up, and the house is quiet. Both Mom and Erick must be asleep. I head for the bathroom and take a quick shower before Rex picks me up.

When I hear him pull up outside, I hurry down the walkway. In the sky, I see silvery clouds clearing away from a bright waning moon.

Once I'm in Rex's car, I slide over and kiss him. He's like a ghost of his usual self. When I pull back and study his face, all the glitter and sparkle has gone out of his eyes, and I'm worried.

"What happened?"

"Can we drive?"

"Sure. Wherever you want."

At first, he drives around aimlessly. But eventually he ends up in the field behind the school. It's spring, and there are other cars there. But I no longer care.

After he parks, he sits there without saying anything.

"Rex. What's wrong?"

"Somebody...died."

"Who? Somebody in the band? Your family?"

"No, they're all fine."

"So, who?" I ask, trying to keep my voice soft.

He mentions a name that's vaguely familiar, then the band the guy played in. The band sounds familiar, too.

"Didn't you do a show with them?"

Rex nods. "They're the ones who took us out on tour, back in October."

I'm afraid to say the wrong thing, but right now he seems incapable of speaking unless I ask him questions. "How'd he die?"

"Overdose. Heroin."

The words give me an ugly feeling. My brain flashes back to the party where people were shooting up in the back bedroom.

I reach out and touch Rex's arm. "I'm sorry. That just... that sucks."

He's quiet for a few moments, then he speaks again. "We weren't super good friends or anything. We had a great time on tour, but I didn't know him like I know Todd or Noah or Theo." He stretches his hands out to the top of the steering wheel. "Things were going so good for them. It's wrong. It feels so wrong."

"I'm sorry," I repeat.

Suddenly he turns to me, and I'm shocked when I see his eyes are full of tears. "That isn't going to be me...is it?" he asks.

I yank off my lap belt and scoot over to him so I can put my arms around him. Then I hold him while he cries. While he repeats, over and over, "It's so wrong." And, over and over, I tell him it's not going to happen. He's not going to die of an overdose.

There's so much emotion flowing between us that I start crying, too. We're holding each other and getting each other's clothing wet. Finally, he pulls back and looks at me.

"Can I stay with you tonight?"

"At your mom's?"

He shakes his head. "She's home, and I don't—I don't want to talk to her. Not tonight."

I'm decisive. "Come home with me. You can stay there."

"You sure?"

"Yeah. My mom will just have to deal." I've never actually thought about how Mom would react to Rex staying over in my room. In a way, I haven't wanted him to, because he's always been an escape for me. From Mom, and from our house.

But he needs me tonight, and I'm going to bring him home with me, whether she likes it or not.

"Francesca?"

"Yeah?"

"I love you."

I reach out and touch his face, like I'm framing it. "I love you, too."

We park a couple of blocks away from my house, in case Erick's still up and watching out the window. As we go in the front door together, I'm preparing myself to find Mom up late, loitering in the kitchen or maybe reading in the living room. But inside, the house is still dark and quiet.

"C'mon." I tug Rex's hand and take him down the hall to my room.

Once we're in there with the door shut, we fall into each other's arms and stay there, sort of swaying back and forth. Eventually we make it over to the bed and lie down. He holds on to me, pressed against my back.

I'm wide awake, and I can feel his heart beating, fast, between my shoulder blades. Eventually it slows, and his breathing becomes more relaxed. He's asleep. I stay awake longer, just listening to the air going in and out of his lungs. But eventually, I fall asleep, too.

When I wake up the next morning, he's hard. I stay still,

not sure if he's actually awake yet. Then I feel his hand move across my stomach, below the waistband of my jeans. He places a kiss on my shoulder.

"Are you awake?"

I nod.

"Can we...?" He pushes his hand further down.

I nod again. "Yeah."

The sex happens fast. We tear off each other's clothes and he enters me without much foreplay. I'm ready and I want it that way. It's like we're both desperate to be as close as we can, to feel as much sensation as it's possible to feel.

As we're coming down from the high of being together, an unpleasant thought grips me. This time, I know, I'm going to have to tell him what's on my mind. Even if it makes him angry.

"Can I ask you a question?"

"What's up?"

"It might piss you off," I warn.

"Ask your damn question."

There's some laughter in his voice, and I'm glad. I was relieved he wanted to fuck this morning. Last night, I was afraid all the life had been permanently squeezed out of him. But he's still in there. He's shaken, but he's still himself.

"There were people shooting up at that party, you know, after you finished the record?"

"I was aware of that," he says. The strain is back in his voice, and I hate that I'm bringing this up. But I have to.

"Is that something you do? Or does anybody else in the band do it?"

He's quiet for several moments. "We drink a lot," he says. "We smoke. Cigarettes. Weed. Acid. That's mostly me and Theo. But hard drugs...no."

"Okay," I say, uncertain. I feel like he's holding something back.

Rex sighs. "I think Noah's tried it. Todd, for sure no. Alcohol's his poison. And I haven't."

I turn over on the bed, so I'm face to face with him. "Please promise me you won't do it. I don't want to tell you what to do, but just please. Promise me."

His eyes soften. There's a sadness in them that wasn't there just days ago, and it makes my heart ache.

"I promise," he says. "I won't touch it. It's not worth it. Obviously."

I believe him. "Thank you."

He touches a finger to my chin, then waves a hand in front of his nose. "You need to brush your teeth, kid."

I pummel him with one of my pillows. "You're not smelling so pretty yourself!"

After we've both got dressed and shared my toothbrush to brush our teeth, I go with him to the door, so I can walk him out to his car. It's still morning, but not too early. Erick should be at school by now. I didn't see Mom when we were going in and out of the bathroom, so I figure we've dodged that bullet.

But I'm wrong. As we head for the front door, I see her in the kitchen. She's leaning against the counter, drinking a cup of something that might be coffee. It kind of smells like coffee. We don't have a coffee maker, so if it is coffee, it must be instant.

"Hey, Frankie," she says, stopping us both in our tracks. "Who's this?"

I look at Rex and decide the best way to handle this is like it's something completely natural. Which it should be —he's my boyfriend, and he needed me last night. I'm not going to apologize for that.

I take Rex's hand and we go into the kitchen.

"Hey, Mom," I say. "This is my boyfriend, Rex." I look up at him again. "This is my mom."

He puts out a hand. "Hi, Ms. Peterson."

After a second, she takes his offered hand and shakes it. "Nice to meet you, Rex. Finally."

"Nice to meet you, too, ma'am," he replies, in this subdued, respectful tone. It kind of cracks me up the way he's gone from a guy in a band to a smooth-talking Eddie Haskell type in a matter of seconds.

I tell Mom, "Well, I'm gonna walk Rex out. I'll be right back."

We start for the door again. Then Mom says, "I sure hope you mean that. It would be good if you did something productive today. I had to make Erick's lunch this morning."

Shit. I forgot to throw his lunch together when I got home last night. Everything else kind of faded after Rex called. Even though I know I should cut myself some slack, I feel guilty, and open my mouth to apologize. But Rex stops me by turning around and addressing my mom again.

"Hey, Ms. Peterson. I don't know you very well, so I'm sorry if I'm out of line. But Francesca works really hard, and she's trying to make something better out of her life. You should be proud of her."

Mom looks shocked. I am too, but my heart is swelling with the most beautiful feeling.

"No disrespect," Rex adds. "But I thought you should know."

"Well, thank you for sharing," Mom says. Her tone is odd. It's a bit sarcastic, and there's something else in it that I can't identify. But I don't care because my heart is still bursting with awesomeness. I nudge Rex and we go to the door. We don't speak until we get out to his car.

"Sorry if I pissed off your mom back there..." he starts.

I reach up and kiss him. "I love you for saying that to her."

"Somebody needed to say it." He twines his arms around me and pulls me closer. "How's that scholarship thing going?"

I smile ruefully. "Seven rejections and counting. I'm waiting on the rest."

"You'll figure it out," he says. It's what he always says. But right now, it's what I need to hear.

For awhile we just stay next to his car and hold each other.

"We're leaving in a couple days," he reminds me.

"I know."

"I want to be with you again tonight."

"At my house?"

"We can stay at my mom's. It's her turn to deal."

"Okay." I grin at him. "That works for me."

When he leaves, I stand on the sidewalk and watch his car until it's out of sight.

He needed me, and I was there for him. And he stood up for me. They're small things, maybe, but they feel gigantic. They're the kind of things that give me the courage to go back in the house and face my mother, no matter what she's going to say.

CHAPTER 32

I'm with Erick at the mall. Mom gave me some money, then let me take her car so we can get him nice clothes for his sixth-grade graduation. When I was his age, we never had a graduation ceremony. But apparently, it's a thing now.

It's still April, and graduation isn't until June. But Mom wants Erick to get his clothes for the ceremony this weekend, because there's a big sale going on.

I don't actually want to pick Erick's clothes out for him. I also have no desire to advise him on the appropriate attire for a sixth-grade graduation ceremony. Though, I have to admit, if we let him wear whatever he wants, he'll probably show up in ripped black jeans and a Metallica T-shirt.

In the boys' section of one of the mall's department stores, I send him to a dressing room with a bunch of pants and button-down shirts in his size. While I'm waiting, I wander around, pretending to shop for more clothes.

Shopping is kind of a good distraction. The band, with Ronnie, has already been on tour for a couple weeks. It's been hard on me. I've barely heard from Rex. He's called me a total of two times, both from a pay phone.

The first time, he was drunk. In a way, it was a sweet call. He kept telling me he loved me, and if I hadn't been so anxious, I might have thought it was funny. The second time, though, was more disturbing. That time he was sober, and we had a normal conversation. He told me the tour was going well, but that some of the audiences had been hostile because they were the wrong brand of metal. "Too slow and too sleazy," he joked. He asked me how things were at work, and if I'd got any more news on scholarships. Then he told me he loved me and missed me. He said everything I wanted to hear.

What freaked me out, though, was that after we ended our conversation, he put Ronnie on the phone. The minute I heard her voice, I knew that something was not okay, but she wouldn't tell me what it was. I asked her several times if everything was all right, and each time she replied, in this tight voice, that everything was fine. But I knew she was lying.

Her caginess sent my imagination into overdrive. Was something going on between her and Theo? Did they break up? Was the tension I'd noticed between Ronnie and Rex getting worse? Or was it something else?

I tried not to let my mind wander in the direction of possibilities that scared me the most. Was anyone in the band doing hard drugs? Was Rex? Or was he cheating on me? But we love each other. And he promised me he wouldn't touch heroin. I had to trust him. Didn't I?

I sense someone at my elbow and turn my head. It's Erick.

"None of those clothes work," he groans.

"What do you mean they don't work? They don't fit? Do you need a different size?"

"No." He's irritated. "They fit."

"So what's the problem?"

"I don't like any of them. They all look stupid."

"It's just a dumb outfit for a graduation ceremony. You don't have to wear it every day."

"They look stupid," Erick insists.

I sigh. "Please don't say you need *me* to tell you if they look okay?"

He gets even more irritated. "No, I don't, because I already know they look stupid."

"Fine. I guess we can keep shopping. Let's try a different store."

"No!" Erick says vehemently. "I don't want to go to any other stores."

Oh God. This is a disaster. If I don't bring Erick home with a graduation outfit, Mom is going to lose it.

"Okay," I say. "Of all the things you tried on, are there any you hate a little less than the others?"

He shrugs. "I don't know."

"Why don't you go back in the dressing room and try the *one* outfit that wasn't as stupid as the others just one more time. Okay? Then come show me, and I'll tell you if I think it actually looks stupid. How's that?"

He gives me a wary look, like he knows I'm trying to manipulate him.

"We have to go home with something," I groan. "So will you just go try on some fucking pants and a shirt and let me tell you if it actually looks stupid?"

"Okay, fine." Erick stomps back to the dressing room. I follow him and hover outside, feeling like his mother instead of his sister. I hate it when Mom puts me in this position.

Eventually, he shuffles out wearing dark blue dress pants and a yellow button-down shirt. I'm surprised. He looks like a different kid. It always makes me cringe when women talk about their sons this way, but he kind of looks like a "little man." My brother cleans up good.

"See?" he says. "Stupid."

"No, actually, it looks really good," I tell him.

He rolls his eyes at me.

"I'm serious!"

Erick folds his arms across his chest. "It doesn't feel right. It's not..." he hesitates. "It's not me."

"It only has to be you for one day," I remind him.

He throws up his arms in an exasperated gesture, and I have to choke down my laughter.

"Fine," he huffs. "I want to get the hell out of here anyway." He goes back into the dressing room.

After I buy the pants and the shirt with Mom's money, I drive down to Seattle, to the nearest Dick's, which is a local drive-in hamburger joint. It's just burgers and fries and milkshakes, but it's good and it's cheap. And Erick loves it.

We sit in the parking lot and devour our food.

"So, Rex is still on tour, huh?" Erick is shoveling in fries at an alarming rate. I'm kind of afraid he's going to choke on one of them.

"Yup."

"Do you miss him?"

"Yeah, of course," I say. "Could you slow down with those fries? It's been, like, a year since I practiced the Heimlich maneuver."

"The *what*?"

"It's something you do when a person is choking on food."

"I'm noff gonna choke on my fooff," Erick says, around a mouthful of fries.

"Okay," I grumble. "Just be careful."

He swallows and takes a sip of his chocolate milkshake. "It must be weird, not knowing what your boyfriend's doing for a whole month."

My response is automatic. "That's how it is all the time. I don't know what he's doing whenever we're not in the same place. It's not different just because he's on tour."

That's what I've been telling myself and what I actually believed up until last week's strange phone conversation with Ronnie. I know she was keeping something from me. I wonder if she'll tell me about it when she gets home. Whatever "it" is.

Erick shrugs. "Whatever you say."

"Thanks for caring, though."

He picks up on my sarcasm and gives me his signature withering look. Then I feel kind of bad. I don't want to be sarcastic about everything. The way Mom is.

"No, seriously," I say. "Thanks for asking about it. I actually appreciate it."

In response to my heartfelt expression of gratitude, he does this thing where he flips his eyelids inside out and makes this horrible, monstrous face. He used to do it more when he was younger. But apparently, he's been inspired to pull that particular kid-brother trick just one more time.

He flips his eyelids back to normal and starts laughing maniacally. I flick my empty straw wrapper at him, and he bats it away.

"We should probably go back now." I put the key in the ignition and start up the car.

"Okay." Erick sighs. "I guess Mom'll want to see if the new clothes fit."

"Probably. Just play along. Tell her we got a great deal at the sale. That'll make her happy."

"Nothing makes her happy," he says, glumly.

He's right, of course. "Just tell her we got a great deal," I say again. Then I back the car out of our parking space.

CHAPTER 33

"I need to talk to you."

It's Ronnie. She's back from tour. The guys are, too. Rex already called me from Todd's and we're seeing each other later tonight. But Ronnie drove home separately, in her own car. I can't believe she took it on a month-long road trip. For her sake, I hope it's still running okay. She has a hard time existing without a car.

"Sure," I tell her. "I'm not working today. Do you want me to come over there?"

"No. I don't want anyone eavesdropping. I'll come pick you up."

When I get in Ronnie's car, it's clean, but I detect the barest hint of an unpleasant odor. I notice it because usually Ronnie's car looks *and* smells squeaky clean.

"How's your car holding up?" I ask.

"Okay." She grips the steering wheel tighter. "But I'm never taking it on a trip like that *ever again*."

Uh oh. It sounds like Ronnie has a story to tell me.

She doesn't get into it right away. Instead, she drives us south, to this park in Seattle at the top of one of the hills where you can look out over the city. The Space Needle is usually visible from here, and on a clear day you can see the nearest snow-covered volcano, Mt. Rainier. Today, though, it's raining, so you can't see the mountain. The city itself is shrouded in grey clouds.

Ronnie isn't talking, which is not typical for her.

"So was the tour...fun?" I venture.

She lets out a long sigh, then looks over at me. "It was so much work. I don't think your boyfriend appreciates just how much I did for them."

So not getting paid *is* bothering her. I have a feeling Rex knows exactly how much work Ronnie's doing for the band. But he also knows she'll put up with a lot because of Theo.

"Can you renegotiate the pay thing?" I ask.

"They haven't released the record yet. So, no." She looks over at me. "I'm good at this, Frankie. I want to keep doing it."

"Do they want you to keep helping them out?"

"Yeah. But being on the road with them was insane. I burned through so much money. Gas. Food. Laundry. Even motel rooms a couple nights. And every time I brought up how expensive it was, Rex was like, 'You can go home if you want to.'" She grimaces. "I guess he doesn't care about what I did for them, but I did a *lot*. I got them so many radio interviews. It wouldn't have been the same tour without me."

"He cares." I feel torn between my loyalty to Ronnie and to Rex. "He thinks the reason you want to be their publicist is because of Theo. He figures that's the 'payment' you want. Being with Theo."

She goes quiet. "Maybe I thought that too, before I actually did this. But it's not enough."

"Why don't you tell Rex? Tell *him* it's not enough."

"He already said they can't pay me until the record's released and starts selling."

I shift in my seat. "I have a hard time believing the label didn't budget for a publicist. Especially once they actually release the record and start promoting it? They might even be planning to hire a professional publicist once that happens."

She gives me a sharp look. "Did Rex tell you they were gonna do that?"

"No. But think about it. It makes sense, right?"

"Maybe," she relents. "But if that's the plan, how can I fight that? I can't compare to a publicist with years of experience."

"I don't know, tell Rex," I repeat. "Ask him to talk to the record label. Tell him it isn't just about Theo, you know, that you want to do this as a job. He might respect that. If he values what you've been doing, he'll fight for you to be their publicist. And if he doesn't, fuck him. He's using you. Go find some other band to work for."

She grins at me. "You realize this is your boyfriend we're talking about, right?"

"It's not just him. The whole band is using you." I sigh. "But, yeah. Rex is kind of an opportunist. I know that."

"And you love him anyway," she says. "I get it. Whatever, it actually isn't just about Rex. The whole tour was a freak show." She glances in my direction. "I caught Theo shooting up."

A cold feeling grips me. "You mean heroin?"

"Yeah. After one of their shows, I found him in the bathroom at this motel we were staying at. He'd just done it. I was so pissed. We went out to my car, and he puked all over. So many times."

I'm consumed by one thought and one fear. "Did the other guys in the band do it, too?"

Ronnie groans. "I have no idea. Theo was alone when I found him, so who knows. The whole thing...it was seriously fucked up, Frankie. I know all the guys had a blast, and the tour was definitely a success. But it's such a... different world."

"But you like it," I remind her. "Don't you? You've always liked it."

"I could skip the part where I watch from the sidelines while a bunch of dudes do stupid shit," she says. "But yeah. I still love being around bands, and I really loved getting them seen and heard by more people. It was...satisfying."

"Then you should keep doing it."

Her eyes are suddenly bright with emotion, and she touches my hand. "Thanks for letting me actually say all of that out loud. I don't think there's anyone else who could even understand." She gives me one of her rare real smiles. "You're a good friend, Frankie."

"That's what you pay me for," I joke. But my gut is churning. Did Rex break his promise to me? I'm looking forward to seeing him tonight, but now my anticipation is tinged with dread.

REX SURPRISES me by booking a hotel room for the night, so we don't have to use his car to be alone. It's not fancy, but it's clean, and I'm touched. I know they have some advance money from the label, but they're not rolling in cash. And any money they spend now will have to be paid back to the label with record sales.

The minute we're alone in our room, all my resolve to ask him about anything drug-related dries up. He's glowing and beautiful. And happy. It's good to see him happy. I love him, and I just want to be with him.

He goes over to the large TV across from the bed. "Want to watch the boob tube?" He takes a brochure off the top of the TV stand and holds it up, grinning. "One hundred cable channels."

"Sure...if you want?"

He drops the brochure and crosses the room to me in a couple quick steps. Twines his arms around me. "I missed you," he says.

I tell him I missed him, too. We sit down on one of the beds in the room and begin to remove each other's clothes, going slow. It feels good. Exciting, but also comfortable. Being naked with him isn't even like being naked. It's like being myself.

"I kinda love you," he says.

"I kinda love you, too."

We fall back onto the bed and sort of devour each other. It's intense. More intense than I expected. I wasn't sure how much he truly missed me, but now I know he did.

Afterward, we both sleep for a couple of hours, but it's not late, and once we get up we're wide awake again. We raid the vending machine in the hotel lobby for snacks, then go back to our room and watch TV.

Rex takes control of the remote, and he's changing the channel every couple of seconds.

I laugh and give him a playful shove. "Will you just pick something and stay there?"

"There's one hundred channels! We have to watch them all!"

"Please?" I lean against his shoulder and look up at him.

"Okay, okay. Oh, yeah, this one." He uses the remote to point at the TV.

I recognize the show. It's *Cops*.

He laughs, a kind of classic stoner laugh. "Have you seen this show? We watched it all the time on tour." Then he rips into a snack-sized package of chips from the vending machine and offers it to me. I take a few chips and keep my eyes on the TV.

After a while, I wish I hadn't asked him to stop channel surfing. One of the cops on TV is asking this person if they're high. If they've ingested any drugs. The actual reason the cops are there—the reason they're in this person's house—is a domestic violence call. But they keep asking the person if they're high.

Ever since we got to the hotel, I've been able to push what Ronnie told me out of my head. How she caught Theo shooting up on tour. But now, because of what's happening on TV, I can't stop thinking about it.

"Hey," Rex nudges me. "You ok?"

I keep staring straight ahead at the TV. "Ronnie said Theo did heroin while you guys were gone."

"Yeah?" He digs into the chip bag, but comes up empty. "Yeah, he did. He did it a couple times, I think."

"So...did anybody else do it?"

Rex is quiet, as the TV goes to the show's theme song. I'm afraid to look at him, but I force myself. When he turns to me, I can already see the answer in his eyes. But I wait for him.

"Yeah," he says. "We all did it. Except Todd."

I feel like I've been dropped in a hole, and I don't know where the bottom is. Obviously, Rex survived. But I'm scared to death anyway. And hurt. Because he promised me he wouldn't do it. I remember how we held each other, and he made a fucking promise. But he broke it.

"Francesca...." He reaches for my hand, and I pull away.

"You promised." As the words come out of my mouth, they sound so childish. I feel like an idiot for believing him. For trusting him to keep his word.

"It wasn't like you think," he says.

"So how was it?"

"I don't know. It was just...around. Like mini candy bars at Halloween or something." He pauses. "And I was curious."

I want to hit something. How could he be curious, after coming to me all shattered because someone he knew died of a heroin overdose? How could he cry and tell me he didn't want to die that way, then risk doing exactly that?

"I don't understand." My voice sounds dull. I'm angry. I'm numb. I'm hurt. I'm all of those things at once. It's confusing and shitty.

But the thing that bothers me most is that he broke his promise. I know that's messed up. I should care about him using drugs, right? If he's going to be okay? I should be thinking about whether he's hooked now, and how to get him some kind of help. But instead I feel betrayed, and it's the only thing I can see.

"I'm not sure I understand, either," Rex admits. "But I had to try it. I had to see if I could beat it. And I did. I did beat it. I'm here."

I feel a sob in my throat but force it down. "You beat it *this* time."

"Lots of people try it and don't get addicted. That's me. I know that now. I'm not gonna get addicted."

He's sincere. I believe he believes what he's saying. But how can it be true? All I've ever heard is how addictive heroin is. That once you've tried it, you never stop wanting it.

Or is my reaction just a throwback to my old high

school persona? Ms. Follow-the-Rules. Taking the "appropriate" amount of time before having sex. Always being safe. Never cutting class. Avoiding the field behind the school. Assuming all recreational drugs are evil.

Ever since I've been with Rex, I've broken most of my rules and I feel more alive than I ever have before. I never knew I could be in love the way I am now, with him. I've never been this happy or this scared.

Maybe the reality of drugs is part of this more *alive* version of the world. I don't know. I don't know anything anymore.

Rex reaches out to touch my hair, starts to speak, then hesitates. He pushes a few strands of hair behind my ear, then says, "It won't be like it was with your dad. I know what I'm doing."

"All I know about my dad is that he's gone."

"Don't cry." Rex wraps his arms around me, and it's not until he does that I realize I'm crying. "I'm not going anywhere. I'm going to be okay. Everything's going to be okay."

He starts kissing me. At first, I'm clinging to him. The fear of losing him is immense. I kiss him back, but my kisses are desperate, like I'm trying to memorize how he feels. How he tastes.

Rex doesn't read it that way, though—as desperation. He reads it as passion. He pushes me back on the bed and pins my arms above my head, kissing me more deeply. And then passion does kick in, and my desperation gives way to desire and the pleasure of being with him.

CHAPTER 34

W e wake up late. Rex says we should get moving, because checkout is at eleven. We're in a hurry, so we take a quick shower together, and it makes me feel close to him. But underneath, there's this growing feeling of dread that I can't shake.

"Want to get breakfast?" he asks as we're getting dressed.

"Sure. They might have free breakfast here. Want to find out?"

He shakes his head. "We're too late." Then he starts laughing. "We stayed in these really shitty motels on tour. Most of them didn't even have breakfast. But this one place tried so hard. They put out slices of bread on a dish tray. And a jar of peanut butter. Grape jelly. Oh, and a toaster."

"So...at least they made an effort?"

"We made a shit ton of peanut butter and jelly sandwiches and took them with us."

It sounds wholesome. Peanut butter and jelly sandwiches. Hungry guys making the best of bad accommodations. I wonder if he's trying to show me touring isn't all about drugs. Or maybe he's just talking.

I feel weirdly detached. Like I'm gathering information for later. *Okay, so you tried heroin. So you stocked up on peanut butter and jelly sandwiches. Interesting. Tell me more.*

Rex starts laughing again. He's in a good mood this morning. "This one time we actually did stay somewhere with breakfast, we all went down to eat without Theo, 'cause he wouldn't wake up. We ate all this fucking food, and when we got back to the room, we found Theo with one of the hotel maids..." Suddenly he stops talking. Like he just remembered he's talking to me. A girl. A girl who happens to be Ronnie's best friend.

"Was Ronnie there?" I ask.

"I think they had a fight or something," Rex says. "She stayed somewhere else."

"Did he cheat on her?"

He gives me a look. I know what it means. He's not going to break the "guy code" and tell me what Theo was doing with the hotel maid. But he doesn't have to tell me. It's kind of obvious.

"Did you cheat on me?" I ask, in a small voice.

"No." He looks defeated. "I didn't."

"Are you sure? Cuz you kind of forgot to tell me about the heroin thing, so maybe you forgot about cheating on me, too?"

"Did you cheat on *me*?" he counters. Even though the question is absurd to me, I can tell it's bothering him.

"No," I say. "But I'm not the one who was out there with lots of willing, you know, devotees." I'm dressed now, and I sink down onto the hotel bed, suddenly exhausted.

Rex sits down next to me. "I didn't cheat," he says, again. "I promise. I wouldn't lie to you about that."

I believe him, and yet there's something reserved in his voice. Like he's still not telling me everything. I look up at him. "There's something you're not saying."

"I didn't cheat on you," he repeats. "But it was...really hard not to."

I feel like I've been punched in the gut. Because it has the ring of truth. And, as they say, the truth hurts.

I remember when I caught the girl with dyed black hair coming on to him. How I stopped her by distracting him with a blowjob. But I can't follow him around the country, policing each interaction he has, giving him blowjobs every time some girl gets pushy. Even if I could, if I did that, I think I'd start to hate him.

"You're gonna be touring a lot next year," I say.

He nods. "Yeah."

"So, do you think...will you be able to...stay just with me? For all that time?"

He holds my eyes for several seconds. His look pained. "No," he says finally. "I don't think I can."

I don't want to cry in front of him, but water squeezes out of my tear ducts anyway. I wipe the tears away.

"Shit," he says. "Jesus, Francesca. What do you want me to say? Do you want me to lie to you, the way Theo lies to Ronnie?"

I stare at him. He's essentially broken the guy code by admitting Theo lies to Ronnie about fucking other girls. I have a feeling Ronnie already knows, and that she's rationalized it somehow. But I've never seen things the same way she does.

"No," I tell him. "I don't want you to lie to me. I want you to not fuck other girls. Can I go home now?"

Without another word between us, we leave our room and check out of the hotel. We continue in silence as he drives me home. When he pulls up in front of my house, he finally speaks.

"What's going on?" His voice cracks a little. "Are we done?"

"I need some time to think. Can I have some time?"

"I'll call you." He reaches for my hand. "I love you."

"I love you, too," I say. Then I pull my hand out of his. "I'll talk to you later." I get out of the car and rush inside, not bothering to notice when he leaves. To my relief, Mom isn't lurking anywhere. I go straight to my bedroom and shut the door.

BY THE WEEKEND, Rex still hasn't called. I'm kind of relieved because I'm in no mood to deal with reality. Saturday night, I have a bad dream.

It starts like a good one. I'm with Rex in his car at the field behind the school. We just fucked, and I feel super close to him. The sun is shining, and it's like the light and warmth of it is filling us both up. We're sharing the sun's energy between us. It's the best feeling in the world.

Then, there's the loud, startling sound of someone knocking on the window of the driver's side.

Rex turns in the direction of the sound, then looks over at me. He says, "I'll be right back, okay?"

Then he scoots over to the driver side door and exits the car.

As soon as he's gone, the sunlight disappears. All at once, it's night. I keep expecting Rex to come back, but he doesn't. I grow restless and scared waiting in the car, in the dark. I can't see Rex through the windows, and it feels like he's never coming back. Finally my fear builds to a point where I can't stand it anymore, and I launch myself out of the vehicle.

Once I'm outside, everything feels unfamiliar, even though it looks the same. But it's so, so dark. There's no moon, and I can just make out the shapes of the trees surrounding the field. I don't see Rex anywhere.

I call out his name.

There's no answer.

I start stumbling across the field, hoping I don't fall. There's no wind, but I can feel a haze of uneasy energy swirling around me in the dark. It's menacing. It makes my stomach hurt.

And then I see Rex. He's with a woman. She's tall, as tall as he is, and she has lustrous, taffy-colored hair. I shouldn't be able to see them so clearly but it's like I've acquired a superpower that allows me to perceive detail through darkness. The woman has her arms wrapped around Rex, and he's clinging to her, too. Seeing them together makes me crazy with jealousy.

Rex's back is to me, and her head is resting on his shoulder. I don't know if the woman can see me.

I keep moving closer, and suddenly, she looks up. Straight at me. Her face is TV beautiful, perfectly proportioned, and she assesses me with an expression of combined contempt, pity, and maybe even hatred. Then she smiles, and her face changes, from beautiful to gaunt, and then, the flesh dissolves from her bones, leaving a skeleton face. The woman is gone.

The skeleton stares at me through eyeless sockets, and I know the destructive, dark energy that's flowing around me is coming from its eyes. My jealousy dissolves into a feeling of horror. I want to run, but I can't move.

Still watching me, the skeleton leans over and whispers

in Rex's ear. He turns around, slow, and sees me. He looks like himself. But his eyes have changed. There's no recognition in them. He's staring straight at me, but it's like he's looking at a complete stranger. And I know that I've lost him.

I wake up, but it takes me awhile to realize I'm no longer in the dream. That I'm not actually in the field with Rex and the creepy skeleton. But I still feel the unnerving energy from the dream state. It's like I brought it back with me, into my bedroom, and it's a long time before I finally go back to sleep.

I spend Sunday morning locked in my room, listening to an old R.E.M. album, doing that angsty, cliched thing where you lie in bed and stare at the ceiling.

Michael Stipe is in the middle of singing "The One I Love" when I hear insistent knocking at my door.

"Who is it?" I ask, even though I'm pretty sure it's Erick.

"It's me," my brother confirms.

"You can come in."

He slips inside the room, shutting the door behind him. Then he moves closer, and sits gingerly on the edge of my bed. "Are you, um...are you ok?" he asks.

I'm about to lie and say I'm fine. That's the role I play, most of the time. His big sister, the one who has it basically together. But today, I'm not up for it.

"No," I admit. "Not really."

"So, like, what's up?" Erick sounds uncomfortable, like maybe he doesn't want to know the answer. But he also sounds curious. So I decide to tell him.

"I think I need to break up with Rex." As soon as I say the words aloud, I know it's true. For months, Rex has felt like this safe place for me. A refuge. But he doesn't feel that way to me, now. I still love him, but I've lost my refuge, and I don't know how to deal with that.

Erick looks over at me. "Life on the road, huh?" As usual, he sounds like he knows all about it. Like he's been there. I have to fight down a strong urge to laugh.

And yet—he isn't wrong.

"Yeah," I admit. I smile ruefully. "I guess, after I break up with him, I won't be your cool sister anymore."

"You're still cool," Erick says. "Especially if you dump him before he dumps you."

Then I do laugh. Because my little brother is his own brand of hilarious. And because laughing feels better than crying.

REX NEVER CALLS. As usual, he shows up at the chicken shack while I'm working.

I haven't seen him in two weeks.

When he comes in, I'm at the front counter. He gets in my line and politely waits his turn. Once he reaches me, he just stands there.

"Can I help you?"

"Can I pick you up after work?"

I nod. "Do you want anything to eat?"

"No. I'll see you tonight."

Then he leaves. I have to fight to put on a cheerful expression as my next customer steps forward in line.

When Rex shows up after my shift, he puts my bike in the trunk of his car, then drives us to the field behind the school. As we sit there, not speaking, it starts to rain. Water runs in tiny rivulets down the windshield.

"I can't do this." Even though I'm not speaking very loud, my voice sounds explosive.

"I think we can make it work," he counters.

For a moment, I feel a rush of hope. Maybe he has some brilliant solution in mind. Maybe he's decided sleeping with other girls isn't worth losing me. "How?" I ask.

He turns toward me. "Ronnie and Theo are making it work."

"I'm not like Ronnie," I remind him. "I told you that a long time ago."

"You told me that last year," he teases.

I'm charmed for a split second. Then I say, "I don't want to make it work the way Ronnie does."

"Is this about drugs?"

"It's not—you promised me you wouldn't do it. And you broke your promise. It's not the drugs. It's...that. You broke your promise," I repeat.

"But you don't like it."

"Drugs scare me to death, Rex. So, okay, maybe it's partly that? And you breaking your promise. And the cheating thing. I mean, I'm glad you didn't lie to me about it, about how you feel, but it's too much, I can't..." I start crying.

He scoots over on the seat and puts his arms around me, and holds me until I stop. Eventually I put my arms around him, too. Then we sit and hold each other.

"I wish my life was somewhere different," he says.

"I wish we lived in a completely different fucking world."

He laughs, kind of quietly. "Good luck with that."

I laugh with him, but I mean it. I wish we lived in a world where drugs and music weren't so intertwined. Where no one ever breaks a promise. Or where people who love each other would meet at the right time, instead of when their lives are moving in opposite directions.

It's easy to blame this on Rex, because it's his life that's clearly taking off. But if I get a scholarship to college in some other state, I'm taking it. I won't stay here and be Rex's girlfriend at home. Even if he promises he'll never do drugs again. Or that he'll never look at another girl. Even if he could keep those promises.

We stay in the car for a long time, watching the water traveling down the windshield as the rain continues to fall. Then he drives me home. He gets my bicycle out of the back of his car, then shuts the trunk and leans the bike against it. He comes over to me.

"You're gonna kill it in college, Batgirl."

"I don't have a scholarship yet. I'm not even enrolled anywhere."

"You'll get in. And when you get there, you're gonna kill it."

I feel tears threatening again. "You're one of the only people I know who even cares about that."

We're standing close to each other. His pale green eyes are full of light, light that's so familiar to me now. I reach up to kiss him and he responds with the sweetest, saddest kiss of my life.

"Bye, Francesca," he says, as we break apart.

"Bye, Rex." I try to grin. "You're gonna kill it as a rock star."

He grins back. "I know! I'm going to be the rocking-est rock star ever." Then he rolls his eyes.

I pound at his shoulder, out of habit. "Guess I'd better get my bike."

"Here." He moves it off the car and hands it over to me. "Take care of yourself."

I take the bicycle's handlebars. "You, too."

He places one more kiss on my forehead. It's hard to

tear myself away from him, but I do, wheeling the bike toward the garage.

There's no moon tonight. Just darkness and the fresh smell of the air after rain. Rex stays in his car until I get the bike inside the garage, then I go through the inside door between the garage and the kitchen.

The kitchen is dark and empty. I stop and lean against one of the counters, trying not to cry again, feeling like I've lost more than a boyfriend or someone I'm in love with. I've lost those things, too. But I've also lost a good friend, and that's what hurts the most.

CHAPTER 35

Life is dull and grating without Rex. My job, which I've always thought of as my financial ticket to freedom, begins to wear on me. My boss starts to call me "college girl" all the time, even though I'm nowhere near going to college. He definitely has a sixth sense for figuring out how to piss me off.

Every time he calls me "college girl" the insinuation is that I think I'm better than everyone else on the crew. I don't think that, but some of my co-workers pick up on the vibe, as well as the nickname. I tell myself it's not severe bullying, it's just annoying. I can handle it. And I need to handle it because I need the paycheck. But it makes work unpleasant.

At home, Mom seems to sense something's up with Rex and me. I don't know if Erick's let anything slip, or if she's noticed that Rex isn't really around anymore. It's kind of hard to miss his big purple monstrosity of a car—either its presence or its absence.

I practice avoiding her. If I'm stuck with her in the same room, I make sure to talk to her about Erick—about his lunches, or making sure he does his share of household chores, or offering to take him to the mall whenever he needs something. It seems to work well as a distraction tactic. I don't want to talk to Mom about my breakup with Rex. She'll be smug, and I won't be able to handle that.

Slowly, I begin to understand that I'm heartbroken. It didn't hit me all at once. I was sad when we broke up, but it also felt like the right decision. Breaking up seemed like the sensible thing to do. The best thing to do.

But I miss him. I miss the feeling of our bodies pressed together. That golden energy he has. Basking in the glow of it. Being in the presence of someone who believes I can actually accomplish the things I want to do.

I'm angry, too. While I'm glad he wouldn't lie to me about the realities of life on the road, I also wish he would rise above it. He said he loved me. So if he loves me, why can't he? Why can't he be with me and no one else?

The more I ruminate on those questions, the more I wonder if he loved me at all. Maybe I was convenient because I was Ronnie's friend. Someone who was available while he waited for his life to start.

Thoughts like these run in the background of my brain constantly. Like when I'm at home. Or driving Erick around in Mom's car. Or at work. It's on my mind on a Saturday afternoon in late April while I take a meal break at the chicken shack.

We're busy, and the dining room is full, so there's nowhere for me to sit. I hide away in our tiny office, squished up against the wall on a folding chair, gnawing on a chicken sandwich that I made with a piece of fried chicken and one of our homestyle biscuits.

Plastered all over the office walls is a hodge podge of food-safety posters. One poster urges, "WASH YOUR

HANDS!" with a picture of cartoon hands being rubbed vigorously together under a stream of pouring cartoon water.

As I'm eating, one of the cooks slips into the office with his own plate of food. He takes a seat at the small desk and balances his plate on the narrow desktop. We always let the cooks sit at the desk and use the office chair. It's an unwritten rule.

He grins at me as he sits down. "Hey, college girl. How's it going?"

This cook, Ben, is one of the nicest guys in the kitchen. I can't bear it if he starts joining in on this "college girl" crap. It's absurd. Just yesterday, I received another scholarship rejection.

"I'm not in college," I inform him sharply. "I can't even fucking afford to go to college."

He looks over at me, curious. "But you want to go, right?"

"Well, sure," I shrug. "But unless a bunch of money drops out of the sky, it's not happening."

"Financial aid?" he suggests.

I shake my head. "I don't want to go in debt."

"You know," he offers, "I have this friend who goes to the local community college? It's way cheaper than going away for school. You could work and keep living at home."

"But I want a degree."

"So transfer to a four-year college after you get your associate's." Ben shrugs. "It's just an idea. But if you're low on cash, you might want to think about it."

I start to tell him why that won't work. If I go to community college and live at home, I'll still be living at home. My main problem is the fact that I live at home. Community college won't solve that.

Still, what Ben's saying is reasonable. He just doesn't know where I'm coming from. I'm not going to confide in him, though. We get along, but it's not like I know him well enough to dump my problems on him.

"Thanks," I tell him. "I'll think about it."

At home, after my shift, I make Erick's lunch for the next day. Then I get ready to go out with Ronnie. I haven't hung out with her since Rex and I broke up, and I'm a bit nervous to see her.

She says she wants to go to this place in Seattle where you can get a ton of food, super cheap. We end up at the diner where Rex and I shared an omelette last fall. I don't think Ronnie knows about that, so she doesn't know that being here makes me kind of melancholy. It reminds me of Rex. I'm actually starting to wonder if breaking up with him *was* the right thing to do.

"How's the chicken shack?" Ronnie asks.

We've ordered a number of breakfast sides, and I'm currently picking at a dry cinnamon roll.

"They're better if you smother them in butter," she advises.

I open one of the foil butter packets and spread it on the roll. I'm starting to gather that this diner is some kind of musicians' hangout. A lot of people here look familiar.

"The chicken shack is fine. I mean, it's the chicken shack."

"Sure you don't want to help me do publicity for the guys?"

I stare at her. "Have you talked to Rex in the last couple weeks?"

"Yeah," she says. "He told me you broke up."

"So why would you ask me to help with publicity?"

She gives me her patient look. The one she always uses

when she thinks I'm not understanding something. "You don't have to be his girlfriend to do publicity for them."

"Why would he even want me to?"

"He's not pissed at you, Frankie. He still likes you. A lot."

"I can't do it," I tell Ronnie. "I can't wrap my head around the drug thing. And the girl thing. Women. Groupies. Whatever. I can't."

"I get it," she reassures me.

"How do *you* deal with it?"

Ronnie lifts an eyebrow. "I don't know if I'm dealing with it. I'm more just kind of...rolling with it."

"Did you talk to Rex about getting paid?"

She nods. "You were right. I told him I want to help them, but I won't do another tour like the last one. I said I'd find a different band to work for if they can't pay me. So Rex talked to the label. They set an amount to pay me for the next tour, the one after the record release? We're gonna re-evaluate after that."

"Are they paying you enough?"

She rolls her eyes. "Enough to cover everything I'll have to pay out of pocket. There might even be some left over. But it's okay. If the band starts doing great and they still like what I'm doing, and you know, if the label's happy, I'll make sure they pay me more next time."

"So—that sounds better?"

"It's better," she affirms. "I mean, they're helping me get my foot in the door. It's not like I'm an experienced publicist."

"I still don't know how you handle...the rest of it." I'm not sure if Ronnie knows Theo's been cheating on her. Or if she does know, maybe she doesn't want to acknowledge it out loud.

She shrugs. "That world they're living in...it's like its own thing, you know? They're one way when they're in it, and they're different when they're out of it. At least this way I get to see both worlds. Maybe it's weird, but that helps me. A lot."

I sense it's not okay for me to point blank ask her if she knows Theo is cheating on her. Still, I feel like she's stronger than me, and I wish I knew her secret.

"You're amazing," I tell her.

"Or a chump," she laughs. "You sure you don't want to come with me? I bet I could cover both of us on what they're paying me."

I shake my head. "I need to keep putting money in the bank."

"The college thing?"

"Right."

She sighs. "Guess you gotta go after what you really want."

I'm startled to realize that, after all this time, I wish I was more like Ronnie. Running toward the specific things she knows she wants. Working for bands. Theo. I've set up college in my mind as the promised land. I've been assuming that going to college will not just get me far away from my mother, but that it will also be the ticket to a better life. But what if it isn't the promised land? What if it doesn't deliver the life I want?

And am I really going for it the way Ronnie does?

After she drops me back home, I have a hard time sleeping. I'm itching to do something stupid. Something like calling Rex and telling him to come get me. Driving somewhere with him in his car and fucking him until it gets light outside. I'm craving his energy and his physical presence. I keep imagining going to the phone in the kitchen, calling him at his mom's house, and asking him to come over.

But I don't do it. I don't even know if he's at his mom's or if he's still crashing at Todd's or if he's God knows where else. If he's screwing someone else already. I decide that's probably what he's doing.

The thought tortures me and keeps me awake. Maybe it's that girl I pulled him away from. The one with the dyed-black hair and thick bangs. He's probably with her in his car right now, using his long, expert fingers on her body. Making her come. She probably gives better blow jobs than I do. Maybe he's glad to be rid of me.

If he's with her, I wonder if he's told her that he loves her.

CHAPTER 36

"Shit!" I yelp.

I'm working the front counter at the chicken shack with LuAnn. A departing customer just spilled half their soda from a to-go order on the counter near my register. I eye the tiny lake of liquid warily, expecting it to start dripping onto the floor, making a worse mess and creating a trip hazard. But miraculously, the soda stays neatly puddled on the countertop. Since we're not super busy, I decide to let my line of customers go down before I clean up the soda.

"Can I help you?" I ask the next customer in line, hoping he didn't notice my foul language. We're not supposed to swear in front of the clientele.

As he gives me his order, our manager, Brodie, comes out front and plants himself next to me.

"How are you doing today?" he asks the customer, as I ring him up. "Thanks so much for coming in."

When I hand over the guy's receipt and order number, Brodie points to the spilled soda.

"Better get that cleaned up, college girl. Somebody

might plant their arm in that mess. It's not creating the most customer-friendly environment."

I'm exhausted from not sleeping the night before, and something in me suddenly snaps. I look up at Brodie and I'm angry. His moon shaped, perpetually smug face makes me even more angry.

"I'm not a 'college girl.'" I spit at him. "And I know you don't mean it as a compliment, so stop calling me that."

He actually looks taken aback. He glances over at LuAnn, then back at me and holds up his hands. "Whoa, sorry. Somebody told me you were going to college. My bad. I won't call you 'college girl' if you don't want me to call you 'college girl.'" Then he eyes the puddle of soda on the counter. "Please do get that cleaned up, though. *Frankie.* Like, now?" He gives me a malevolent grin, then goes back in the direction of the office.

I reach for our sanitizer bucket under the counter, grab a rag, and start mopping up the spilled soda. "Sorry," I tell the next customer in line. "I'll be right with you."

"Take your time." It's a young mother with her daughter. They have a sort of patient energy about them, and I drink it in while I finish mopping up the mess.

Later, after the mini-rush has passed, LuAnn comes over to me.

"I'm sorry," she says, in a low voice. "I told Brodie you were going to college, because he was making jokes about how long you've been working here. I was so pissed. I just said it to shut him up. I never thought he'd make such a big deal out of it."

"It's okay," I tell her. "He's a jerk."

"He's probably worried he's gonna lose one of his best employees."

I snort with laughter. "Or maybe he's just a jerk."

That night I sleep some, but it's still not enough. I stumble into the kitchen the next morning, yawning, around nine. Mom is already there.

"I had to make Erick's lunch again this morning," she says, without preamble.

I forgot. Again. I was so tired when I came home, I fell right into bed.

"I'm sorry," I mumble.

"What's going on with you, Frankie?" she asks. "You haven't been very dependable lately."

"I'm sorry," I say, louder this time. "I was super tired last night. I forgot." I go to one of the cupboards and find a box of cereal, then start hunting for a bowl and a spoon. I'm still groggy. I need a real night of sleep.

"Are you taking drugs?" she asks. "Is that boyfriend of yours getting you into drugs?"

I slam a cereal bowl down on the counter. "No. I'm not taking drugs." I start pouring cereal in the bowl.

"Are you sure?" Mom presses. "Because that Rex person —is that his name, Rex?—looks like the type."

"I'm not doing drugs, Mom, okay? I'm just tired. Like I said, I haven't been sleeping." I open the fridge and get out the milk.

"Why aren't you sleeping? What's going on that's making you not sleep?"

I still don't want to tell her I broke up with Rex. Even though we're not together, in my mind he's still a buffer against my mother, and I'll lose that if I tell her about the breakup.

I lean against the kitchen counter and start eating. "I guess I'm worried about the future or something."

"I bet you are," she agrees. "Because you're just drifting. With that dead-end job. And *Rex*." The way she says Rex's name, it's like she's putting it in quotation marks. Like he's a thing instead of a person.

"I'm saving money for college," I remind her. "I'm not drifting."

"And how is that plan going?" she scoffs.

"It would be going better if I wasn't having to pay you rent *and* provide child care for your son," I retort.

Mom is unfazed. "Life's expensive, Frankie. You're an adult now. If you want to live in this house, you need to pitch in."

"I've been pitching in my whole life. I've been helping you out with Erick since he was a baby. Doesn't that count for anything?"

"I appreciate your help," Mom sounds grudging. "But he's your brother. He's *family*. I'm not charging you that much rent. You'd have to pay at least four times as much if you tried to rent somewhere else."

My frustration is building, and I'm afraid I'm going to start yelling at her. That could get ugly. "I want to go to college," I say, trying to keep my voice calm. "Why can't you support me?"

"Support you how? How would I support you?"

"I don't know." My voice gets louder. "How about just care? Say that you know I can do it if I put my mind to it. Something like that. Or tell me I can accomplish anything I want to. You know, the kind of things a parent is *supposed* to say?"

She gives me this look I know well. It's a look that tells me I'm too young to understand life. That I couldn't possibly know what a parent should say to her child. Now she says, "I just want you to be realistic."

"How am I not being realistic? I graduated from high school with a 4.0 GPA. I got 1450 on the SAT. I won an award for my work on the school paper. Those things matter when you're applying to college. Me getting into college *is* realistic!"

I wait for my argument to sink in. For her to get it. To register "4.0 GPA" and "1450 SAT" and "award." She *has* to get it.

"If you wanted to go to college so bad, why didn't you work harder on making that a reality during your senior year?" Mom asks.

Her question stops me. I've wondered that myself. Why didn't I? As the answer surfaces in my conscious mind—slowly, painfully—it makes me feel ashamed. Weak. I should have been more focused. I should have applied for the schools and scholarships on my own. But I felt like I needed Mom's help and approval—even though I knew I would never get it. And then, I let that knowledge paralyze me.

"I wanted to talk to you about it." As soon as I say it out loud, I feel close to tears, but I force them down. "I needed you to be on my side."

Mom just stares at me for a few moments. Then she starts shaking her head and laughs. It's her sarcastic laugh. "No way are you going to put this on me," she says. "If you want to go to college, go to college. Figure it out. But don't blame me if you can't."

"I don't mean I wanted you to do it for me, I just wanted some support—"

"You want to talk about support, kid? Support is what I've been doing ever since your dad took off. Support is working at that damn store, that place I hate, every damn year, so you and your brother have a roof over your head. Hell, maybe I'd like to go to college. But I can't, because I'm here, providing you with goddamn *support*."

We stare at each other for what feels like an ice age. Then the words come hurtling out of me. "But I'm your kid, *Mom*. That's what parents do, they put a roof over their kids' heads! It's what you signed up for when you decided to have kids."

She opens her mouth to dispute me, so I yell over her unspoken words. "It's not wrong to want to go to college! It's not wrong to want to do better for myself. I want to do better!"

"Do better," she sneers. "Better than what? You mean better than me, right? You want to be better than me."

And then I get it. She doesn't want me to have the opportunities she never had. It's what Aunt Carrie told me back at Thanksgiving. Mom doesn't like herself, and she doesn't have it in her to want better things for me. Which means I *will* have to get them without her help. I guess I always knew that. But now, it's in my face and undeniable.

"Isn't that what you want?" Mom repeats. "To be better than me?"

"Forget it," I mutter.

"No, I won't forget it." She points at me. "Have you ever thought about what will happen to your brother if you go gallivanting off to college and leave him here? He looks up to you. He's going to fall apart if you leave. How could you live with yourself if you do that to him?"

I stare at her. "I'm not Erick's mother! You are! I can't stay here and be his proxy mom until he graduates from high school. That's six years from now. That's fucking *crazy*. I have to live my own goddamn life!"

"All you think about is yourself," Mom spits out. "*My future*," she mimics. "*My dreams. My need for support.* Not everything is about you, Frankie. You have a family. Your brother and me. Maybe we're not good enough to fit with your dreams and your plans for the future, but that doesn't mean we're not here."

"You're twisting everything!" I yell. "You always do that. Just because I want to make my life better doesn't mean I don't care about you or Erick!"

"You don't care about Erick! Putting bad ideas in his head. Giving him that stupid guitar. What the hell were you thinking? Do you want him to end up a deadbeat loser like that Rex person?"

"Rex is not a loser!"

She just rolls her eyes, like the whole world knows different.

I'm furious. I'm sick of her sarcasm. The way she mocks everything that matters. I stare her straight in the eyes. "If I stayed here to protect Erick from anything, it would be you! So you don't kill his dreams the way you're trying to kill mine. But you're not going to kill them! I won't let you kill them!"

My words seem to vibrate between us for a long time. Mom seems to be in shock. Then she fixes me with a hard look.

"So that's what you think of me. You think I'm trying to hurt my own kids. Well, fine. You just remember you said that the next time you're eating the food *I* bought while depositing your paycheck in the bank for your *college fund*."

She moves past me and snags her purse from the counter. "I have to go to work. Please don't forget to make Erick's lunch again." Then she slams out of the house.

It isn't until I hear her car drive away and down the street that I realize my hands are shaking.

CHAPTER 37

I go for a bike ride in a fruitless attempt to shake off how shitty I feel. First, I coast down to the Food Mart, then pedal back up the hill, hoping the climb will use up the energy that's been coursing through me since my fight with Mom. But by the time I get back to the top, even though I'm panting and sweating, the agitation from the fight is still with me.

I ride through different neighborhoods, an easier ride since most of them are level. As I zip by each house, I wonder what life is like inside. If the family living there gets along with each other. Is the atmosphere tense, or warm and friendly?

Soon I realize I'm riding through Rex's neighborhood. I feel an overwhelming urge to go by his house, so I pedal in that direction.

When I get close, I spot his purple car under the carport. Is he home? If I knock on the door, will he talk to me? I stop my bike in front of his driveway and plant my feet on the ground. Somewhere nearby, there's the sound of someone mowing their lawn. I stay where I am, and stare at Rex's house.

I'm pathetic. I'm just as bad as my brother. Stalking Rex. Hoping to catch a glimpse of him, like an obsessed fan.

I get back on my bike. But then, miraculously, he appears. He comes around from behind the house and walks toward his car. It's quiet now. Whoever was mowing their lawn has stopped.

He goes right for the driver's side, and I figure he doesn't see me. But then, before he opens the car door, he turns and looks. For a few seconds, we stand still and stare at each other.

Rex moves in my direction, walking until he's in the street, standing right in front of me.

"Hey, Francesca."

"Hi, Rex."

His eyes glitter. "You lost or something?"

"Why are you here?" I ask. "I thought you moved in with Todd."

"Mowing my mom's lawn. I was just heading out."

"Oh, right. Okay. Well." I feel awkward. "Guess I should go."

He gives me a probing look, then sort of half grins. "My mom's at work. You want to come inside?"

We lock my bike outside, then go straight to his room. As I sink down on his bed, I marvel at how comfortable I feel. I've only been in his room a handful of times, but it's still a more friendly environment than my own home.

Rex takes his chair, turns it around backwards, and sits down facing me. "What's going on?"

I wave a dismissive hand in front of my face. "Just a fight with my mom. No big deal. Happens all the time."

"Kind of seems like maybe it was a big deal this time?"

"Maybe," I admit.

I've been afraid, if I saw him again, that he might look like he's been using drugs. Unhealthy skin, maybe, or track marks on his arms.

But he looks the same. Better even. Healthy. Glowing with the promise of the future ahead of him. With that light in his eyes that's somehow older and wiser than he actually is.

"I miss you," I tell him.

Rex studies me for a second. Then he gets up off the chair and sits next to me on the bed. He squeezes my knee. "I miss you, too."

"I'm glad."

"Nothing's changed," he says, watching my face.

"I know. I wasn't planning on coming here. It just kind of...happened."

"And I was here."

"Here you are." I laugh, looking up at him. There's sweetness in his eyes, the same sweetness that surprised me the first time I saw it in him.

"Francesca..." he warns. "I should take you home."

"I don't want to go home." I reach up and touch his face. "I want to stay here."

"Nothing's changed," he repeats. His voice sounds hoarse.

"I don't care. I need you." I lean closer to him and put my hand on his leg. Then I kiss him. I feel him hesitate for a split second. But then he's responding, kissing me hard.

A rush of relief moves through me. I've missed the connection between us so much. I'm hungry for him. For that feeling of belonging that came over me the moment I walked into his room. I want as much of it as I can get.

We fall back on his bed and start pulling off each other's

clothes. He slides his hand between my legs, and I close my eyes with pleasure and happiness.

"You're so fucking beautiful," he groans, and kind of collapses on me. "Goddammit."

I can feel his erection pressing against my stomach, so I know he wants me. But everything else about him is vibrating with confusion. "Don't you want to?"

"No," he groans again. "Yes. Yes, I want to." He lifts himself up and goes to his dresser for a condom. He rolls it on, then positions himself over me again, and I open my legs wider.

I'm breathing hard, and I can feel him listening to me, like he's getting in tune with my energy. He's kissing me again, and I move underneath him, impatient.

"Batgirl. I always want to," he says in my ear. Then he slides his hand down to my hip and enters me.

"WHAT ARE you gonna do about your mom?" Rex asks. "What was your fight about?"

We're lying together on his bed, under a blanket. I'm pretending we can stay here as long as we want. Days, even, if we feel like it. I'm one hundred percent relaxed.

"The usual," I sigh. "College. Although...I don't know. I think it's more than that. It's about her. She doesn't want me to... She's not happy. It's just really hard to live there."

"Maybe you should move out," he suggests.

"I've thought about it. But if I do that, I can't save as much money for college."

"Couldn't you get some help from... I don't know, the government or something?"

"You mean financial aid?" I ask.

"Sure, that. Can't you get that?"

"You have to pay it back," I sigh. "I don't want to go in debt."

"We're going in debt," Rex points out. "Like, serious debt with the record company. Unless we sell a shit ton of records."

"Yeah. I guess."

"No guessing about it. It's for real." He shifts a little on the bed. "Sometimes you just have to make a move, you know? And maybe it's not the move you planned on, but life kind of forces your hand. So just make your move, then make the best of it."

I'm quiet as I let his words sink in.

He runs his hand over my hair in the way I love. "If your mom is making you feel like you owe her something, it's just gonna get worse the longer you stay in her house. She was responsible for you until eighteen, but now, anything she does for you is a favor, right? She can always hold that over your head."

I know he's right. "I just wanted her to be on my side."

"I want that for you," he agrees. "But if she's not, you need to get out of there. Make a plan to do it. As soon as you can."

I snuggle against him. "Thanks for listening to all this... stuff. About my mom. And everything else."

"I care about you." The words are sweet, but his voice is pained. And just like that, the spell—the one that made me feel this moment between us would last forever—is broken.

"How are things with the band?" I venture.

"Francesca. We can't do this again."

I feel my stomach drop.

"I love you," he says. "But if we keep doing this, you're gonna hate me, and I'm gonna resent you. We have to stop."

It's not like he tricked me into this. He was honest about the situation before we had sex. Nothing has changed. He tried hard drugs after he promised me he wouldn't. And he won't promise not to mess around with other girls while he's on the road. I'm still not okay with those things. I will never be okay with those things.

"I shouldn't have come here," I whisper.

"No," he tightens his arms around me. "I'm glad you're here. But we can't do it again. Do you... Do you get it?"

Tears fall from my eyes, and I try not to shake with the sobs that are fighting to force their way out of me. I'm afraid he'll push me away. He's probably pissed that I'm so emotional right now when I'm the one who ended things in the first place.

"Hey," he says, holding me firmly against him. "It's okay."

I finally let the sobs escape, and he doesn't let go of me while I cry. When I'm spent, I twist around in his arms so I can look at him.

"I get it," I tell him. "We won't do this again."

We're eye to eye, and the connection between us feels so strong. But there's also so much sadness in it. It's a huge, unfamiliar feeling. I'm not sure I understand it.

Rex offers to take me home, but I tell him I'd rather ride my bike. He walks with me out to the street, and we stand there together, almost awkward. As if we just met.

He's so beautiful. He's glowing from us being together, and I feel that glow all over me, too.

"Things are going to work out for you," he tells me.

"For you, too."

He reaches out and frames my face with his hand. "Ride safe."

I'm too overwhelmed with emotion to answer him, so I

get on my bike and begin to pedal down the street. When I look back, he's still there, watching me go. Something about that kills me. It's a relief to turn around and face forward. To keep my eyes on the road.

I have the night off work, so instead of going straight home, I keep riding for a while, around nearby neighborhoods. When I get hungry and thirsty, I turn back in the direction of our house.

Mom's car is in the driveway when I get there. After stashing my bike in the garage, I go straight for the kitchen. I'm starving. I haven't eaten all day, so I make myself a sandwich.

Erick walks in the kitchen while I'm eating it.

"Hey," he says, on his way to the refrigerator.

"Sorry about your lunch today."

"I can make my own damn lunch." He rummages around in the fridge and brings a bunch of sandwich stuff out. He spreads it all on the counter. Then he takes out two pieces of bread and looks at me.

"So you're gonna do it from now on?" I ask.

"Yeah." He raises his eyebrows. "How hard can it be?"

"It's not," I confirm. "But Mom has rules you should know about."

He groans. "What are the rules?"

"You can use as much American cheese as you want. But only use three pieces of deli meat per sandwich." I grin at him. "Bet you thought I was skimping on purpose, didn't you?"

Erick points to my sandwich. "What about the one you're eating right now?"

I show it to him, so he can see how sparse the meat is inside it.

"Got it." He peels three slices of deli meat from the

package and slaps them down on a slice of bread. "Wait, should I put mayo on first?"

"No. I mean, not unless you want a super soggy sandwich. That's why I always send it in one of those little containers."

"Oh, right."

"I'll show you where they are." I open the cupboard where the small food storage containers are and wave him toward it. "Go ahead and grab one of those."

Erick nabs one out of the cupboard and tosses it to me. I catch it and toss it back. We grin at each other.

Mom's voice cuts across the room. "What's going on?"

"I'm making my lunch!" Erick announces.

"I'm helping him," I tell her. "Don't worry, I let him know about the three-slice rule."

Mom crosses the room to the fridge and retrieves a diet soda. "Where have you been all day?" she asks abruptly as she closes the refrigerator door. I know she's talking to me, but I don't answer.

"What about the lettuce and stuff?" Erick asks.

"Put those in a separate baggie, too." I open a drawer. "Baggies are in here."

Mom tries again. "Frankie," she says, with an edge to her voice. "Where were you all day? Erick said you weren't here when he got home from school."

I look up from the sandwich stuff. "I wasn't. I went for a super long bike ride."

"Where?" She gives me a knowing look. "To see Rex?"

"No," I lie. Then I tell her the truth. "Rex and I broke up."

"Oh," she says. "Oh. I didn't know."

Erick holds up a baggie with lettuce and sprouts inside it. "Like this?"

"Perfect."

"Make sure he remembers to put both fruit and cookies in that lunch sack," Mom advises.

I look up at her. "Of course."

"Well, guess I'll read my book for a while," she says. "Don't forget to clean up the kitchen when you're done."

"We will!" Erick yells. "Or I mean, we won't forget!" He goes to the pantry and grabs the package of sandwich cookies. "How many of these?"

"Four," I tell him. "In a baggie."

From the kitchen, I watch Mom as she settles on the couch with her book. Somehow, it's like I'm seeing her through a picture frame. Like the moment is already in the past. And right then I decide, if I'm not in college by the fall, I will no longer be living in this house. One way or the other, I'm leaving.

Rex is right. Sometimes you just have to make a move, then make the best of it.

CHAPTER 38

I'm looking for an apartment—or at least, I'm attempting to get an idea of what's out there and how much it will cost. Currently, I'm holed up in the office at the chicken shack, perched on the uncomfortable chair against the wall and combing through the apartments for rent in the newspaper. I've circled a few available places already.

Ben walks in with his meal and sits down at the desk. He looks over at me, and grins. "Catching up on today's headlines?"

I peer around the edge of the paper. "No. Looking for an apartment."

"I thought you wanted to save money for college?"

"I do. But I can't... I have to get out of my house first." I hope he doesn't ask more questions because I don't feel like explaining myself.

"Got it." He smiles at me, then stands up. "Why don't you take the desk? It'll be easier to look at the paper if you have a flat surface."

"Oh, it's okay..."

"Take the damn desk," Ben laughs.

So I do.

I HAVE THE LATE SHIFT, and when I get home, it's close to midnight. I open the refrigerator to see if there's any left-over apple juice, which I've been craving. Erick's lunch is on the top shelf, packed and ready to go, and it makes me smile. There's some juice left, so I pour myself a glass and drink it down quickly.

The pile of mail on the kitchen counter catches my eye. I consider waiting until morning to look through it, but curiosity pulls me in, and I flip through the envelopes. Most of them are bills. Something I'll be dealing with myself, soon, when I get my own apartment.

Then I stop. There's an envelope from NYU. At first, I feel a tinge of excitement. Then it dies. Because of course, it's another rejection.

I have to accept that I waited too long to apply for scholarships. I should have been on it my senior year. Or even before that. Maybe there's something I can do to make myself an attractive candidate for scholarships again. Maybe a different job, or some kind of volunteer work. But for now, I have to accept that my scholarship plan is a dud.

I turn the envelope from NYU over in my hands. Another annoying surge of hope rushes through me, but despite my GPA and SAT scores, I don't think I'm the kind of person who gets accepted to a fancy East Coast school. I'll do better locally, once I get my shit together again.

Finally, I open the envelope and pull out the letter. "We're sorry to inform you, blah, blah, blah..." I intone. And then I stop. Actually read the first sentence of the letter. Read it again. Rub my eyes.

It starts:

Dear Ms. Peterson,

We are happy to inform you that we have awarded you a journalism scholarship for the 1990-91 academic year. After a careful review of your academic record, as well as your accomplishments in journalism at your high school, we have decided you are the perfect candidate for our program at NYU.

"Holy fucking shit." I drop the letter on the counter. It doesn't seem real. I look at the envelope, at the return address, expecting to discover it's a joke. It didn't actually come from NYU. Maybe it came from somewhere else, like someplace in the Midwest. Or somewhere local. It's pretending to be from NYU.

But after thoroughly inspecting the envelope, then reading the letter one more time, I finally believe that it's real. The rest of the letter includes brief instructions for how to accept the scholarship.

I stand there in our kitchen, the same old kitchen I've known for almost nineteen years, and begin to feel a surge of deep excitement. I'm holding the ticket to my future in my hands. It's going to be real. It *is* real. I made it real.

All at once, the house is different. Less stifling. It's losing its power over me already. I stay where I am, just savoring the feeling. Then I start to make a plan.

In the morning, I'll call my aunt. I need to talk to her first, to get advice on how to handle this with Mom. And who knows, maybe she'll have some suggestions on how to handle the rest of the situation. I need to talk to someone who I know supports me. Then I can take the steps to accept the scholarship and make my move. To New York City.

I put the offer letter back in the envelope and take it to my room.

. . .

When I call Carrie, she's full of great advice. She says to accept the scholarship before I tell anyone else. That way, the decision will be made, and no one will be able to plant doubts before I set the plan in motion. Then she says that if Mom won't do it, she'll take a trip with me to New York to visit NYU.

"I don't know if Mom would do that," I confess. "I can't picture her doing it."

"Well, ask her," Carrie says, briskly. "But if she says no, then I guess you and I have a date."

I'm speechless.

"Oh, and don't worry about how much the trip will cost. My treat."

"I have savings," I protest. "And I have a scholarship now, so I can use my savings for the trip."

"Think of it as your going-away present," Carrie says. "And in case no one else tells you, I'm so proud of you, Frankie."

"Thank you," I manage. My voice is suddenly shaky.

"You deserve this opportunity." Her tone is firm. "You earned it. Don't let anyone tell you different."

For almost a week, my scholarship stays a secret between me and Carrie. I write back to the school to accept the offer. Then I start looking at possible dates for taking a trip to New York, so I can plan it around my work schedule.

I keep the secret from Ronnie, even though I want to tell her. She's still dropping hints about me helping her do publicity for the band. They're busy, she tells me. They've been doing photo shoots. They've picked a first single. They're filming a video. The single will be released in June, and the album comes out at the end of July.

When she tells me all this, I'm kind of glad Rex and I aren't together anymore. I'm sure with everything the band has going on, I'd feel like a distraction again instead of his girlfriend. But I still miss him.

Sometimes I want to call him and tell him I got a scholarship. That I did it. I'm going to college. I want to thank him for believing in me. But after the last time we were together at his house, it feels wrong to call him. I love him. But it's over. First, I decided it was over. And then he agreed with me. I can't go back.

When I'm certain that NYU has received my acceptance of the scholarship and that everything is set, I finally tell Ronnie.

She's shocked. "I thought you wanted to go to school around here?"

"I did. But I didn't get a scholarship offer from anywhere around here, so..." I shrug.

We're at Ronnie's house. I didn't want to be at my house when I told her, because I'm not ready for Mom to know yet. Or Erick. I know Carrie's keeping her mouth shut, waiting for me to tell Mom about my plans when I'm ready. Not that she and Mom talk to each other much, anyway.

"Wow," Ronnie says. "New York City."

"It's crazy," I agree.

"Did you tell Rex?"

"We broke up," I remind her.

"I know. But he'd still want to know—"

"I don't think so," I cut her off. "I went to see him awhile ago. He doesn't want to keep dragging this out, and I agree with him. He's right. We both need to move on."

Ronnie gives me a look. "Well, if you change your mind, if you want to go to the CD release show, I'm sure they'll put you on the list."

"Maybe," I say.

I finally do tell Mom, after I've already arranged to take

time off work for my trip to New York. Carrie went ahead and booked the plane tickets and a hotel. She said if Mom wants to go, she can use her ticket.

I approach her on a morning in early May, before she leaves for work. "Hey. Mom. I need to talk to you about something."

"Is it about Erick again?" She sounds defensive.

"No," I say. "It's about me."

She leans against the kitchen counter and folds her arms over her chest. "Okay. What's going on?"

It's been a rainy month. It's drizzling outside right now, and it's dark even though it's the middle of the morning. There's a bit of a damp chill permeating the kitchen.

"Well, you've probably noticed a lot of mail coming from different colleges and stuff...."

"I've seen that, yeah. You never talk about it."

"There wasn't anything to say until now." There's no way to ease into this. "So, I applied for a scholarship at NYU? In New York. And I got in. I got a scholarship."

Mom blinks. "You got into college in New York?"

"Yeah. A scholarship. And I was talking to Carrie about it, and she thinks I should go out to New York City and visit before school starts."

She frowns. "How are you going to afford that?"

I take a deep breath. "Well, that's the kind of cool thing. Carrie bought tickets already so—I don't have to pay for it."

Mom just stares at me, and I keep talking, nervously. "She said she'd go with me, but she was thinking, I mean, I was thinking, too, that maybe you could go with me instead? So you can see where I'll be going to school? Carrie and Jared would take care of Erick, so no need to worry about that."

At first, Mom says nothing. She just keeps staring at me.

Then she lets out one of her signature sarcastic laughs. "You told Carrie about all this, and you didn't tell me?"

There's not much point denying the obvious, so I just nod.

"When did you know you got in?" she asks.

"Couple weeks ago."

She shakes her head slowly. I'm tense, waiting for what she's going to say. And then, suddenly, I'm sick of it. She should be happy for me. I want to be happy for me. Before she can say anything else, I speak up.

"Do you want to go with me when I go to New York? Or should I go with Carrie?"

"What about work?"

"I already have the time off," I tell her. "The trip's all set."

Mom goes quiet. Maybe she's thinking about it. Considering it. Then she says, "I think you should go with Carrie."

I'm surprised when her answer feels like a punch to the gut. I've actually been dreading the idea of going on this trip with Mom. Sharing a hotel room with her sounds like a nightmare. I've even thought it would be better if I *did* take the trip with Carrie. But now that Mom has refused to go with me, it hurts.

"When are you moving out?" she asks.

"Sometime in August. I can still pay rent for that month—"

"I have to go to work," she interrupts, and starts for the door. I watch her grab her purse off the kitchen counter. She begins to open the front door, then turns around and looks at me. "I hope this is what you really want." Then she goes out.

I listen to her get in her car, then drive away.

"Congratulations, Frankie," I say out loud.

I wish Mom was happy for me. Or proud of me. But she doesn't seem to have that in her. It makes me kind of sad.

Still, I'm not going to let that stop me.

WHEN I TELL Erick that I'm leaving, it's hard. He's actually happy for me—excited even. But I'm worried sick about him.

"New York City!" he croaks. "That's fucking awesome!"

"Yeah, all the way across the country." It's hitting me just how far away from home I'm going to be. Even if I were going to a school several hours away, coming home to visit once a month would be possible. But that's not going to be an option with me living in New York.

"I'll have to come visit you," he says, hopefully.

I have no idea how that would work. But I decide we need to make it happen. Somehow. "Yeah," I agree. "You'll have to fly out and visit."

"Have you told Mom yet?" he asks.

I nod. "I did."

"Was she pissed?"

Was she? I'm not sure *pissed* is the right word. I shrug. "She was Mom."

He gives me a look. "Yeah."

"Listen," I say. "Speaking of Mom. Since I'm not going to be here, you're going to have to learn how to deal with her. And I'm sorry. It shouldn't be...the way it is. You know that, right?"

"Yeah, I know," Erick agrees, like it's old news. Then he grins at me. "I figure when you're gone, she won't have as much time to mess with me. I'll probably get to do whatever I want."

My brother. Mr. Incorrigible. For once, I'm glad he's like

that. I think he's going to need that part of himself to survive.

"As soon as I know where I'm living, I'll give you my phone number, okay? You can call me in New York anytime. I'm not going to disappear."

"Mom will probably get pissed about all the long distance," he points out.

"So call collect."

"Sure, Ms. Moneybags."

"I just want you to know you can talk to me if you need to."

Erick rolls his eyes. "Yeah, okay. I get it."

"You're going to be okay," I tell him.

"So are you!" he shoots back.

And I really hope we're both right.

CHAPTER 39

Fern on Fire's CD release show is tonight. It's a hot evening in late July, and I'm going, but not as the band's guest. Ronnie told me I'm on the list, and I said I'd be there, but I didn't want them to waste a spot on their guest list for me. Tonight, I want to be a regular person. Pay my cover, then leave whenever I feel like it. After all, I'm not "Fern on Fire's girlfriend" anymore.

Earlier this month, Carrie and I went to New York to visit NYU. It was exciting and overwhelming, and I was so glad she was with me. It also made everything real: *I'm going to do it. I'm going to move to New York City for school.* The trip gave me more confidence and a sense of certainty that a chapter of my life was truly coming to an end.

When I got back home, it felt like the end of a lot of things. Including my relationship with Rex. It kind of surprised me that something simple like flying across the country and back would be the dividing line between the past and the future. But it did that for me.

Tonight, though, I'm still living in the past. Ronnie tried to set it up so I could meet with Rex before the show. But I shut that down, too. Part of me would love to hear him tell me again that I'm going to kill it in college. Or feel the way I always feel when he smiles at me. It would be nice to kiss him one more time. For luck.

But trying to get something from him now would be like opening a wound. And after what he said the last time we were together, I'm not so sure he wants to see me. Ronnie seems to think he does. But I also know she has a tendency to ignore things she doesn't want to see. Like Theo cheating on her.

So I'm going alone. Ronnie already drove down to Seattle. I'm going to call a cab to get there, so I can leave the venue whenever I want.

When I walk out to the phone in the kitchen, I find Mom in the living room reading.

"Hey, Mom."

She looks up from her book. "Well, look at you, all dressed up. Are you going out?"

"Yeah, I'm going to meet Ronnie in Seattle." I don't tell Mom I'm going to a show, since I'm still using a fake ID to get into most shows.

She puts her book down. "Ronnie's not picking you up?"

I shake my head. "I'm taking a cab. She probably won't drive back here tonight, and I don't want to get stuck. I just want to make an appearance and come home."

Mom looks at me, considering. I wait for her to say something upsetting, and remind myself that, in less than a month, I won't be living here. Whatever she says, I can take it.

"Why don't you take my car?" she offers.

I stare at her, incredulous. "Are you serious?"

"Sure. You're going to bring it back tonight, right?"

"That's the plan."

"Keys are in my purse. Go have fun."

"I... Thanks, Mom." I grab her purse from the counter and dig out her car keys.

As I start for the door, she calls out, "Would you mind filling it up with gas before you come home?"

I actually feel like laughing. Of course, there's a catch. But that's okay. I was planning to spend money on a cab. Filling up her gas tank will probably cost the same or maybe even less.

"Yeah, Mom," I say. "I'll put gas in it."

I stop at the gas station on the way down, because later it's going to be too creepy to be there. Mom's car is under a quarter tank, and I fill it up all the way. Then I drive to Seattle.

The show is happening at The Showbox near the Pike Place Market. After I find a place to park, I walk toward the venue. I'm feeling good about my decision to pay for the show. It's like taking back my independence. But when I get to the ticket window, they tell me it's sold out.

"Are you sure?" I ask, feeling my stomach sink with disappointment.

"Yeah, sorry," the guy shrugs. "It sold out fast. They're kind of the most popular band in town right now."

I feel like an idiot. Of course they are. Based on everything Ronnie's been telling me, it makes sense.

"I might be on the guest list?" I steel myself to be humiliated, in case my name isn't there. I hate that it still matters to me. But it absolutely does.

The guy kind of smirks. "You think you're on the list, huh?"

"I said I *might* be."

He picks up a clipboard, and glances at it. "What's your name?"

"Francesca or Frankie Peterson." When he raises an eyebrow at me, I tell him, "I go by both Frankie and Francesca."

He scans the list, then gives an incredulous laugh. "Yep, you're on it. Exactly like that, in fact. 'Francesca or Frankie Peterson.' I guess you're in."

I give him my wrist so he can stamp it, and he tells me to enjoy the show.

Enjoy the show. Right. For me, this show feels more like some kind of ritual. Exactly what kind, I'm not sure yet. But "enjoyment" is not the main reason I'm here.

As I move into the room, it looks like a road crew is setting up the stage for the next band. The place is packed, and I'm sure I won't find Ronnie. But somehow, she finds me.

"Hey," she bumps hips with me. "You made it."

"Barely." I smile at her. "The show was sold out when I got here. Thanks for making sure I was on the guest list."

She gives me a probing look. "It wasn't me, sweetie. It was Rex."

"Oh. Well. That was nice of him." I'm not sure how to feel about this. I want it to mean something. Then again, it's just a guest list. It means he doesn't hate me, but it doesn't have to mean anything more. For instance, it doesn't mean he wants to see me again.

So of course, Ronnie suggests it. "Want to hang out after the show?"

"Probably not," I say. "Mom let me borrow her car. I should get it back to her. She won't be thrilled if I'm late."

"You don't have to be late, you can just come say hi, then go home."

"We'll see." And then, to my relief, the lights go down,

and the crowd starts cheering as Fern on Fire takes the stage.

I'm in a strange state of mind for watching a show. I want to be done with this part of my life, but the band keeps breaking through my resolve. They're so damn good. It's their moment, and this is a *thing*. A phenomenon. How can I say no to being a part of it? To being a part of history, even?

I get caught up in the experience, screaming and cheering them on right alongside Ronnie. Feeling like I'm a part of it all, the way I have been for nearly a year. The euphoria lasts through almost two encores.

But at the very end, I begin to see the stage the same way I've been picturing scenes at my mom's house. Like I'm snapping a photo in my mind, filing it away for later. Turning the present into the past.

When the lights go up, Ronnie asks me again if I want to go backstage and say hi to the guys.

It's on the tip of my tongue to say yes. Why not? Just one last time. Then I wonder how the other guys feel about me breaking up with Rex. If they're pissed at me. Maybe they don't give a shit one way or the other. Still. However things were before, they're different now.

"No," I say to Ronnie. "I'm going to try to get Mom's car back before midnight." I give her a hug. "Let them know they were amazing. And please tell Rex thanks for putting me on the list."

"It'd be better if you tell him yourself," Ronnie says, as we break apart.

I shake my head. "I have to go. Talk to you soon!" Then I turn around and leave. I can feel Ronnie staring after me. Not understanding me or my behavior.

I'm not sure I understand it myself.

When I get to Mom's car, I'm desperate to drive away, fast. I want to go, just in case Rex tries to come out and speak to me one last time. Of course, he won't do that. He's probably already reveling in the success of the show with the band and their friends.

But whatever he's doing, I need this chapter of my life to be done. Now. Tonight. So as soon as I've maneuvered out of my parallel parking spot, I speed away without looking in the rearview mirror.

New York City
1995

CHAPTER 40

Here goes nothing.

I follow Jeff, the tour manager, inside a room that's neither big nor small. There're some couches set against the wall, and a large round table in the middle of the room. An ashtray on the table is overflowing with cigarette butts, and someone is sitting there, smoking.

It's Todd.

He looks up, and I see hesitant recognition in his eyes.

Jeff says, "This is Frankie, with *Rags to Bitches*."

Todd grins. "Is that you, Francesca?"

"Yup, it's me."

Todd looks at Jeff, and gestures to me. "Whatever you say to this woman, do not call her a groupie. She is not a fucking groupie."

"Okay?" Jeff looks puzzled. "You know each other?"

I give Jeff my most professional smile. "A long time ago. In Seattle. Thanks for all your help, I really appreciate it."

He takes the hint. "I'll leave you to it."

I sit down at the table, and Todd states the obvious. "So, you're a journalist, huh?" He sounds friendly but also wary, and maybe even ready for a fight. I get it. The band doesn't like journalists, so I'm the enemy now.

I'm not in the mood to play the game where I pretend to know what I'm doing or even why I'm doing it. "I'm barely a journalist," I say. "I started working for *Rags to Bitches* to get into shows for free. So. Here I am."

He smirks. "You know, if you wanted to get in touch, you could have just talked to Rex's mom or something. I'm sure she would have hooked you up."

"I didn't get this assignment until this morning," I inform him. "The person who was supposed to do it couldn't make it, so I'm just filling in last minute."

I'm not sure he believes me. Still, he seems to relax a little. But just a little.

I pull my voice recorder out of my bag and set it on the table. Then I look up at Todd. "I use this for every interview," I apologize.

"I'm familiar with those." He takes another drag of his cigarette, blowing the smoke up toward the ceiling.

"So, am I interviewing just you, or is the rest of the band going to show up? I mean, if it's just you, we could get started now."

"No, they'll be here." He gives me a smile that feels almost like old times. "You trying to work any particular angle? Any way we can help you out?"

I decide to be honest. "I have no idea what the fuck I'm doing. Like I said, I just found out about this today. I have zero questions prepared. Right now, I am the least professional journalist you've ever met. Lucky you."

Todd's face lights up. "This oughta be fun then." He raises his eyebrows at someone behind me, and I turn around. Noah and Theo have just walked into the room. Rex isn't with them.

"Look who it is!" Todd greets them, gesturing to me. "Blast from the past."

They sit down at the table, and Theo recognizes me immediately. "Holy shit! It's Francesca! What the hell?"

"She's a rock journalist now," Todd tells him.

"Barely," I repeat.

Todd grins, and blows more smoke up at the ceiling.

"How the hell are you?" Theo asks.

"I'm good."

"How's Ronnie?"

"She's...married."

Ronnie never told Theo about her wedding. When their relationship ended, it did not end well. She convinced him to go to rehab for his own addiction issues, years ago. He's supposedly been sober ever since. But after he finished rehab, he got involved with someone else. He still wanted to hang on to Ronnie, but she'd reached her limit of what she was willing to tolerate and dumped him.

Now, he looks a bit rueful. But then he shrugs. "Well, good for her. She always wanted to get married." He gestures to Noah. "This guy got married too."

"Really?" I'm kind of surprised. It's hard to picture any of them married, but especially Noah.

I guess Rex isn't going to be here. I'm disappointed, but also relieved. I have no idea what I would say to him, and if he were here, it might be difficult to do my job.

The guys don't seem that different. They're cautious, but they're not acting like they're better than me, which is something I've definitely experienced interviewing other bands. Even bands who are nowhere near as successful as Fern on Fire.

They *are* more confident. All of them used to have an edge of hungry desperation about them, and that's gone. I know not all bands get great deals from their record labels, and not every successful band is rolling in money. But I have a feeling they're no longer worried about money. Whether they're rolling in it, or not.

"Can I turn on my voice recorder?" I ask.

"Uh oh," Noah says.

Todd laughs. "It's getting serious."

"Like I told him," I say to Theo and Noah, "I just found out I was doing this interview this morning. I have zero intelligent questions to ask you."

Noah doesn't smile, but his mood seems to lighten a bit. "Turn it on, then," he says, gesturing to the voice recorder. "We'll give you the best interview ever."

I can do this, I think. *Or at least I can get through it. I've been doing this for almost five years. I can make it work.* I hit the record button on the machine and look up.

"So," Todd says, mock serious. "What questions do you have prepared for us today?"

We all crack up, but my laughter is the most nervous. For a moment, my mind is a complete blank. Then a generic question bubbles to the surface.

"How do you feel about the reaction to your new album? Is it what you expected? Or has anything surprised you about your fans' response to it?"

Phew.

Noah turns to the other guys and widens his eyes. "I think they're buying it? Is anyone buying the new record? Or did it bomb?"

"We try not to burden Noah with the business details," Todd confides. "It ruins the purity of the rock n' roll experience for him."

"I'm here for the good times," Noah affirms.

"We're super happy with this record," Theo says,

looking directly at me. "We've expanded our fanbase since it was released, so I figure we must be doing something right."

I take Theo's actual answer to my question as a sign to move on.

"The subject matter of the songs seems a little dark—"

"Uh oh!" Now Theo laughs. "It's the dark lyrics question!"

Noah rubs his chin theatrically. "Why does everybody ask that question?"

"Everyone asks it!" Theo agrees. "Rolling Stone asked it, MTV asked it..."

"...and that chick at the local TV station in Denver asked it." Noah looks at me. "And now you're asking it. Do you all coordinate with each other? Because I can't figure out why everybody keeps asking the same question."

Todd says, "If you want a straight answer, you should probably ask our wordsmith."

He means Rex, of course. I want to ask where he is. Why he's not here. But I don't, because I'm not sure I want to know the answer.

The interview continues in the same vein. I manage to dredge up questions from my years of experience talking to bands. The guys make tons of jokes in response. But every once in a while, one of them gives me a real answer. The questions I'm asking are standard, at best. I'm hardly in award-winning or career-advancing territory.

At one point Jeff comes back in and speaks in Todd's ear. Todd answers back, just as privately, so I have no idea what they're talking about.

"Sorry about that," Todd says, after Jeff leaves. "Did I miss a question?"

Noah looks over at him. "She wants to know if we're

enjoying the level of success we've achieved, or if there are any pitfalls we didn't expect?"

I wince. Hearing Noah repeat my question makes it sound like a borderline asshole thing to ask. I always think of that question as an invitation for a band to dish some dirt *if they want to*. But they can answer it however they want. Nobody has to talk about the pitfalls of success if they'd rather keep that private.

Todd gives me a shit-eating grin, and says, "What I really dig about the level of success we've achieved is that now, we actually *do* have groupies."

"I call them admirers," Theo supplies.

"I call them whatever the fuck they want to be called," Noah adds.

This is what they're infamous for. Messing with journalists. I could be touched that Todd remembers my aversion to being called a groupie. But mostly, I feel gently ganged up on by the three of them.

I attempt to gather my thoughts. To move on to my next unprepared question. And then I hear the door to the hallway open again, and someone walks over to Todd. I'm expecting it to be Jeff.

But it isn't the band's tour manager.

It's Rex.

CHAPTER 41

The minute Rex sees me, his face lights up. "Holy shit! Is it actually you, Batgirl?"

Without thinking, I stand up. He moves back across the room and comes over to me. Immediately, he pulls me into a hug.

Old feelings come screaming to the surface. And, as he holds on to me, they just keep coming. It's an explosion of emotion.

He feels thinner than I remember. But good. It's so good to feel the unique Rex-energy again. To have his arms wrapped around me.

When we finally break apart, he holds me at arms' length, then smiles and asks, "What are you doing here?"

"She's interviewing us for *Rags to Bitches*," Todd chimes in. "She's a journalist now."

"Barely," I repeat, for what feels like the umpteenth time.

"No shit?" Rex says. "You did it, right? You came here for college?"

"Yup." I nod. "Graduated last year."

300

"Good for you." His eyes glitter at me. "I always knew you could do it." He motions for me to sit back down, so I take my seat. Then he goes and stands behind Todd with his arms folded, still looking at me. Smiling.

I reach over to my voice recorder, because I'm no longer sure this is an interview. I want to turn it off if it isn't.

"Already got it," Todd says, meeting my eyes. "It's off."

Noah gets up from the table. "You know," he says, in this theatrical manner, "I *just* remembered I have to talk to somebody about something very important. So, I'm leaving. I'll see all of you later."

"Oh yeah. Wasn't that your drum tech?" Todd suggests.

"Yeah. I need to have a spontaneous heart to heart with my drum tech. We do that all the time. All the time." He nods at me, then goes for the door.

Rex takes Noah's vacated seat. Now it's him, Todd, and Theo at the table with me.

Todd glances in my direction. "Have any more questions lined up for us? Don't want to cut your interview short."

I give him a look. I already told him I wasn't prepared for this interview, and I'm sure my generic questions confirmed that. "No," I say, "I don't have any additional questions."

He grins, amiably. "I hope you got enough from us to put something together for your magazine."

Rex is still looking at me. I like it, but it's unnerving, too. I've forgotten about that quiet focus he gets, sometimes.

"I'll figure something out," I tell Todd.

"Well, then, I don't think you need us anymore." He gets up from the table.

Theo stands up, too. "Tell Ronnie hi for me. And tell her congratulations on getting married."

301

"Sure, I'll tell her."

Todd turns to Rex. "Okay, man. Guess you two are off the record now, so I'll leave you alone." Then he levels a pointed look at me.

"One hundred percent off the record," I promise. "Thanks for doing the interview. I really appreciate it."

"You're welcome." Todd nudges Theo, and they leave together.

All at once it's quiet in the room.

I'm nervous. There was a time when Rex made me feel more comfortable than anyone else. But now his presence is making me fidgety.

He's beautiful. There's no other word for it. When I first met him he was a ratty long-haired guy in a band. He became beautiful to me over time, as I got to know him. As I fell in love with him.

But now he's objectively beautiful. His haircut shows off the compelling bone structure of his face. Just the way he sits there, the light behind his eyes shifting between warmth and sharp perception, is devastating. And his hands. Looking at his hands unearths long-buried memories of him putting them on me. How good that used to feel.

Only now, millions of people know who he is. How many other women have felt his hands on their own bodies? It's overwhelming. Even if we were on the record, I doubt I could manage to interview Rex if I'd had days of preparation.

Finally, he breaks the silence. "I wasn't going to show up," he confides. "But they told me Todd said Batgirl was here, so I had to come see what was up."

He digs a pack of smokes and a lighter out of his pocket, then offers me a cigarette.

"No, thanks," I say.

"Do you mind?"

"Go ahead."

Rex lights a cigarette and scoots the ashtray on the table a bit closer to him. Then he takes a drag, exhales, and grins at me. "So, how the hell are you doing, Francesca?"

I shrug and grin back at him. "I don't know. Okay, I guess?"

"You're living in New York City," he points out. "That's pretty fucking cool."

"I s'pose," I say. "I mean, I still can't believe I'm here. Sometimes I feel like I'm just dreaming."

"What's not working for you?" he asks. "'Cause it sounds like something isn't."

He's still in tune with me. I haven't had a chance to tell him a thing about how I feel directionless, but he's picked up on it anyway. Or at least, he's picked up on the fact that something's wrong.

I was already pretty honest with Todd, so I figure I might as well go all the way with Rex. "So, I'm here as a journalist, right? That's what I'm supposed to be. But I don't think I actually want to be one."

He raises his eyebrows, but he's still listening, so I keep talking.

"I came to New York on a journalism scholarship, so it feels like that's what I'm supposed to do. I don't know. I love working for *Rags to Bitches*, but they pay by the piece. It doesn't exactly cover my bills. And everyone in this city is so ambitious, you know? You're supposed to do big things here."

"Why don't you try to get a job with a bigger magazine?" he suggests.

"Like I said, I'm not sure it's even what I want."

He leans back in his chair and aims a shrewd look at me.

"If it *is* what you want, this interview will help you out, right?"

"Well, sure," I say. "It was amazing to get an interview with you guys, now that you're..."

His eyes crinkle up with amusement. "Now that we're super hot shit?"

"Right. I mean, of course it helps. I wasn't at my best, though. I didn't have a ton of time to prepare and...I asked pretty standard questions."

"Standard?"

"Boring," I confirm.

"Why don't you ask me some questions?"

"I just promised Todd we're off the record."

He smirks. "So, I'm officially revoking that sacred vow you just made to Todd. You have my permission to ask me three questions. On the record. You want to?"

"Um, okay." I reach for my voice recorder. "They probably won't be good ones," I warn him.

"Right, I know. You didn't have enough time to prepare."

"Exactly," I agree. I hit the record button on my machine and look back at Rex. "Okay. Are you ready?"

He blows smoke up toward the ceiling, like Todd did earlier. Then he grins. "Ready and willing."

"Okay. Okay, so, the new album feels like maybe you guys went about it in a different way. There're sections that sound kind of improvised. Did you actually approach the recording of this album differently? Or does it just sound that way?"

Rex has been watching me while I speak, and I feel silly when I'm done. Like I'm playing the role of a rock journalist in a comedy sketch. Not like I am one, for real.

He stubs out his cigarette in the ashtray. Then he

reaches for another one, and lights it. Once it's lit, he asks, "Have you listened to the new album?"

"I did," I nod. "Today. Before I came here."

"Then you picked up on a lot. We *did* approach it differently. We did most of the writing in the studio, which was new for us. And, yeah, that resulted in some improvising. So, good ear."

"Thanks. Um, can I ask a follow up question, or will that use up another question?"

He grins. His sweet grin. The one that used to turn my insides all melt-y. As it turns out, it still does.

"You can ask a follow up question," he says. "*And* your other questions."

He's still smiling at me, and it's starting to mess with my concentration. But I push forward. "Okay, so, did you prefer making the album in this new way? Or would you rather have the songs worked out ahead of time?"

"I preferred it this way," he says, decisive. "It felt looser and freer and more creative. You'd have to ask the other guys how they felt about it, but the way we did it this time gets a definite thumbs up from me."

"Okay, thanks for that. So, next question. The lyrics for this record seem kind of dark. Is there a reason for that?"

I'm afraid he might get angry, but he just looks patiently amused. It's probably like the other guys said: everybody asks this question. I'm just one of a multitude to bring it up.

"I was talking about what was going on—with me—at the time we made the record," Rex says, keeping his tone even. "If that hits people as dark, then it hits them that way. But I didn't sit down to write dark, scary lyrics."

"That's just how they came out?"

He nods.

I sense he's not going to say anything more on the subject, so I move on. "All right. So for my last question, um..." I hesitate, then decide to go for it. "How do you feel about the level of fame the band's achieved? Are you comfortable with it? Or not?"

Rex shrugs. "I'm not comfortable with it or uncomfortable with it. I mean, it's different. It's strange to get recognized every time you go somewhere. But you know, in ten years, that could all be over." He looks directly at me. "No one is ever gonna know you like the people who actually know you."

For a moment, I forget I'm interviewing him, and get kind of lost in the pale green light of his eyes. Then I recover, and say, "Thanks for answering my questions."

"You're welcome."

"I'm going off the record." I hit the stop button on my voice recorder, and look up at him. "Was that okay?"

"Totally fine. You're good at this."

"It's just asking a bunch of nosy questions."

We're looking at each other, and neither of us is breaking eye contact. I can't possibly know who he is, now. Too much time has passed, and our lives are wildly different. But I feel like I *do* know him. I feel the same way I did the first time Ronnie dragged me to one of their shows and left me stranded with the band. Like me and Rex were already connected, even though we hardly knew each other. The connection is still there.

"How have you really been?" I ask, quietly. "Is everything...okay?"

He looks like he's thinking about what to say. I wait. I want to know how he is. For real. But when he speaks, he asks me another question, instead.

"How come you didn't have enough time to get ready for this interview?"

"Because my editor told me about it just this morning. And I was supposed to work at this coffee shop for half the day before I could even start thinking about it. And because..." I hesitate, then look him in the eye. "Because I wondered if I was going to see you again, and that made it hard for me to think about anything else."

Something in his eyes shifts, and he grinds out his second cigarette in the ashtray. "You want to go somewhere?" he asks.

"With you?"

"Yeah, with me. You and me. Let's get out of here. You game?"

Of course I am. Because it's Rex. And despite everything that has changed—fame, addiction, success—there's still something magic about Rex.

"Yeah," I say. "Let's go."

CHAPTER 42

To get out of the venue undetected, Rex shrugs off his leather jacket and puts on a nondescript grey hoodie, instead. He pulls the hood up over his head, so it's harder to tell who he is.

I feel like any fan who's super into him would still know he's the person under the hoodie. And he's carrying his jacket over his arm. Anyone who saw the show tonight would probably recognize it.

Still, we manage to get a cab without anyone bothering him. He leans toward the divider and tells the driver to head to Lower Manhattan.

"Where are we going?" I ask.

"I was thinking we could just drive around. Talk. And then I'll have the cab drop you off wherever you live."

"Sounds good."

I wonder if he's planning to follow me to my door. Or inside. That could be awkward, if we run into Mark. But I can't believe Rex wants that. It's been such a long time. Given everything he must have experienced by now, I can't possibly have anything he would want or need.

There's something intimate about being in the backseat of a cab together. We're not sitting too near each other, but I feel close to him, just being confined in the same small space. However, now that we don't have the pretext of an interview for conversation, it's hard to know what to say.

"How's your mom?" I ask, finally.

"She's good. My sister had a kid, so she's all into being a grandma now."

It's weird for me to think of people our age, or close to it, having kids. I'm not sure how to respond, so I ask him another question about his mother, instead.

"Is she still religious? Your mom?"

"Oh, yeah." He laughs. "Still going to her conferences. Gives her something to look forward to."

I laugh with him.

Our driver is slowing down. The traffic seems to be getting heavier.

Rex smiles at me. "How are things with your mom? I remember she used to be kind of hard on you."

"That hasn't changed." I sigh. "But it's been a lot better since I moved here."

"Only so much damage she can do from three thousand miles away?" he guesses.

"Yeah, pretty much. When I left home I was worried about my brother, but he seems to be handling things okay. Better than I did, anyway."

"I remember your brother." Rex grins. "He still playing the guitar?"

"Yep," I nod. "And he's playing in a band, too."

"So he *was* serious about guitar then, huh?"

"Very serious," I agree.

"What kind of band?"

"Oh, I don't know," I groan. "That's another thing I hate

309

about rock journalism. How we have to put everything in categories. But I guess they're sort of nu metal meets punk. Except their singer writes good melodies, so they're also kinda pop. So that's what they are. Nu pop punk metal."

Rex's laugh is obliging. Then he leans back on the seat. "So, you still want to know how things *really* are?"

"Yeah. I do," I assure him. "Tell me anything you want."

"Mostly, things are good," he says. "The new record's doing great. We're playing two sold out shows at Madison Square Garden. The label's happy. No complaints."

"Sounds like lots of...positive stuff."

He looks me in the eye. "I'm sure you heard about me? Addiction, rehab. Relapse rumors?"

"It's kind of everywhere," I agree.

"It's all true." He gives me this vulnerable, naked look that goes straight to my heart. "You could say I told you so."

Just like that, all the turmoil I felt when we broke up, all the feelings I thought I put behind me, all of it is in front of me again. It's like this stuff was just hiding in my brain, or my soul, or wherever stuff like this hangs out, waiting for Rex to show up and bring it back to life.

I look at him and shame courses through me. "I was pissed you broke your promise. That's all I cared about. But I never said anything, and I should have said something. I should have tried to get you some help. You were more than my boyfriend, you were a friend and...I wasn't a good friend."

Rex gives me a sidelong glance. "My addiction stuff is not your fault."

"No, I know that. But I wish I'd pushed harder or something. I don't know. I think I gave up on you—because I couldn't handle it."

As soon as I say it, I know it's true. I *did* have to stop

being his girlfriend, because I didn't want to share him with other women. I don't feel bad about that decision. But I also gave up on him as a person because I didn't want to deal with his budding addiction. Because of that, I wanted to erase him from my life. For good. It hurts to admit it.

He hooks one of my fingers with his and tugs on it so that I look at him. "Listen," he says. "There's nothing you could have said that would've changed my mind. I was gonna go there, no matter what anyone told me. I'm glad you took care of your own life. I just would've dragged you down."

I choke down a sob, then fight to control myself. It doesn't feel like losing it would be a helpful thing to do.

"I shouldn't have made promises," he goes on. "To you or anyone else. I knew I wasn't going to keep them."

"So how are you now?" I manage to ask. "Are you okay now?"

Rex doesn't answer me right away. When he does, he speaks slowly. "You learn a lot about yourself in rehab. It gives you a shit ton of self awareness and—don't get me wrong—that's valuable information to have."

He's still holding on to my fingers, and I squeeze his, encouraging him to go on. When he looks at me again, his eyes have that haunted look I noticed during the show.

"Self awareness is great," he says. "But having that and sharing it with some well-known magazine doesn't mean shit in the moment when you want to use. Self awareness doesn't take away cravings. You can be one thousand percent self aware, understand the implications of the choice you're making, and still decide to go there." He shrugs. "At least, that's how it is for me."

"I'm sorry." I'm holding on to his hand tightly now.

"No, I'm sorry," he says, trying to joke. "That was really heavy."

"I asked," I remind him. "I wanted to know."

He interlaces his fingers with mine. We're connected. As much as we used to be.

"What are you thinking?" he asks.

I don't have words for my thoughts, and I have more emotions than actual opinions. But I try to answer his question. "I'm not sure. Maybe...maybe I don't want to be a rock journalist because it seems like there's this constant obsession with the problems of...brilliant people. With whether they're going to fall down or not. It's kind of gross."

"*Brilliant people*," he repeats. "You mean addicts. People like me?"

I go quiet, as what he said sinks in. This isn't the cocky kid I used to know, who believed he could handle himself around heroin. Rex knows he's an addict. Or, it's how he sees himself, now.

I look at him. "I love my editor. When I do interviews, he doesn't expect me to get dirt on anyone's problems. He just wants me to write about music. But everywhere else I look—like, the places where I could get a 'real' job?—they seem obsessed with those kinds of stories. I don't know, maybe I'm wrong."

"You're not wrong. Sensation and scandal are easy to sell."

I hesitate. "Can I ask you something?"

"Ask me anything."

"When you did that interview, over the summer? The one about addiction and rehab and everything? Was that on purpose?"

His eyes flash in a way that reminds me of Rex six years ago. I can almost hear him say *What do you think, Batgirl?*

"People like a story they can understand," he says. "And what they understand is a story about someone who falls from grace and goes under. Or a story about someone who beats the odds and makes a comeback. It's a lot harder to tell a story about how addiction really is. You know?"

"So you went with the comeback story?" I guess.

Rex shrugs. "Gives me something to live up to, right?"

But I see that haunted look flash in his eyes again. And for a moment, I have a sense of the pressure he must feel. The tension between the story he sold the press and his real everyday struggle with addiction.

"I don't think I want to tell stories like that," I blurt.

He pulses his fingers around mine. "Sounds like you know what you don't want. Do you know what you *do* want?"

His question makes me go still. He's having his old effect on me. Forcing me to focus on what's going on inside. It's another gift of his.

"I guess I just...want to do something that builds people up." I feel self-conscious the moment the words come out of my mouth. "That sounds so naive."

"It is," he agrees. "Making music can be kind of naive, too, though. I feel like a chump most of the time. And then someone will tell us our music helped them in some way. I still take that to heart. It's a good feeling."

I smile at him. "That's kind of awesome."

"I'm not the best person to give advice," he says. "But can I give you some?"

"Sure. Give me advice." I know I'm falling under his spell. He doesn't have to do anything special to win me over. He just has to be himself.

Rex takes both my hands in his own and gives me this earnest look. "Don't focus on all these things you don't want," he says. "Don't let that stuff stop you. Focus on doing that thing you said you want to do—something that builds people up. Maybe you *will* find a better magazine. Or maybe it'll be something else. But you won't find it if you're not looking for it."

I wonder how I've gone six years without talking to him. I've missed the way he sees things. I'm about to tell him that when he turns and looks out his window, then all around us.

"What's going on?" I ask.

"We're not moving." He lets go of my hands and leans forward to talk to the driver. I hear a muffled reply about traffic.

Rex sits back. "Bad traffic jam. We could be stuck here for a long time." He studies me for a moment. "Why don't I just walk you home?" Then he tells the driver he wants to pay for our ride.

So...I guess he's coming home with me.

CHAPTER 43

W hen I open the cab door, Rex is right behind me. On the street, we're surrounded by a sea of unmoving cars. He puts his arm around my shoulders, and we step around the cars until we reach the sidewalk.

"So where are we going?" he asks.

I tell him the address of my apartment in Brooklyn, and we start walking. I still don't know what he intends to do. Even though our connection feels good, I find it hard to believe he's doing anything more than catching up with an old friend. At least, I hope we're friends.

It's starting to rain. It's light, but relentless. He shrugs his leather jacket back on, over his hoodie. He still has the hood up.

I decide to ask what he wants. We're comfortable enough with each other. There's no reason to spend the rest of the long trek to my place guessing if he wants to spend the night with me, or if he's just walking me home.

I look at him. "Hey, Rex..."

All at once, this strange guy is up in our faces. He must

have been walking in the opposite direction, because he's right in front of us. But it feels like he came out of nowhere.

"Hey, you're Rex Thornton, aren't you? I can't believe it, I knew you guys were gonna be in town, but here you are, just walking down the street. Just like that! This is so fuckin' crazy!"

Rex takes my arm. "Nope, got the wrong guy. Wish I was him. Just hanging out with my girl."

"Nah, you're him," the guy says. "I know you're him. Hey, is all that true about rehab and stuff? Did you really go to rehab?"

"You've got the wrong guy," Rex repeats. "Sorry to be rude, but we need to be somewhere." He moves us past the guy, who keeps yelling after us down the street.

"I know you're him! I recognize your face!"

Rex is walking very fast, and I'm struggling to keep up with him. He veers down a side street, tugging at my sleeve, and I follow. We make a couple more zigs and zags and then, finally, he slows down, and looks at me.

"I think we lost him."

"Does that happen a lot?" I ask.

"More than I want it to. I don't mind talking to people, but that guy was aggressive. Didn't like his vibe."

"I didn't, either."

I wonder if we'll continue to run into people who recognize him while we walk back to my place. I can only imagine how invasive and exhausting it must be if he deals with shit like this all the time.

"You know," I say, "I could just take the subway home. I mean, I do it all the time. It's nice of you to walk me back, but the subway works too."

He turns his head to me, abruptly. "Is that what you want? You want me to take you to the subway?"

"I was just thinking it might be easier for you if we—"

"Yeah, okay," he says, like he's made his mind up about something. "That's what I'll do."

Shit. He's pissed, or hurt. He thinks I don't want him to come home with me. And the truth is, I'm conflicted. I do want him to come with me. But I don't want to get hurt.

The nearest subway stop is close, and it's a good one. I can get a train from there straight to my neighborhood. At the top of the stairs to the subway, we stop and stand off to the side, so we don't block other people from using the stairway.

Rex turns to me, and he's smiling. Not angry. But something between us has shifted. "I'm glad I got to see you," he says. "I always wondered how it turned out with college and everything."

"I'm glad, too."

"Don't freak out too much about your job stuff. You'll figure it out."

"Hey," I reach out and touch his arm. "Thanks for talking to me. I mean, about how you're doing and everything. Please know that it's all off the record. It was just good to talk to you."

"I trust you." His eyes glitter at me. Then he says something strange. "I'm going to leave you alone, okay?"

Before I can think of a response, he reaches out and frames my face with his hand, the way he used to. "Take care of yourself, Francesca."

"Yeah, Rex. You, too."

And then he's gone, walking so fast that it's only seconds before I lose sight of him in the dark.

I go down the stairs to the subway, feeling numb. What just happened? One minute, I was sure I'd have to decide if I wanted to spend the night with him, and the next, he disappeared into the wet and chilly New York City streets.

I push onto a subway car with a small crowd of people. It's not as full as it was when I traveled to the show earlier, so I find a place to sit. As the train rumbles forward, I try to make sense of the last hour or so.

Did I want something to happen? What if we'd hooked up? I would have wondered where I stand with him again, and that would have sucked, right? Especially if he only wanted to do it once, for nostalgia or whatever. I can only imagine what sleeping with him would have done to me.

Plus, haven't I been saying I don't want to devote my life to a particular guy ever again? Because I always lose myself when I do that. As much as I loved Rex—and maybe still do—I lost myself when I was with him. And he was just the first of many similar experiences.

Or is that true? *Do* I lose myself when I'm with Rex? Because there's that thing he does, how he helps me clarify what I really want. What my next step should be. That's more about finding myself than losing myself.

But I also remember feeling like I always had to stake my claim to him. To fight off rivals. That was exhausting. And then, there's that broken promise.

I ache for him and his troubles with addiction. I want him to win his fight against it. But I can still picture the haunted look he got in his eyes tonight when he talked about the urge to use. Am I emotionally capable of dealing with that, even as some kind of friend? Or would I push him away again because I can't handle it?

The light inside the subway car is garish, and I'm unsettled. I don't know if I've just escaped an emotional train wreck, or if I've missed the chance to reconnect with someone I care about on a level that's difficult to explain. Even to myself.

I remind myself that he's famous. His life is different than it was when I first knew him. All the weird shit that comes with fame would make me crazy. If I want a guy in my life at all, I want a "regular" guy.

And it doesn't matter that the connection between us was raw and explosive, with our fingers intertwined in the back of the cab. Even though it's been six years, I'm sure it's still true that, fundamentally, nothing has changed.

I'm running the same thoughts over and over in my head as I get off the subway, then start up the stairs to the street. It's still drizzling, and I feel the water hit my face as I emerge from the tunnel.

I exited the subway couple stops early so I could stop at this bodega I like, because they carry a rare brand of clove cigarettes. I still don't smoke, but I tried a clove cigarette at a party the first year I lived in New York, and loved the taste. That first year was exhilarating and terrifying and ultimately a triumph. Cloves are terrible for your lungs. But now and then, I'm willing to do some damage to recall the euphoria of that first year in the city.

I don't light up right away, and instead slip the pack of cigarettes in my bag. I'm used to walking through the city alone, but it's late and I want to stay alert. It's not an ideal time to be distracted with nostalgia.

But I'm distracted anyway. Because of Rex. Less than an hour ago, I was talking to him. He was here. Real. Now he's gone again, and I feel empty. I don't want to feel that way.

Even though the rain is light, I'm getting soaked, slowly, as I trudge back to my building. When I start down the last block, I pick up the pace, eager to go inside, dry off, and smoke one of the cloves. Nostalgia, here I come.

And then, as I approach the building, I stop dead at the foot of the stairs. Rex is at the top of the staircase. Waiting for me.

I walk up the steps to reach him. "How'd you find me?" I ask.

"You gave me your address, remember? It wasn't hard."

I'm bewildered. "But...the traffic jam?"

"I ran pretty hard, all the way to the bridge. Traffic was okay once I got there. Caught another cab." Then he grins. "But I guess I also got lucky."

I'm at a loss for words. Finally I ask, "Why are you here?"

Rex stares down at me, and his face is shrouded by his grey hoodie. It almost makes him look like a monk. Which makes me want to laugh, because of course, he's not.

He gives me a determined look. "I shouldn't have run away from you. I didn't intend to do that. I got...scared."

"Scared of what?" I ask, keeping my voice low.

"Just—everything. I wasn't sure you wanted to associate with me based on...how things are."

"I wasn't trying to get rid of you," I tell him.

"I know. I panicked."

Looking in his eyes, I believe him. I want to touch him, just to make sure he's real. I found him then lost him again, all in one night. And now he's on my doorstep? It's hard to believe I'm not dreaming.

"I was a little scared, too," I admit.

I see understanding flash in his eyes, and he straightens his posture. "Look," he says, "I don't know who you're with or what you want. I don't want to mess up your life. But I didn't want to leave without...could I kiss you? Just once. Then I swear, I will leave you alone."

I step forward, so close that the lapels of his coat are touching me. "Yeah," I say. "You can do that."

He slips his arm around me and pulls me close. It feels good. Better than anything I've felt in years, and he hasn't even kissed me yet.

We watch each other intently for a few seconds, a minute, maybe more. I have no sense of time. We're vibing on each other, and it's a thousand times better than the lift I would have got from smoking one of those clove cigarettes. I don't want the buzz to end, ever. And then he kisses me.

It feels right.

Even as I fall in deeper, I'm running reasons in my head like a tape loop. Reasons why anything beyond this one kiss is a bad idea. *Nothing has changed.*

But I feel so good, and all that tape in my brain starts to tangle and melt. This is what Rex does for me. There's nothing and no one else who can make me feel this way.

Rekindling anything real between us is impossible. I know it deep in my gut, the way I knew it when I broke up with him six years ago. But it doesn't matter. Maybe all I'm looking for are more moments like this one. Moments, however long they last, where every part of me feels like it fits inside the fabric of this harsh and beautiful world.

END

ACKNOWLEDGMENTS

I would like to thank Matt Cory for the fantastic book cover that captures the essence of this story so perfectly. I would also like to thank Michelle Meade for her insightful and incisive editing assistance.

Much gratitude to every single one of my friends who have been supporting my foray into writing actual books. I would be remiss if I didn't specifically mention Amy Crum, Anna Kagley, Matt Menovcik, Louis O'Callaghan, Kelly Skore, Marlese Webb, Beth KS Whiting, and Dana Whitney.

A special shout out to Joe Murphy for reading early drafts of this book and providing invaluable feedback.

And Dad, a huge thanks to you. I wish you were here to see me publish my debut novel. I still remember the first time you told me, "I love your writing." You created a monster. But that's all right.

About the Author

Andrea Maxand was born in Seattle, WA. She has been many things: a singer/songwriter, a paralegal, a baker, and a receptionist. However, the one constant in her life has always been writing.

Andrea lives in the Pacific Northwest with a menagerie of robotic cats. When she's not writing or spending time with the robo-kitties, she's likely up to something a bit odd and random. (Aren't we all?)

The 2019 novella "Boxing Day" was Andrea's first published story. "Dreams Fall Like Rain" is her first novel.

Also by Andrea Maxand

Boxing Day